"YOU'RE A GIRL."

Belatedly, Alec realized how inane that remark sounded. It wasn't as if she didn't know.

A flush touched her cheeks. "So wot's it to y'?" Her voice came out a squeak. She frowned and cleared her throat.

Alec had to blink a few times to snap himself out of the daze he was in. "I'm just surprised. I wasn't expecting it."

She braced her legs apart in a defensive stance, hands on the swell of her softly rounded hips. "Well, get used to it."

How had he thought her a boy? The only excuse was that he hadn't been looking for it. "It wasn't an insult—simply a moment of shock. Especially after Anthony mentioned you were a . . ." He stopped.

Folding her arms across her chest, she leveled him with her exquisite sapphire gaze before finishing his sentence. "A thief?"

"Well . . . yes." He stared at her, suddenly uncomfortable.

"Now, wot's that look fer?" she snapped. "Don't y' dare pity me! I'm just as good as y' are—and maybe even a damn sight better!"

BOOK YOUR PLACE ON OUR WEBSITE AND MAKE THE READING CONNECTION!

We've created a customized website just for our very special readers, where you can get the inside scoop on everything that's going on with Zebra, Pinnacle and Kensington books.

When you come online, you'll have the exciting opportunity to:

- View covers of upcoming books
- Read sample chapters
- Learn about our future publishing schedule (listed by publication month *and author*)
- Find out when your favorite authors will be visiting a city near you
- Search for and order backlist books from our online catalog
- Check out author bios and background information
- Send e-mail to your favorite authors
- Meet the Kensington staff online
- Join us in weekly chats with authors, readers and other guests
- Get writing guidelines
- AND MUCH MORE!

**Visit our website at
http://www.zebrabooks.com**

LIKE NO OTHER

Melanie George

Zebra Books
Kensington Publishing Corp.

http://www.zebrabooks.com

ZEBRA BOOKS are published by

Kensington Publishing Corp.
850 Third Avenue
New York, NY 10022

First Printing: April, 2000
10 9 8 7 6 5 4 3 2 1

Printed in the United States of America

This book is dedicated to my son, Andrew, my inspiration, who has shown me I can be anything I want to be . . . but what I'll always want to be most is his mom. You're my greatest accomplishment, Andrew.

Chapter One

London, England

"For the love of God, get to the point!" Alec fairly bellowed as he looked up from the papers he had been studying on his desk. He narrowed his eyes at his friend, who leaned negligently against the mahogany sideboard holding a glass of Alec's best Scotch in his hand. "You're blathering again, Whitfield, and as you can see, I have work to do."

"As if you're the only one," His Grace, Anthony Whitfield, muttered sourly, plucking a clinging strand of his blond hair from the sleeve of his pristine black jacket. With a grimace of distaste, he stared at the offending hair as if its very presence was a personal affront.

Alec cocked a brow. "Certainly you're not i̶̶
I think you're implying?"

"I don't believe I like the tenor of that question, Breckridge."

Alec shook his head. Even with all Anthony's pompous titles—the Duke of Glassboro being his most illustrious—the man lacked the ducal glare, bearing, and wherewithal required to be taken seriously. The only ducal quality Anthony had in abundance was a bloated sense of self-importance.

"Enlighten me, if you will, on this work you've been doing."

Anthony shrugged airily, causing some of the contents of his glass to slosh over the rim and onto the new Persian rug beneath his shiny black-booted feet. He took notice only insofar as discerning if any of the liquid had marred his perfection. Satisfied he had only stained the carpet, he proceeded to answer the question put to him. "I've a contingent of females clamoring for my amorous attentions. Keeping them all satisfied is a lot of bloody work, I'll have you know."

"I wasn't referring to your harem."

Anthony made an expansive gesture. "Well, I have a standing appointment with Huntley and Thornton at Boodles. At least twice weekly, I must trounce them at whist. Not the most difficult task, I admit, seeing as they are rather pathetic at the game. Yet they insist on playing, and I, as their friend, feel obligated to embarrass them in public."

Alec leaned back in his chair and eyed his friend. "I meant *real* work. You know, as in making decisions and following through on things?"

Anthony looked aghast. "Good God, man, are you daft? Why would I want to do anything so personally repugnant d positively against the grain as having to think? Remem-
ʿ you will, that I have been left a considerable pile of

blunt by the Elder, may he rest in peace. It's all I can do just trying to squander it before I cock up my toes and ascend to ye olde mansion in the sky."

"I wouldn't be so sure you're going that way," Alec felt obligated to point out. "Decadence and a morally depraved life-style aren't usually rewarded by the Almighty."

Anthony barked with laughter. "Oh, please"—he waved a dismissive hand—"I'm too damn wealthy to go anywhere *but* up. I've paid off the devil, don't y' know."

Alec figured the devil wasn't in need of enticement where Anthony was concerned. Whitfield was unrepentant, outlandish and a blighted pain in the ass on a regular basis. Nevertheless, Alec liked him—although he would deny it until his dying breath.

He and Anthony were polar opposites, as different as two people could be, positive to negative, black to white, oil to water. Whereas Anthony went to every party, drank too much, gambled too much and did just about everything in excess, Alec, on the other hand, worked.

And worked.

It was hard for him to believe only fifteen years had passed since the day his father fell facedown into his breakfast plate, dead. It seemed more like fifty. But who was counting?

One minute they had been talking, and the next, Edward Breckridge, seventh Earl of Somerset, was gone. No warning. No goodbyes.

Although Alec had been fated for the yoke from birth, he just hadn't expected that yoke to clamp around his neck so suddenly—or so soon. He had only been seventeen at the time and had thought he had at least a few more years of frivolity ahead of him.

Even though he had felt ill-prepared at the time, without

hesitation he had stepped into the shoes of all those who had come before him.

It never crossed his mind to shirk his responsibilities. With four estates, two textile mills, and a shipping company, he didn't have the time or energy to be a ne'er-do-well. He also had his mother and sister to care for. Besides, playing the idle wealthy wasn't in his nature. He was considered an oddity. That didn't bother him, though. He rather liked being a round peg in a square hole. If he wanted to take a walk on the wild side, he need only spend ten minutes in Anthony's presence. The man could provoke a saint.

"Need I remind you," Alec said, "that along with all the blunt, you have inherited a title. Thanks also to your dearly departed father."

Alec wondered why he bothered saying anything. It would only succeed in opening the door for Anthony to drive him to the brink of insanity that much quicker. The man lived on a different mental plane than the rest of the world.

"Ah, but I do sorely miss the old scoundrel," Anthony intoned, his words sincere. "The Elder was a card. And there are so bloody few of them out there."

"He was a good man," Alec agreed soberly.

Anthony stared past him, a thoughtful expression on his lightly tanned face. At length he said, "I'd rather the money come without the title since dukedom brings with it all those hideous responsibilities I so loathe." He stared down at the mirrorlike shine on his boots. When he glanced up, he wore a crooked smile. "Still, the money does give me the power to employ someone else to take care of the mundane details so that I can enjoy life." He shrugged. "Well, either way, I win."

And the lunacy begins, Alec thought with a mental sigh.

"You excel at delegation, Whitfield. Let no one say you're not a dyed-in-the-wool elitist. But heed my advice, I wouldn't allow anyone complete control. You may find yourself the victim of someone unscrupulous."

"You don't give me much credit," Anthony replied with a scowl. "I'm smarter than that. Like that dead French chap, Monty something, I have a system of checks and balances in place."

Alec heaved a sigh. "It's Montesquieu. He also said, 'Power without knowledge is power lost.' Since you have no knowledge, Whitfield, your system is doomed to failure."

"One day, sir, I may take offense to your particular brand of humor and refuse to speak to you."

"One can only hope," Alec muttered.

Anthony refilled his glass. "But I digress. We were talking about you."

Alec blinked. They were? Since when? Something told him he was probably better off not knowing.

He pulled in his chair and then picked up his papers. "You are always entertaining, but I have to get some work done today. You know where the door is."

"Oh, no. You'll not rid yourself of me that easily." Anthony's words were like a death knell ringing over the newly turned soil of Alec's grave. In a long list of irritating qualities, Anthony had mastered the art of being a tenacious sonofabitch. He would dig in his heels until he had said what he had come to say.

"So, what were we discussing?" Alec asked in a bored tone, not looking up from his papers.

"Your lack of charitable contributions to Society," was the blunt reply.

Alec slowly elevated his gaze and stared at Anthony over the top of his papers. Had the man left his mind along with his coat at the front door?

"My lack of charitable contributions? What sort of tangent are you on now?"

"Not a tangent, old man . . . more like a mission, if you will." Anthony plopped himself down on the corner of the desk. "Charity is all the rage right now, you know. Society has found itself a new cause *du jour*—not that any of these inane twits know the first bloody thing about charity."

Alec was loath to remind Anthony that what he knew about being charitable was the distance between nil and zero. But that would just get the man going on another subject, and then they might never get to the point, the possibility of which was enough to make Alec shudder. Therefore, in the interest of sanity, Alec kept his comment behind his teeth and continued to stare at Anthony with his usual mask of disinterest, hoping for a quick and painless end to his suffering.

Undaunted, Anthony pressed on. "More than half the *ton* believe a charitable deed consists of hiring servants to wait on them hand and foot."

"Much like you, Whitfield," Alec murmured dryly.

Anthony harumphed and smoothed an imaginary wrinkle from the lapel of his exquisitely tailored evening jacket. "Do not mock me during my speech, if you please. Now, where was I? Oh, yes . . . well, people are trying to outdo one another. It's really rather amusing."

Alec suppressed a yawn. "A veritable laugh riot, I imagine."

Anthony glared, but otherwise ignored the sarcasm. "I, too, have been pressed into duty. One must do what one can to help the less fortunate."

Alec lifted an eyebrow. "I believe I have just witnessed one of the biblical signs of the Apocalypse."

"Anyway," Anthony drew out the word, "with you being

so cloistered these days, I thought I should let you know what is happening outside yonder door.''

"These conversations always make me dizzy. Now, if you don't mind?'' Alec looked pointedly at the door.

"Have you not heard a word I've said?''

Alec realized his friend was on his high horse and nothing short of tossing him bodily out the door would topple him from it.

Putting his papers down, Alec calmly folded his hands on top of them. "I heard you. So, what is it you want me to do? If it is a donation to the cause you're looking for, why not just say so?''

Opening a side drawer, Alec withdrew a metal box. Removing a small key from his vest pocket, he unlocked the box, revealing a great deal of money. "Here,'' he said, pulling out a stack of bills and placing them in front of Anthony, "take this with my blessing to the poor unfortunates.''

Shaking his head, Anthony picked up the money, snorted, and then tossed it back into the box. "You just don't get it, do you?''

"I have yet to figure out exactly what *it* is,'' Alec replied, resisting the urge to grind his teeth. "And just as a reminder, since you seem to have forgotten, it is not like this family isn't charitable. Both my mother and sister donate their time at several orphanages. And there is the Somerset wing at the hospital, made possible by my father. So it isn't as if we are a bunch of misers.''

"Ah yes, but what have *you* done?''

"Me?''

"Yes, you.''

Alec needed a drink.

Rising from his black leather chair, he made his way to the sideboard to pour himself a glass of Madeira. He needed to fortify himself while he continued to wait for Anthony to get to the point, *if* there even was a point. Sometimes his friend started down a road that went nowhere or—and more frequently—he just talked to hear himself speaking.

Tipping his head back, Alec downed the contents in his glass. The rich wine slid smoothly down his throat. He only hoped it would dull his senses long enough to deal with Whitfield.

"So this conversation is specifically geared toward me and my supposed lack of charity?" he asked. "Is that correct?"

"Now you've got it, old boy," Anthony replied as he checked his manicure. "Just what have you done for your fellow man recently?"

If that wasn't the bloody pot calling the kettle black.

"*You* are asking *me* what *I've* done?"

"Correct."

"Well, I could ask you the same question. What exactly have *you* done for your *fellow man?*"

"My, but aren't we a bag of snakes today?" Anthony muttered as he got up off the desk, taking himself and his now empty glass over to the sideboard.

"As much as I wish this evening could be sixty-five days long," Alec said, his head beginning to throb, "I have a pressing problem that requires my full attention."

Refilling his glass, Anthony drolly inquired, "And what, pray tell, is that?"

"How I can get you to walk backward and keep going until you're out the front door."

Anthony sighed, loudly. "We live in a crass world with no sense of shame."

"Self-pity, Whitfield?"

Anthony nodded. "I wallow in it. I devote my entire

being to it. I drown myself in utter self-pity." He downed the contents of his glass in one swallow as if to prove his point.

Alec figured if he ever wanted peace again, it would behoove him to bring this inane conversation to its culmination.

"So when did you become such a paragon of virtue, Your Grace?" Alec dryly inquired. "I thought all signs of human kindness and benevolence had been thoroughly eradicated from the Glassboros."

Anthony ignored the sarcasm. "Drollery is *my* forte, Breckridge. Please refrain from treading upon sacred ground."

Alec refused to allow himself to laugh, therefore usurping the rather childlike enjoyment he received from annoying Anthony.

With nary a twitch of an eyebrow, he said, "Forgive my insolence. Do go on."

"Well, as I was *trying* to say, there are certain things required of those of us with money. Charity, old man, begins at home. Ergo," Anthony went on dramatically, "I have hired on a poor chap from the streets and given him a position in my very home. If that isn't a damnably good deed, then I bloody well don't know what is."

Alec remained unconvinced. "Prompted by what, I wonder."

"I told you. One must do what one can to—"

"—help out the less fortunate," Alec finished for him. "Yes, I heard that part. Now I'd liked to know the *real* reason."

Anthony appeared to find the Persian rug beneath his feet of great interest. "I don't know what you're talking about."

"Yes, you do. Now out with it."

Anthony lifted his head and glared. "You really are a rotter, y'know."

Alec folded his arms across his chest. "I know. Now speak."

Anthony ran an agitated hand through his blond hair and said in an exasperated tone of voice, "Society, man!"

Alec quirked a brow. "Well, that explains everything. You don't hear bells, do you?"

Anthony's expression conveyed his annoyance at having to explain something that apparently he presumed should have been patently obvious. "I would not be able to show my face at another soiree if I didn't do my part to aid the cause of the suffering masses. This whole damn thing was decreed by the grand dame of the *ton*, making all the women absolutely frenzied to do the old hag's bidding. I couldn't get close to a single blasted woman without her asking what charitable thing I had done. And when I nonchalantly said, 'Nothing,' damn if they all didn't freeze me right out, like I didn't even exist for Christ's sake! My money and my illustrious title didn't do me a bit of good." He refilled his glass, a petulant twist to his lips. "There are a lot of things I can live without, Breckridge—like mornings, for example, and hangovers. But I can't live without women. I need them like I need air."

Alec rolled his eyes heavenward. "I shall assume that is when your generous nature came to the fore and you hired on the chap from the streets."

Anthony merely grunted in reply, looking none too happy to be reminded of his new employee. "But I tell you now, when this deuced nonsense is over I will send the man packing. Frankly, the creature gives me the willies. I fear I will be murdered in my bed."

As if that were possible, Alec thought. Whitfield might enjoy high drama, but he was a dead-on marksman and a rather good pugilist as well. He was just looking for a reason to be rid of the poor chap.

"I see," Alec murmured. "In that case, I only have one question for you." He paused, making sure he had Anthony's full attention before going on. *"Why the hell are you here?"*

"No need to shout. My hearing is just fine."

"It's not your hearing that worries me. It's that your train of thought has no caboose." Alec didn't give Anthony time to retort with one of his droll witticisms. "If you have accomplished your goal and are once again the golden child of the *ton*, why are you pestering me?"

Anthony shrugged. "Well, it doesn't hurt to have a spare good deed in one's pocket. By enlisting your help in this farce, I'm spreading the word, advancing the cause for humanity ad nauseum."

"Alas, the truth has finally been revealed."

"My hand was forced!" Anthony scowled. "I thought this was a one-time thing only to find out it's a bloody continuous thing. If the women didn't need me to pleasure them, I might take to my country estate until this has all blown over." He glanced upward. "Dear Lord, let it be soon."

Alec couldn't help himself; he chuckled. "I'm glad I don't suffer from the same problems as you," he said, striding toward his desk, intent on getting back to work now that this all important discussion was in its final phase.

"So are you going to help?"

The desperate appeal in Whitfield's voice was really too much.

Alec figured if he could deal with Anthony, he could deal with anything. Besides, Anthony's whims changed on a daily basis. Today, he would attempt to save the world. Tomorrow, he would be back to saving himself. Alec decided to humor him. Really, what was the worst that could happen?

Shrugging, he replied, "Why not?"

Anthony rubbed his hands briskly together.

"You can make the arrangements," Alec went on. "I've no time. But don't go overboard. Fight the urge to listen to those strange voices in your head, if you can."

Anthony pretended to be writing. "Don't . . . go . . . overboard. Leave . . . other . . . personalities . . . on . . . bedside . . . table. Got it."

"If you muck this up, I'll hunt you down and feed you to a slavering pack of wolves."

"Leave . . . country." Glancing up, Anthony flashed him all teeth. "Only joking."

Alec wasn't laughing. "You owe me one."

"Have no fear, you'll get one."

Chapter Two

"Now, there be a fruit wot's ripe for the pluckin'," the tall, lanky individual said to his compatriots, pointing to the fancy gentleman across the street from them.

Hunkering down next to a dilapidated building in a slim, dank alleyway, the group eyed their quarry.

"The nabob looks like his pockets is far too weighted down, don't y'think?"

"So why ain't we over there riddin' him of his personals, eh?" another voice piped in. Two obsidian eyes peered out of a dirty face underneath a hat pulled down low, the would-be thief's body covered from head to toe in clothes that were far too big. "He's all alone, lads."

"He's kinda big—"

"—an' younger than most of our unwittin' donors, mind y'."

"He's just askin' for trouble, though," came a voice as yet unheard, subtle, sly, and willing to take the risk. "An'

I'm the one wot's goin' t' give it t' the bloke." The figure, in black, form-fitting clothes, stood up and looked down at the motley crew. "Sit back and watch the way an ace does the job."

"Christ almighty!" Anthony exploded in a fierce whisper as he took his engraved, gold pocket watch out of his vest, trying to look at the dial in the growing darkness. "Where the bloody hell is Huntley?"

Glancing up and down the street, Anthony shifted restlessly, eager to be on his way so he could begin what was sure to be another night of debauched revelry.

He eyed the riffraff littering the streets, shiny, swill-infested bottles clutched to their bosoms. Strange, but it made him thirsty. Yet were he desirous of a drink at that moment, he would either have to have brought his own bottle or divest one of the supine street patrons of his. The idea gathered merit the longer he waited.

Damn! Where was Huntley?

Had it really been necessary for the man to pick the seediest tavern on the outskirts of civilization? Why this godforsaken place?

Because of Huntley's horse-faced wife, that was why.

The woman, Anthony knew, hated him—not without reason, of course. Whenever he and Huntley went out, inevitably they got themselves into hot water, due, Anthony suspected, to his own godless, unrepentant behavior and those places he liked to frequent, such as brothels and other dens of iniquity. But dukedom, as Breckridge was fond of saying, brought certain responsibilities. Being a dissipated lout topped the list of Anthony's duties.

Tonight, he had to go out of his way because Huntley knew too many people in town—people who wouldn't hesitate to tell his wife *where* he had been and *with whom.* If the missus found out her husband had lied, *again.* . . .

Anthony shuddered at the thought. He considered himself rather fearless, but Huntley's wife was built like a blacksmith and had a shrill voice that when raised in anger could paralyze the entire body.

Anthony peered into the murky hole that was the tavern, tempted yet unwilling to step inside. The gap-toothed denizens might foolishly decide they didn't like the cut of his exorbitantly expensive clothing or the shine on his high-polished Hessians. All hell could break loose—not that he didn't like a good brawl. He did, immeasurably. Four or five of the patrons he could take on easily enough, but even his capabilities with his fists couldn't win the day over the twenty or thirty people packed inside the tavern like powder in a snuff box. He had to have himself one drink too many to be in the mood for such rabble-rousing. And since his friend had yet to arrive so he could begin his alcohol consumption in earnest, such an intriguing thought did not come even remotely close to becoming a genuine possibility. But Huntley, the irritating cuss, had better arrive in the next two minutes or Anthony would go on to greater glory without him!

"Ah-choo!"

"What the . . . ?"

Anthony swung around just in time to see a figure dressed in black merge with the gathering shadows. A boy was slinking away—and holding Anthony's wallet in his thieving hands, no less!

Damn, he hadn't felt a thing!

Lunging after the boy, Anthony grabbed the back of his shirt. "Stop squirming, baggage!" he hissed as a foot swung out with the intention of damaging his unmentionables. Quick reflexes managed to save him.

"Get yer lousy mitts off me, y' blue-blooded bastard!" a low voice hissed in return, arms swinging wildly but not connecting with anything solid.

"Good God!" Anthony guffawed, easily holding the lad at arm's length. "What language for such a little package!"

"Little package! Just let me get me hands on y'. I'll knock y' solid, I will," the thief shouted indignantly, continuing to struggle. "Y'll be seein' stars circling yer head the likes of which y' ain't never seen in the sky if y' don't let me go right this very minute!"

The lad had brass—and was sensitive to boot. Apparently the grimy pickpocket didn't appreciate being reminded of his diminutive stature. Most likely he considered his size a detriment. The lad was not alone in this. Size was something of which most men had an issue. Not Anthony, however. He was amply endowed—in all areas.

"Aren't you frightening?" he mocked. "I'm fairly shivering."

"Leave off or I'll slice y' so bad I vow yer own mum won't recognize y'," the lad swore, reaching into his pocket.

Anthony raised an eyebrow at the item the boy produced. "With a fork? My, you certainly are full of surprises. I can only wonder what other gems are hidden on your person. What would shake loose if I held you by your ankles? Perhaps a full compliment of dishware to go with your fork?"

"Bugger!" The lad scowled viciously at the offensive item and then heaved it down the street. It hit the ground with the dull clink of cheap metal.

The thief's companions watched in growing horror as their leader wrestled with the dandy.

"Blimey, the bloke has captured the Fox!" one of the

older youths exclaimed, pointing out the obvious. A slack-witted expression ruined what could have been a handsome face.

"No one has ever trapped the Fox," a skinny, short lad added to the cacophony of angry voices around him. "I swear I wouldn't have believed it if me own eyes were not now beholdin' the very sight. Gawd almighty, I thought there were more chance of the earth openin' up an' swallowin' me whole afore the Fox got fingered."

"Wot are we gonna do?"

"We're gonna rescue our leader, that's wot!" the tallest of the bunch, and second-in-command, told them with authority. "Now get up off your blinkin' arses and let's go!"

Murmured assents were heard all around as the group collected their wits and planned to rush the double-damned aristocrat and save the Fox. They were a gang that stuck together come thick or thin. They certainly weren't going to let one of their own go down without a fight.

Crouching low and single file, they were about to head across the street when a voice boomed out and a fat man came running toward the blond-haired chap holding the Fox.

"Whitfield! I'm coming, man! Just hold on!"

Anthony looked up, holding on to his recalcitrant captive with one hand and adjusting his cravat with the other. Huntley puffed his way toward him, late as usual. Hearing his friend's serious tone, Anthony shook his head in amusement. Overweight and out of shape, Huntley couldn't help anyone, except himself to the dining room table. But he was a good sort. Anthony almost felt ashamed that he got Huntley in such messes on the home front. *Almost.* It was just too much fun for him to feel a significant dose of remorse over it.

Anthony opened his mouth, intent on informing Huntley he was a little too late to be of assistance, but changed his mind. That would only deflate his pudgy friend's good intentions. Dragging the unwilling ragamuffin down the street and in the direction of the nearest gaol should convey to Huntley he had the situation well under control. The scamp was going to be turned over to the authorities. Maybe it would cure the foul-mouthed little cretin of his bad habits. Anthony had never heard such a slew of trash come out of such a small package. And Anthony thought *he* had the creative language market covered. He didn't come close! The little guttersnipe's array of colorful verbiage and stinging epithets made even Anthony's cheeks flush—and he was a jaded roué, no less.

Huntley came to a staggering stop in front of him. "Don't . . . worry . . . Wh-Whitfield," he said between gasping breaths, his jowls heaving. "I . . . will . . . save . . . you."

Anthony clapped his friend on the back. "Good God, man, take a breath, will you?"

The wriggling thief in his arms chose that moment to attempt another getaway, obviously under the misguided impression Anthony was distracted.

This time, however, Anthony wasn't so lucky or so quick. A booted foot connected solidly with his kneecap. He fell to the ground, taking the little bugger with him.

"Why, you blighted worm!" Anthony hissed, holding his knee with one hand and his captive with the other. "I ought to throttle you. Let's see how tough you are when you have to spend some time incarcerated behind the dank walls of Newgate. The chaps there would certainly enjoy a morsel like you."

Beneath the brim of the cap, the boy's eyes widened in

fear and alarm. "I ain't goin' t' Newgate! I'll kill y' first!" The lad struggled wildly to get away.

"Huntley, for God's sake, now would be the time to do something!" Anthony exclaimed as a small fist glanced off his nose.

So of course Huntley did the only thing a man of his immense size could do.

He sat on the lad.

Air whooshed from the boy's lungs, and he gasped like a landed fish.

"You are killing the lad, Huntley," Anthony pointed out as the throbbing in his knee abated and he slowly stood up.

Huntley looked chagrined. "Well, I'm having some trouble rising, you see."

Anthony put a hand out to his corpulent friend and quickly realized he would need both hands and a lot of back muscle to move a mountain. Finally, he managed to get Huntley to his feet, but the thief still did not move.

"Sweet mother of Jesus, you've done in the brat!" Anthony accused as he knelt down next to the motionless body. Then the boy drew in a deep, shuddering breath, and Anthony felt a great deal of relief.

"Mock me, Whitfield," the big man returned, "but I saved your blasted hide, and I don't intend on letting you forget it."

Anthony spared his friend a brief glance. "Remind me to thank you later."

Huntley harumphed as he cast a nervous look at the captive. "Should I get the constable?" he inquired. "That grimy lad has murder in his eye."

Anthony was about to say no to getting the constable, that he would take the boy to the authorities himself. Then a single beam of moonlight shined down upon the pale, frightened face staring up at him. "Well, I'll be double damned," he murmured, dumbstruck.

Huntley leaned over his shoulder. "What is it? What's the matter?"

Slowly, Anthony reached out a hand, but the thief backed away. "Calm yourself, lad." Then he whisked the dark cap off his attacker's head. "Or should I say, calm yourself, *lass,*" he corrected as a mass of silky black hair spilled out of its confinement. The girl glared at him through a fringe of thick, dark lashes that framed beautiful, wide-set, *angry* blue eyes. He shook his head. "Bloody hell, I was felled by a girl. I say, that is indeed a blow to my masculine pride."

"I'll give y' another blow, an' this 'n will hurt a lot more, y' piece o' pig offal!"

Anthony roared with laughter. "Oh, boy, this is a hoot!"

"Wot's so funny?" the girl demanded.

"You are, sweet," Anthony returned in a deep voice, unable to stifle his male appreciation for the delicate beauty before him. But if looks could kill, he would be dead by now. "Oh, yes, you certainly are. You are a delightful, heaven-sent gift."

"Don't get no ideas, mister." She scooted back another inch. "I've cut the bollocks off men bigger than y'."

Anthony arched a mocking eyebrow. "You have, have you? Well, I will endeavor to keep that in mind."

"Y' takin' me t' Newgate now?" She raised her chin and tried to keep her bottom lip from quivering at the thought of such dreadful incarceration. Every criminal knew about the worst prison in England. One was effectively considered dead if sent there. "I ain't afraid of you or the law!" she declared, but Anthony was able to clearly see the lie for what it was. Her show of bravado impressed him.

He put his hand out to help her up, but she slapped it away. Brass. A goodly supply of it.

"I don't need yer help," she told him curtly, rising up on shaky limbs.

With the girl now standing in front of him, Anthony looked at her with new eyes, trailing his gaze down and then up. "How could I have possibly mistaken you for a boy?" He circled around her. He stopped and backed up to take another glance at the nicely rounded buttocks accentuated by the male togs she wore. "How, indeed?" he murmured. "You're quite a petite thing, aren't you?"

"So wot? I don't need t' be a big lummox like you t' take care of business."

Anthony ignored her sarcasm and gave her a lazy smile. "I would imagine your size comes in handy. You are small and most likely quite a slippery package."

"Bet yer blasted hide I am!" she told him with a confident nod of her head. "An' I woulda given y' the slip, too, if I hadn't sneezed." She ran a finger under her nose, obviously trying to bring her point home. "Y' were bloody oblivious until then. It was probably that stinky perfume yer wearin' wot caused me t' sneeze," she added, wrinkling her nose at him.

"That stinky perfume, as you refer to it, baggage, is called cologne, and it is one of the best and most expensive scents in all of England, perhaps even the world."

Her look told him she was clearly unimpressed. "Well, la-de-da. It still stinks."

Anthony couldn't help being amused. The girl was indeed a piece of work, and he knew exactly what he wanted to do with her. Surprisingly, it didn't involve anything sexual—a rather startling revelation for a renowned lecher. He resisted the urge to check his trousers and make sure all his parts were in working order.

He studied his captive. "Being a common pickpocket is not the type of profession I can picture someone like you being in."

"Oh, yeah?" She raised one rather shapely brow. "An' in yer high-and-mighty opinion, wot profession should I be in, then?"

"One with a lot less clothing, of course," Anthony returned bluntly.

"Y' lousy sod!" she hissed, her fists clenched at her sides.

"My, but you are a testy little thing." Taking her cap, Anthony put it back on her head and tucked her hair underneath. "Perfect."

"For wot?" she demanded.

"For a hanging," he replied, silently chuckling when her mouth dropped open. "Now, be a sweet lass . . . hmm, that does stretch the bounds of one's imagination, doesn't it?" He shrugged. "Well, just come along."

Taking her by the arm, Anthony dragged her along before she regained her senses and started another fight. Her wits came back to her before they took six steps.

"Where y' takin' me?" She struggled futilely in his grasp. "I have a right t' know!"

"You have no right to anything, criminal, so keep walking."

Huntley came up behind him. "Where *are* you taking her, by the by?"

"To a friend," was all Anthony would commit to.

"So why not tell the girl, then?"

Anthony shrugged. "Don't bloody well feel like it, that's why. Let her sweat it out." Not stopping, he looked over his shoulder and said, "I'll see you later, Huntley. I have no time for an evening of joyful debauchery at present. But I'll catch up with you tomorrow. We can get corked and see how many of the good Lord's commandments we can break in one night."

Chapter Three

"Ah, Holmes, good evening!" Anthony said jovially to Alec's stunned butler as he swept into the dimly lit foyer dragging the reluctant, dirty, and extremely angry thief behind him.

"My lord?" croaked the gray-haired butler. "May I help you?"

"Yes, my man, I would like to see Breckridge. Is he at home?" Anthony cocked a thoughtful brow. "By jove, how remiss of me to ask such a question. Since when is the jolly toiler not home? He would probably get the dry heaves if he went too far away from his paperwork." Anthony didn't give the butler a chance to reply as he headed resolutely down the hallway. "Never mind, Holmes, I'll find him. I'm sure I know exactly where he is."

A swift knock on Alec's office door was all Anthony gave before barging in. To his complete and utter amazement, Alec was not in the room. The man's day ran like clockwork; it was so routine ... and so boring it could make Jesus weep.

"Well, don't I just look the jackass?" Anthony murmured. He threw over his shoulder, "Say one word, brat, and you will find yourself getting closely acquainted with Messrs. Cockroach and Spider and wearing shiny metal ankle bracelets."

When blessed silence reigned, Anthony turned back to continue the search, confident his command would be heeded and the girl would not dare defy him. But defy him she did, digging in her heels and refusing to move.

He tossed a look over his shoulder telling her what he thought of her defiance. Her expression told him she didn't give a rat's ass.

"I'm warnin' y' to stop draggin' me around or I can't be responsible for wot I'll do."

Anthony swiveled on his heel. "Is that a threat, my sweet flower of happiness?" She glared, and he grinned. "And just what might you do to me, I wonder?"

"No need t' wonder anymore, y' blusterin' bully."

She smiled at him. The mere gesture should have sent off alarm bells in Anthony's brain, but he was momentarily transfixed, which was why he didn't notice when she lifted her knee and rammed it into his private parts.

He howled and crumpled to the ground. "I ... say ... ," he groaned, "not well done ... of ... you."

"Serves y' bloody right," she told him, fierce satisfaction making her almost giddy. That would teach him to mess with the premiere pickpocket in all of London. "Maybe next time y'll think twice."

She turned to make a grand exit, freedom beckoning her—and walked right into a human brick wall. Strong hands grasped her upper arms, keeping her from falling on her bum.

"For criminy sake! Watch where yer goin', y' big oaf!" she huffed, shaking off the manacles which gripped her and taking a step back.

Head angled downward, she noticed the legs in her line of vision. One brow rose in curiosity, and a slight shiver ran through her at the muscular thighs now set out before her—muscles not even the elegant and obviously expensive trousers could hide. God almighty, they really were indecent—those legs, that was. What normal man had legs like that?

Slowly, her gaze moved upward, taking in every detail: the lean waist and flat stomach, the huge chest and arms, the incredibly broad shoulders, a strong, chiseled jaw with a curious little dent in the center—which for some odd reason she found captivating.

From there her gaze moved along the slope of a perfect nose and touched here and there on equally perfect bronzed skin. At last, her perusal came to a halt at his eyes.

Oh, those eyes! God's teeth, they were as black as pitch—piercing, intense. Beautiful.

He cocked a brow. "Hello." His voice was low, deep, and it vibrated along her nerves in the strangest way.

"Hello," she returned in an equally low voice.

Who are you? Alec wanted to ask, but decided it was better to gird his loins for whatever insanity Whitfield was preparing to spew.

He tilted his head to the side to look at Anthony, who was on the floor with his back against the wall, appearing somewhat pale. No surprise there. Alec had seen the entire incident, and frankly, he was more than a little amused. The scrawny lad was daring; he would give him that. But what had caused the fracas? And what exactly was going on? Who was the lad and why was Whitfield here with him? Why was Whitfield here at all, for that matter?

"Having trouble?" Alec dryly inquired, staring dispassionately at Anthony.

"Of course not, old man," Anthony returned in a sardonic voice. "What would give you that ghastly impression?"

"Your current position, perhaps?"

Alec was treated to a withering glare.

"I happen to be admiring your floor, is all. Is that a crime?" Anthony ran a hand over the smooth surface. "Italian marble?"

"I never asked."

"Pity."

Alec crossed to his friend and put his hand out. "What are you doing here?"

Anthony clasped it and stood up, then proceeded to brush himself off. "You always were one to get right to the point."

"It's a good thing at least one of us can," Alec muttered. "Now, about that point?"

"Ah, there's the rub." Like a whip, Anthony reached out and grabbed the back of the lad's shirt as he began to creep away. "Not so fast, baggage. You're the guest of honor here."

"Ooh, I hate y'!" Anthony's captive told him through clenched teeth.

"I'd like to say the feeling is mutual, but oddly enough I find myself entranced by your viper tongue with those creative epithets you spew like little pearls of wisdom, and those hostile glares which tell me you'd like nothing better than to boil me in oil." He shrugged. "Call me crazy. I guess you just remind me too much of myself."

If it was possible for someone to look like a thundercloud, Alec thought, the lad did.

"Now y' crossed the line comparin' me t' a silver-spooned, momma's boy, don't-know-when-t'-stay-off-a-dark-street fool like yourself."

Anthony's face darkened. "Listen, you bloody little roughneck, I'll—"

"Leave the lad alone, Whitfield," Alec cut in, positioning himself between the two combatants. "He's far too young to be exchanging barbs with you."

Anthony barked with laughter. "Oh, don't get taken in." He nodded at his blue-eyed captive. "This one's as cunning as they come—a veritable gem of the underworld."

Alec scowled. "What the hell is up your ass? He's a child. I've known you to do things I can't quite comprehend, but I've never known you to make war on those who were not your social equal—or at least old enough to take their licks."

"You've got this all wrong, my friend," Anthony returned with righteous indignation. Pointing to the lad, he added, "This one could wipe the floor with me. I'm a babe in the woods in comparison."

"What happened to being charitable?" Alec asked. "You gave me a long-winded speech about it, remember?"

"Yeah, be charitable why don't y'?" the lad chimed in.

Alec was amused. Anthony, however, was not. "I *am* being charitable—little do you know. But that brings us back to the crux of the matter, doesn't it?"

"Which is?"

Anthony put his hands on Alec's shoulders and turned him around to face the lad. "*This,* old man, is your charity case."

Alec shrugged off his friend's hands and wheeled around. "What in God's name are you talking about? What are you up to now?"

"I ain't no bleedin' charity case!" the lad practically shouted in Alec's ear.

Something in the boy's voice caught Alec's attention. Before he could figure out what it was, however, the child lunged at Anthony. Alec barely caught the lad before he began pummeling his friend. As aggravating as Whitfield could be, and as much as Alec sometimes wanted to lay his hands around the man's throat and squeeze until he gurgled, he really couldn't allow Anthony to be attacked while in his home. Now, if they went outside. . . .

Alec shook his head as a string of epithets poured from the child's mouth. He couldn't prevent a slight smile. The lad was inventive.

"I rest my case," Anthony drawled as he sauntered past Alec.

"And just where the hell do you think you're going?" Alec demanded as he watched his friend move to the front door.

"Look around you, old boy. There's chaos, panic, and disorder—my work here is done."

"You aren't leaving this child here with me!"

Anthony stopped. "Oh, but I am," he replied with a wicked grin as he turned halfway around. "You said, and I quote, 'You pick the poison, Whitfield. You can figure out what would be a worthy thing for me to do. I leave it up to your good judgment,' end quote. Well, I have done that very thing—*boy, have I ever.* I should earn a knighthood from the queen for this one."

"I bloody well did *not* say that, you imbecile!"

Anthony shrugged. "I was interpreting. Besides, I can't be expected to read your mind, can I? My mission has been accomplished, and I am free, I tell you, happily, blissfully unfettered." He made it to the front door, which was promptly opened by Holmes, who then averted his gaze, staring at the ceiling as if studying a fresco at the Sistine Chapel. "Oh, I almost forgot to impart the most important information!"

Alec shot a glare in Anthony's direction. "And that hopefully would be what dark alley you'll be in later so that I might beat you to within an inch of your life?" he asked through gritted teeth, irritated by the perpetual humor etched on Whitfield's face.

"Touchy, aren't we?" Anthony taunted in a droll voice. Alec growled.

Anthony raised a placating hand. "Don't get your hackles in a knot. I just thought I should tell you to be ever vigilant of our little friend and perhaps hide your valuables—only for the time being, I'm sure. At least until the child is sufficiently repentant." To the individual in question, he said, "If you're thinking of running away, baggage, just remember the dark walls of the gaol beckon you. I wouldn't press the extent of my good nature."

"What are you talking about?" Alec asked, a slithering suspicion creeping along his spine.

"Let's just say your guest has a tendency to take that which does not belong to him."

Alec shot a quick glance down at the child in his arms, completely missing the soft features, silky skin and crystal blue eyes, before looking back at Anthony. "Are you saying he's a thief?"

The lad stiffened. "I ain't just any thief! I'm the best thief in all of London!"

"You heard it from the horse's mouth," Anthony dryly remarked.

"Bloody hell," Alec muttered.

Anthony turned to leave, but stopped once more. "Oh, and one last thing!"

"What now?" Alec grumbled. "Is he an axe murderer, as well?"

Anthony shook his head, unholy amusement lurking in the depths of his eyes. "How you do go on. No, he's not a murderer of any sort." Then Anthony wrinkled his brow, his gaze moving to the thief. "You're not, are you?"

"Wouldn't y' like t' know," was the saucy reply, promptly followed by a tongue.

"Oh, now, that's delightful. Perhaps some day I can teach you a place where you can put that thing to better use." His gibe earned him a ferocious scowl. Looking at Alec, he said, "Well, friend, the only other thing I can say is that you're in for a big surprise."

"What kind of surprise?" Alec demanded.

A sly smile curved the corners of Anthony's lips, as if his surprise was something that could change the entire course of history. "Remove the hellion's cap and you'll find out."

With that said, Anthony bid them a fond fare-thee-well and strolled out the door, whistling merrily as he went.

Chapter Four

"Someday I'm going to throttle him," Alec muttered angrily as the door closed after Anthony.

"Not if I get the bloody rotter first."

The words brought Alec up short. He had almost forgotten the child he still held.

Releasing the lad, Alec stepped back. Apparently, Whitfield had grated on someone else's nerves, if the slitted glare aimed toward the front door was any indication. Alec didn't doubt the boy's vow was quite sincere.

Alec ran a hand through his hair, feeling decidedly uncomfortable. What was he supposed to do now? Anthony had to be crazy—well, that was a given. But what could the fool have been thinking to drop the lad off here? And a professed thief, at that? Did Whitfield actually think Alec would be able to rehabilitate the boy?

Well, he thought grimly, he had asked for this, courted it with every rotten word out of his mouth. He should have known Anthony would take his words and twist them to suit his own end. Regardless, Alec couldn't blame anyone save himself for this mess. He must have been insane to let Whitfield make such a decision.

He gave the strange child a hesitant smile. Now what?

Furrowing his brow, Alec eyed the lad closely. Something wasn't right, but he couldn't quite put his finger on it. The boy's head barely reached Alec's chest. He was skinny in a puny, defenseless sort of way, making Alec fairly certain the lad had to fight for every scrap he got. Under those circumstances, Alec could well understand the need to steal, though he couldn't condone it.

The boy's limbs appeared almost . . . what? Too delicate? Soft?

His face was the real puzzle; smooth skin, slightly tan— and not a whisker in sight. How old was the lad?

Narrowing his eyes a shade more, Alec took in the pert nose, dark brows, high cheekbones and wide-set eyes— blue eyes, the most unusual shade of blue. They were . . . beautiful.

Anthony's words hit Alec with screaming force.

Remove the hellion's cap.

Slowly, his arm rose, his hand reaching for the cap. The boy stepped back, out of his reach.

"I'm not going to hurt you," Alec softly vowed as he reached out once more.

The boy flinched as Alec's fingers touched the edge of the cap. Staring into the wide, wary eyes before him, Alec slowly pulled the knit cap upward.

A mass of silky, blue-black tresses spilled down over slender shoulders and framed a petite, exquisitely sculptured face. The effect was devastating.

Now Alec knew what that *something* was that he couldn't put his finger on: *He* was a *she.*

And bloody lovely, at that.

Had Whitfield said he was in for a surprise? It was far too mild a description for what Alec felt.

In dumbfounded fascination, he watched the girl put a hand up to her hair as if she, too, were surprised by the revelation. Appearing charmingly self-conscious, she grabbed the heavy tresses and swept them off her shoulders. Stray tendrils escaped and framed her delicate face, accentuating high cheekbones and exotic eyes. She blew the silky wisps away out of the corner of her mouth.

Without realizing what he was doing, Alec brushed back the wayward strands of her glossy dark tresses with the tips of his fingers. She flinched, and he pulled back, his senses returning.

Distancing himself, he said, "You're a girl."

Belatedly, he realized how inane that remark sounded. It wasn't as if she didn't know.

A flush touched her cheeks. "So wot's it to y'?" Her voice came out a squeak. She frowned and cleared her throat.

He had to blink a few times to snap himself out of his daze. "I'm just surprised. I wasn't expecting it."

She braced her legs apart in a defensive stance, hands on the swell of her gently rounded hips. "Well, get used to it."

How had he thought her a boy? The only excuse was that he hadn't been looking for it. And there was Whitfield's presence, which had the ability to sap rational thought.

"It wasn't meant as an insult," he said. "It was simply a moment of shock. Especially after Anthony mentioned that you were a . . ." He stopped.

Folding her arms across her chest, she leveled him with her sapphire gaze. "A thief?" she finished for him.

The young woman appeared touchy about the subject.

Alec decided a subtle retreat was in order. "Do you have a name?"

"Yeah."

"And?"

"And wot?"

"What's your name?"

"Why d'ya wanna know?" *It's not as if I'll be around long enough for you to use it.*

"Necessity. Unless you'd prefer 'hey you.' "

He was a right clever one, she thought, eyeing the good-looking stranger. Without wanting to, she had begun to develop a grudging respect for the mountain of muscle who had defended her, a stranger, to his friend, Lord Muck. Then again, who wouldn't respect such a big piece of man, even if he did seem oddly gentle for his size. What somebody like him could do in a gang like hers would be nothing short of a miracle. No one would dare bother them with him around. Unfortunately, he looked every inch the aristocrat. What a bloody shame.

Well, if nothing else, he certainly was an improvement over his boorish friend.

From the looks of his surroundings, he was a rich bugger. She had already eyed a few items that she decided to make her own. All and all, the day wasn't turning out so bad.

"M' friends call me Fox," she finally replied. "I guess y' can call me that, too."

Alec stared at her for a moment, gauging her expression to see if she was fooling him. The look in her eyes said she was telling the truth. But Fox? What kind of name was that?

"Fox is your given name?" He hoped it wasn't.

"Yeah, it's m' given name. The one the lads gave me."

"The lads?"

"M' gang."

"Your gang?"

"Are y' goin' t' keep repeatin' everythin' I say?"

"Yes." Alec shook his head. "I mean, no." He was starting to confuse himself. "So Fox isn't your real name, then?"

She took umbrage to that question. "M' real name? Wot are y' gettin' at? That it ain't a good name?"

"No, that ain't—*isn't* what I'm saying." *Yes it is.* It wasn't the right name for such a winsome child-woman. "I just wanted to know what name you were given when you were born. I'm guessing it wasn't Fox."

Her face turned mutinous. "I wouldn't know. M' mum died when I was born, and m' pa run off after that."

"I'm sorry to hear that."

The girl shrugged.

"So who took care of you then?"

The wary look in her eyes told him that she was uncomfortable with his line of questioning. "Why?"

She gave him her back and made a point of studying the artwork on the walls. He wondered if she was familiar with Renoir. Then he realized how idiotic that thought was. Of course she didn't know the painter. He had to remind himself this particular belle inhabited an entirely different social circle than all the people he knew.

"I'm just trying to find out more about you," he replied as he moved to stand beside her, studying her profile.

She shrugged. "I stayed at a bunch of orphanages until I was old enough t' take care of m'self."

Curiosity made him ask, "How old was old enough?"

Another shrug. "Seven or so."

"Seven?" Alec choked, trying to comprehend what it must be like to be a child out on the mean streets of London at such a young age.

She added, "Give or take a few months. I don't know

exactly how old I was 'cause I don't know when I was born. The nuns at the first orphanage could only guess."

He felt sorry for her. He had known only the finest things life had to offer, the best schools, gourmet food at every meal, servants to anticipate his every whim, society galas to attend where people had no more to worry about than the latest gossip and the cut of their clothes. And he had money—lots and lots of it. But what did this girl have? And who or what decided that one person should have it all while another person had nothing? Somehow it just didn't seem fair. Look at what such a life had wrought for the girl. She was a common thief. No home. No family. A daily struggle for survival, just waiting for her next mark, and living hand-to-mouth.

"Now, wot's that look for?"

Alec's eyes met her snapping ones. "To what look are you referring?"

"That look!" She swung around to face him. "Don't y' dare pity me! I'm just as good as y' are! Maybe even a damn sight better!"

"I wasn't pitying you."

"Y' bloody well were! That's it, I'm outta here!"

She marched past him. She didn't need or want anyone's pity. She had done just fine on her own, thank you very much! She wouldn't allow herself to think about the fact the man had thus far been nice and hadn't looked down his nose at her like most of his class.

She stopped at the door, and the damnable butler promptly opened it for her. Oh, yeah, the gray-haired snob was just dying for her to leave, probably worried she would take off with the family silver. She should stay just to spite him. But she didn't have time for this fancy place or its inhabitants.

She stood on the threshold, hoping her high dudgeon

would continue to take her feet down the stairs and out to the streets she knew so well. Oddly, she remained where she was, her limbs suddenly leaden.

Turning around, she asked, "Well, aren't y' goin' t' tell me I have t' stay or somethin'?"

Alec hid a smile. The girl was reluctant to go. Good. He, for reasons unknown, didn't want her to leave just yet. She was a rather intriguing package. But he would prefer that she stayed because she wanted to.

He sunk his hands into his pockets and shook his head. "No."

"No? Just like that?"

"Just like that. I'm not your keeper. I can't tell you what to do."

"But wot about yer friend?" she asked, and then frowned. "He said I was t' stay here t' pay m' debt for tryin' t' filch his wallet. He said either I stay here or I go t' Newgate. It was m' choice. It weren't a hard decision t' make."

"This isn't a jail and you didn't try to rob me, so I have nothing to say in the matter."

"Oh," she said in a small voice.

Into the lengthening silence, Alec asked, "Would you like something to eat?" The girl could obviously use a good meal. She was little more than skin and bones. "Cook is preparing duck," he added when she hesitated. "And I will honestly tell you that no one makes it as succulent as he does." He shrugged. "But I'll understand if you want to go. I'm sure you're a very busy girl."

"Bosh. Yer coddin' me, right?"

The thunderstruck look on her face was beyond charming. "No, I'm not *codding* you."

She glanced around the room. Alec followed her gaze as it moved to the massive chandelier above her head and then to the darkly paneled walls where huge oil paintings hung. Her gaze traveled up the red, deep-pile carpet on the stairs, then to the gleaming brass rods securing the carpet, before finally coming to rest on him once more.

"Yer sure?"

"Yes." He grinned. "I am."

She stared at him a long moment before finally shrugging. "Well, all right, then. Why not? A meal's a meal, I always say."

"As do I," Alec murmured, amused. He was sure that had to have been the most ungracious acceptance of a dinner invitation he had ever received. But he was also sure that the evening was bound to be more interesting than he had originally anticipated. The girl had a certain freshness about her that he found appealing. He had long since grown tired of the mundane conversation and frivolity of the women of his acquaintance.

He turned to Holmes, who still held the front door open. "Please inform Cook that we are having a guest for dinner and have a place set for Miss . . . ?" He looked at her expectantly.

She stared back at him with a raised eyebrow, contemplating the repercussions of telling him to take a flying leap off the bloody Bow bells if he was so against calling her Fox. But the persistent growling in her stomach reminded her that she hadn't eaten in a long while and it would behoove her to hold her tongue. Besides, what was a name anyway?

"Kate," she barely pushed past her lips. That was the name she had been called up until the day she had taken to the streets. She didn't feel like a Kate, though. That name sounded like it belonged to someone refined, a lady, not some urchin from Whitechapel.

"Please prepare a place for Miss Kate at the table, if you would, Holmes."

The request, Alec noted, had Holmes sniffing, his expression dubious as he peered at Kate. His butler couldn't completely mask his disapproval as he turned his attention back to Alec.

"As you wish, my lord." Holmes hesitated. "Does Miss Kate want to, er, freshen up before dinner is served?"

Holmes's question was met with derision from one lively urchin who glared at him as if willing the floor to open up and suck the butler into the black abyss.

"Why y' askin' him?" She pointed in Alec's direction but glared at Holmes. "Y' afraid t' speak to me, y' overbearin' windbag?"

Alec hid a grin. The hellion had certainly put Holmes in his place. His butler wasn't a bad man, not by far. But he did have the tendency to look down his nose at people who were not of a certain social station. Most likely he didn't realize what he was doing—or at least Alec hoped he didn't. He hated to think he had a snob for a butler.

Yet Holmes had asked a legitimate question. Perhaps the girl *did* want to get cleaned up.

As if knowing he, too, had a questioning look in his eyes, she slowly swiveled her head in his direction.

"Yes?" she drew out the word.

Alec hesitated. She had taken offense at Holmes's suggestion, so she would probably lop his head off should he ask it as well. But her look told him that she already knew the tenor of the situation, so he said cautiously, "You're certainly welcome to . . . use the facilities."

Kate found her anger abating in light of the big man's obvious discomfort. How could such a giant appear so boyish? She wouldn't have believed it possible if she hadn't witnessed it with her own two eyes. And she knew he wasn't trying to be insulting—unlike his uptight and annoying butler. No, he was just trying, in his own way, to be courteous. It was a rather sweet gesture—if one liked sweet gestures, that was. For her, she didn't care one way or the other. She was used to the rough side of life where people only took and definitely never gave. And as much as that tough part of her said she didn't need or want to *freshen up*, another part of her thought it would be divine to feel clean again. It had been so long since she had been able to bathe in anything other than the rain or an occasional fountain. To be able to do so at leisure would be pure, blessed heaven.

Her clothes, however, were an entirely different matter. She glanced down at her patched shirt with the new tear at the collar and her made-over men's trousers with grime from her tussle in the streets stained on them. Blast, she had just scrubbed them in the fountain near Westminster two nights prior! Now they were ruined, and she doubted they would last through another washing.

Her eyes rose and locked with pools of liquid chocolate, melting and undeniably sweet. Her self-consciousness flew away in the face of an unnamed sensation that began to swirl in the pit of her belly.

"Look, you don't—"

She cut across his words. "Where do I go?"

He furrowed his brow. "Excuse me?"

She gave him an impatient look. "Where do I go t' get cleaned up?"

"Oh . . . upstairs," he replied. Then he turned to his butler, who still had the front door open as if he were hoping his employer would change his mind about having her stay for dinner. "Holmes, please show our guest to my room," he instructed.

"Your room, my lord?"

"Yes, *my* room, Holmes."

"Are you sure?"

He scowled. "Yes, Holmes, I'm sure," he replied in a clipped undertone.

Kate wanted to tell his lordship she didn't want to go with his rotten snob of a butler. The man grated on her nerves. She could find a bowl and some water on her own. However, she doubted the giant would want a stranger roaming around his house. And frankly, the place was much bigger on the inside than it appeared on the outside. She would probably only succeed in getting lost.

With complete ill grace, Kate marched along behind the butler, following the pompous ass up the stairs. She cast a quick glance over her shoulder to find herself the object of close scrutiny. She looked away, suddenly discomfited and not knowing why.

Once she and the butler reached the top of the stairs, her thoughts moved elsewhere. Ten years of living on the streets had molded her into a cunning criminal. With an expert eye, Kate catalogued the expensive knickknacks lying out on an ornate half-moon table in the hallway, a huge, equally ornate mirror hanging over it.

A beautiful porcelain figurine of a young woman in a gown of white with small pink roses graced the table—as well as many other objects that were just asking to be taken. But the figurine was what held Kate's attention. The woman's little mouth was red, and on her cheeks there was just a hint of color. Her glossy, dark hair was pulled back off her delicate face by a single pink ribbon. Her expression was thoughtful, as if thinking of a beau—or maybe a good burglary, Kate amended to suit her own lifestyle, silently chuckling.

Without thinking, she reached for it. She just wanted to

touch it, to hold it perhaps. But before her fingers could even wrap around it, the bloody butler slapped her hand.

"Do not touch the valuables," he dictated in his oh-so-superior tone of voice.

"Ye'll keep yer bloody paws off me if y' know wot's good for ye. I don't take kindly t' people touchin' me."

The man was completely undaunted by the threat. "Do not touch anything. I shan't tell you again." Then he continued on down the lengthy hallway.

Kate heaved a resigned sigh, taking one last look at the pretty figurine before reluctantly following Holmes.

Chapter Five

"I'll be standing right outside these doors, so don't think to remove anything. Do you understand?"

Kate returned Holmes's glare. His complexion was bilious. Obviously, he was distressed at having to do his employer's bidding. *Good!* She hoped he choked on it.

With some muttering, he pushed open the double-door entranceway to the master bedroom, leveling her with another look that she assumed was meant to intimidate her.

When hell freezes over.

Obviously under the impression she wasn't listening, he repeated, "Do you understand?"

"Yeah, I understand," she replied as she breezed past him and entered the room, too irritated to take notice of her surroundings. Swiveling around to face him, she added, "I understand that y' are a pompous, pig-headed, pain in the arse, and I would like nothin' better than t' toss y' as far as I can throw y'. Now, if y' don't bloody mind, *I* have a dinner t' attend." With a self-satisfied smile, she slammed the doors in his face, quite pleased with the resounding noise it made. She could still hear him muttering on the other side that she had better be out in five minutes or he was coming in to get her.

"Yeah, yeah, yeah." She waved a dismissive hand at the door and turned around, getting her first good look at the master bedroom. "Sweet Mary in heaven," she whispered in awe, making the sign of the cross.

Kate had always believed she possessed a rather creative imagination, but in all her wildest dreams she had never pictured anything as glorious as his lordship's bedroom.

It was a huge, dark-paneled affair. Deep-burgundy velvet drapes, tied back with gold tassels from two tall windows, revealed panels of ivory silk shot with threads of gold. The massive four-poster bed was saturated in shades of rich, dark wine, as were the chaise and wing chair. A bookshelf lined one entire wall from floor to ceiling, and a toasty fire blazed in the hearth.

Moving to the bookshelf, Kate ran a finger over the smooth, leather-bound volumes as she walked along, peering at the titles but not knowing what they were because she couldn't read. His lordship had no doubt read every book on the shelves and then some. He probably had the best education money could buy, going to one of those fancy boys' schools where you had to dress up all the time and bow to everyone.

She walked over to the marble fireplace, ablaze with crackling logs shooting up orange and blue flames. Kneeling down, Kate warmed her hands. Many a cold night she had wished for a roasting fire to lie in front of, to gaze into its glowing embers and dream of a better life, one where she had the security of a home and loving parents.

Instead, she had been cursed to wander the streets, always wondering where her next meal would come from. It was a day-to-day battle, one that made her feel much older than she was.

She had imagined the kind of homes wealthy people lived in, feeling envious and sometimes bitter, asking herself why some people got everything while others got nothing. It just wasn't fair. It hurt to be looked down upon, as if she were at fault because she was an orphan. She felt somehow to blame for her circumstances and wondered why being poor meant she was a lesser being. There had been a few times when she and the lads had tried to improve their lot in life, without success. People continued to kick them back down, never willing to give them a chance.

She hadn't wanted to be a thief, hadn't planned to live that kind of life. But what else could she do? No one would hire someone like her for a regular job. She couldn't read, couldn't speak right, didn't know which fork to use or how to hold a knife. Basically, that left her with three options: a life of crime, begging, or becoming a street trollop. The second option didn't sit well with her. She wouldn't be a charity case! And she wasn't going to be one no matter what the blond-haired bugger said! As to the third option . . . she didn't want anyone pawing her. No, she would rely on the one thing she had learned to do well, which was to pick pockets with a stealth that had earned her the name Fox.

There was only one misconception she had fostered, and that was the belief she was really tough and mean. In truth, she was scared more times than not. And she was tired of being hungry, and wondering where her next meal would come from, and living every day repeating the last, for things had not improved as she had gotten older.

The changes in her body—as meager as those developments were in her eyes—had started attracting unwanted attention. She had found it necessary to hide whatever female attributes she had under binding, male togs and a dirty face. She tucked her hair under a cap because she couldn't bear to cut the one thing that made her feel feminine.

Standing up, Kate stared at her reflection in the mirror above the fireplace. The face looking back at her was drawn and pale, and her eyes, which had seen far too much brutality and unhappiness, appeared much older than her young years.

She was a mess. She ran her hand over a smudge of dirt on her cheek, rubbing it briskly to get rid of it, but seeming to do nothing more than make it worse. She dropped her hand in disgust.

Her hair, which was in the same shape as the rest of her, hung limply around her shoulders. It needed a good cleaning, but that was a luxury she rarely got.

Kate turned away, not wanting to see any more. Instead, she let her gaze roam.

In the center of the room lay a mountainous bed—and mountainous was the only apt word she could find for it. One actually needed stairs to climb up onto its lofty height. Kate imagined sleeping on it would be akin to sleeping on a cloud. She had the greatest urge to nestle herself in its comfort. She couldn't imagine having the bed all to herself. At least six people could fit on it and probably have room to spare. But that was six normal-sized people, she thought, revising her original body count down to the one rather large and well-muscled man who rightly was the actual occupant of the bed. Heat rushed to her cheeks as she found herself picturing him in the bed, wondering what kind of nightclothes he wore. Did he wear any at all?

Where did that thought come from?

Certainly the man was tall, dark, handsome, and yes, somewhat intriguing, but lord in heaven what possibly had possessed her to think of him in his natural state? Probably the fact that she stood in the middle of his bedroom staring at his bed.

Kate berated herself for her silly thoughts as she moved around the bed, its looming presence hard to ignore. Nonetheless, she walked over to another huge piece of furniture, the bureau. She imagined its size was a necessity in light of the enormous bed. Anything on an average scale would be dwarfed next to that bed.

God's teeth! Why did her mind keep returning to that bloody bed? It was unnatural!

She concentrated on the bureau, running her fingertips along the fine wood, admiring the workmanship that had gone into it.

Without thinking, she picked up a beautiful, gold-handled brush off the top. What kind of money the man must have to own something as frivolous as a hairbrush that looked as if it had been dipped in gold. She wondered if it would fit underneath her shirt without making too large a bulge. How much might such an object get her on the streets?

Shaking her head, Kate put it down, deciding it really wasn't a practical item to steal. In the world she lived in, who would be interested in such a thing?

Next, she stepped over to the armoire, not realizing her time was ticking away and she hadn't even begun to clean up. Curiosity got the better of her. She had never seen the inside of one of these fancy homes, and most likely, she never would again; so she had to take the opportunity afforded her. Who knew, perhaps behind that drawer or in that closet would be a treasure worth taking, something that would make her little sojourn into the lives of the West End upper class worth her time.

Opening the doors of the armoire, Kate sucked in her breath. Never had she seen such an extent and array of clothing, stunning emerald greens and sapphire blues and pristine whites. How many black jackets could one man own? It seemed black topped the list as his favorite color.

With reverence, she removed one of his shirts. It was silky and cool to the touch. She rubbed the material over her cheek, forgetting the dirt on her face. Kate was sure it would be pure bliss to wear something so wonderful against her skin.

A faint scent rose up to greet her, musky and very masculine, invoking pictures of the man who wore it. The fragrance suited him.

Closing her eyes, she inhaled deeply, reveling in all the new sights and smells she was experiencing in her temporary haven.

Tapping his finger on the arm of the chair, Alec glanced out the window, then to the mantel clock, stopped tapping, thought he would have a drink, decided against it, began tapping again and then heard the bong of the clock tolling the quarter hour. He stood up and just as quickly sat back down.

Where was the girl? She had been gone more than a half hour. What could be taking so long?

He debated going to check on her, but reminded himself that she was with Holmes. . . .

Holmes, who had taken an immediate dislike to her.

Taking two stairs at a time, Alec hurried above stairs, fairly certain he would find blood had been shed, and wondering who, besides himself, would mourn Holmes's passing. Alec refused to acknowledge that he was behaving like a besotted schoolboy—and an overprotective one at that. Lively little Kate could be *his* protector; she was that fiery-tempered.

Holmes was nowhere to be found when Alec reached the hallway, and that surprised and somewhat alarmed him. It was passing strange not to see the man standing sentinel outside the bedroom. Perhaps, then, he was inside the room with the girl? That was not beyond the realm of possibility. It was patently obvious Holmes didn't trust Kate. It would be just like the man to stand over her shoulder while she tried to freshen up.

Belatedly, Alec realized he should have asked Mrs. Dearborn to take charge of the girl. His housekeeper was unflappable and one of the most likeable people he had ever known. And from the look of things, the girl could use a woman's gentle ministration. She was beleaguered and far too hardened for her young years. How old was she? he wondered yet again.

Things were too quiet, Alec thought, more than a bit panicked by the images that presented themselves as he neared his bedroom.

Stepping up to the door, he pressed his ear to it, not stopping to think how ridiculous he looked or how he would explain himself should he be caught with his ear to his own door.

No sounds of mayhem came from inside. Then again, he didn't hear *any* sounds coming from inside. Was the girl still in there? Had she perhaps ducked out? But why would she do that? He had offered her a decent meal, and from the looks of things, she probably hadn't had one in a long time. The promise of food should be incentive enough for her to stay, at least until she had eaten her fill.

Alec's concern grew as the silence lengthened. He hesitated, uncertain of his next move. For a man that supposedly reeked of decisiveness and action, he was decidedly *indecisive*.

He considered his options: stand in the hallway like an imbecile and pretend he had lost the diamond stickpin in his cravat should someone come upon him *or* raise his knuckles to the door and hope for a response.

However, the last thought came after his hand was already on the knob and he was slowly opening the door.

The sight that greeted Alec halted him in his tracks. Kate stood before his armoire, the doors flung wide, holding one of his silk shirts to her nose. It should have struck him as odd, perhaps even alarmed him, to find that she had been rifling around in his things. But it didn't. He could hear Holmes reminding him that she was a professed thief and that her person should be thoroughly checked for valuables before she was allowed to exit. But at that moment Alec could not have cared less. He had no desire to break her reverie. He wanted just to watch her.

Eyes closed, she was oblivious to his presence. Her expression was angelic, serene. He took that unobserved moment to study her, realizing he hadn't imagined the soft curves trying unsuccessfully to hide under the rags she wore. He specifically remembered the gentle sway of a beautifully rounded backside that he had watched with rapt fascination as she walked up the stairs with his butler. He had been frankly shocked at his unusual behavior. He had often admired the allure of the feminine figure but had always behaved respectfully, not blatantly ogled a woman like a drooling moron. The worst thing was the dark-haired waif should be about as far from enticing as one could get. She was dirty from head to toe. Yet her delicate beauty was unmistakable. Again, he found himself wondering her age.

He suddenly realized his thoughts of work had disappeared. Though he certainly had plenty to do, at that moment, it didn't seem so urgent. His responsibilities would still be there later, and the next day, and the next. His life was about as routine as it could get. His zest for living had been sucked dry by a mountain of paper.

Kate was so absorbed in her whimsical thoughts that she didn't realize she was no longer alone until a slight chill prickled her skin.

Her eyes snapped open, her gaze flying to the doorway to collide with the amused dark eyes of his lordship.

With an inward groan, she realized she still held the man's shirt in her tightly clenched hand. She whipped the offending garment behind her back as if he might have possibly missed the fact she had it *and* missed the fact she had been sniffing it like a fool *and* missed the fact she had been going through his things.

"I hope I'm not disturbing you." His voice was low and calm.

Kate released the breath she hadn't realized she had been holding. He wasn't angry.

She cleared her throat and then licked her suddenly dry lips. "No, y' ain't disturbin' me."

He stepped into the room. "I should have knocked."

"It's yer room." Kate saw him flick a glance down to her arms. Knowing she was acting foolishly, she released her hands and brought the shirt in front of her. She had been trying to manufacture an excuse as to why she had been in his closet and why she had taken out his shirt. But what possible reason could she give? She decided on the truth—in a much abbreviated fashion. "I guess yer wonderin' why I have yer shirt?"

He leaned his shoulder against the doorjamb and crossed his ankles. "No, I wasn't wondering."

Kate was dumbfounded. How was it possible he wasn't wondering what she was doing in his closet? Nobody liked a snoop. Certainly *she* couldn't tolerate them. And why wasn't he mad? He knew she was a thief, after all. He could easily assume she had been trying to steal something.

"I shouldn't have been in yer stuff," she rushed out, hastily moving to the closet to hang up the now thoroughly wrinkled shirt. "I was just, er, lookin' for a towel." Not original, but it would do. "Yeah, I needed a towel, so I decided t' look around for one."

The man pushed away from the door with the grace of a predatory cat, and Kate thought he must have finally lost his temper, seeing her concocted story for the lie it was. His expression gave nothing away, however. She wondered if he was the kind of man who didn't raise his voice or show any outward sign of his anger, but instead struck like a viper. She had seen that type—and they were the most dangerous.

Unconsciously, she took a step back. She couldn't have blinked if she wanted to. He lifted his arm. Was he going to hit her now? She watched in horrified fascination as he came closer and closer, his arm outstretched. . . .

And he walked right past her and opened the door behind her.

Kate hadn't paid that door more than scant attention. There were too many other things that had caught her eye.

Her shoulders sagged with relief. She willed her limbs to move as he gestured a hand to the room now revealed— the room Kate had come up to use but had forgotten about in light of other more interesting pursuits.

Her mouth dropped open to an unbecoming extent. She had never seen a bathing tub inside a house.

Kate didn't know how to describe the various fixtures

because she'd never seen them before. When his lordship turned the knob over the tall, bowl-shaped contraption and water gushed out, she jumped back nearly a foot, certain he had performed a miracle.

"Inside plumbing."

"Inside *wot?*" Kate took a tentative step toward the spout that poured water.

He chuckled. "Never mind. It isn't important."

He ran his fingers under the spigot . . . and then splashed her with cold water. Little sprinkles rained over her face.

"Hey! Cut that out!"

The smile on his face was positively wicked—and dash it all if he didn't have a pair of crescent-shaped dimples!

"What? Afraid of a little water, are you?" he teased. "And here I thought you were so tough."

Arms akimbo, Kate replied, "I am tough."

She tried to paste a mean expression on her face. She even narrowed her eyes in the hopes of proving her point. But the dastardly man had the nerve to merely smile wider—a smile that certainly had a devastating effect on her senses. He had such an innate sense of humor. "An all-around good sort," she could hear Weasel say.

Another spray of water hit her in the face then.

"Ooh! I said t' stop!"

That should have ended it.

It didn't.

He splashed her again. "This is what you came up here for, isn't it?"

Two can play at this game! Kate decided.

Marching over to the sink, she swiped her hand through the water. Not very elegant, but it got the job done as droplets smacked her antagonist in the face and sprinkled over his pristine clothing.

As soon as the deed was done, she couldn't believe that

she had acted in such a manner. She wasn't some child to be playing a silly game. She was the leader of the toughest gang in the East End—or so she liked to tell people. She had an image to uphold, a certain standard, even if no one could actually see her cavorting like . . . like what? A normal person? Enjoying herself for one moment? Really, where was the harm in that?

The harm was that his lordship's home was a temporary haven, and she wasn't the lady of the house or even some honored guest. She was just a scruffy street urchin living hand to mouth and, for a few hours, relying on the kindness of a massively built member of the ruling class with a charming, boyish smile.

Kate's eyes darted from the faucet to his face. "I can't bloody well believe I did that," she said in a voice barely above a whisper.

He brushed the few droplets off his jacket. "I'll survive, I assure you."

The sound of someone clearing his throat had Kate whipping around to see who had entered the room. The scowl returned to her face.

The double damned butler.

She had hoped the smarmy blighter had gotten sucked out into the universe never to be seen again. And his steady glare told her that he had wished her the same unhappy fate.

"I apologize for leaving the young *lady,* my lord, but I had to settle a squabble between two of the maids."

"That's all right, Holmes," his employer said as he turned off the spigot.

"Is aught amiss?" the butler then asked, his look saying he wouldn't doubt if there was.

"No, everything is fine," he replied, his gaze lifting to Kate's. He stared at her rather oddly, as if she had grown another head. "But I've disturbed our guest, and she hasn't had time to freshen up. So I will adjourn to my office. If you would be so kind as to bring me a bottle of wine from the cellar, Holmes, I would appreciate it."

The mountain stepped past Kate and ushered his reluctant butler out of the bedroom. He stopped in the doorway. Knob in hand, he looked over his shoulder. "Take your time, and feel free to use anything you need." Quietly, he shut the door behind him.

Kate stood there and stared at the closed door.

Chapter Six

Alec gazed aimlessly out a window in his office. His papers lay forgotten on his desk. He still couldn't believe he had engaged in such a ridiculous act as splashing water on the girl. He wasn't quite sure what had come over him. He wasn't known for his spontaneity. His sister was fond of telling him that he needed to loosen up a bit, to stop working so hard and relax. She would be surprised at the manner in which he had taken her advice.

"My lord?"

Alec turned to find his butler and the cause of his confusion framed in the doorway.

"*Miss* Kate has finished freshening up," Holmes informed him, casting a quick, disparaging glance at the person in question.

"Thank you, Holmes." When his butler remained standing there, looking as if he had no intention of leaving, Alec added pointedly, "I'll call if I need you."

Holmes hesitated another moment. Then, with one last chilling look at Kate, he turned from the room and closed the door.

Alec shook his head, torn between annoyance and amused exasperation. Was this Holmes's way of showing his loyalty? By thinking to protect him from a slip of a girl? Alec had never seen the man so bent out of shape. But his thoughts about Holmes lasted no more than a second as he found himself alone with Kate.

"Please, have a seat."

He watched her closely as she moved to the nearest chair and plunked herself down unceremoniously. She didn't look at him. Instead, she eyed the room slowly as if cataloguing its belongings. Well, he couldn't expect that just because she had washed away some of the dirt from her face and hands, she was no longer a petty criminal.

She had certainly cleaned up quite nicely. Beneath the smut that had so recently covered her face lay a creamy complexion with skin as smooth as a summer peach. She had managed to obtain a ribbon and had tied her hair back with it, which only emphasized her sculpted cheekbones, pert nose, full lips and big, blue eyes. As for the rest of her, namely her clothing, there wasn't much that could be done.

Alec suddenly pictured her wearing his silk shirt that she had been clasping so tightly. Of course, the shirt would fall to her knees, and the sleeves far past her wrists. She certainly would look devilishly cute in it, though. Of that, he had little doubt. That startling observation made him wonder where his general ambivalence to all things unrelated to work had flown off to.

Mentally, Alec shook himself to clear his unproductive thoughts. Still, he couldn't help but speculate about the girl, which again brought up the question of how old she was. He decided that would be the first thing he would ask her—delicately, of course.

Should he offer her a drink?

He strode to the sideboard, intent on at least getting himself something—something strong. He poured a healthy glass of whiskey, took a swig and then turned to his guest. "Can I offer you anything to drink?"

Kate pretended to be looking at a picture on the wall next to him when his dark gaze swiveled in her direction. She tried not to stare at him, but ever since she had been in the man's presence she had felt odd. She really didn't know how else to describe it. Whenever his gaze settled on her, her stomach flipped over. Maybe it was just nerves. She was in a strange environment, far out of her element. As well, the only men, or rather *boys,* she knew were the lads in her gang. And she didn't think of them as being different from her; their basic goals were the same.

So what was with this giant anyway? And where did he get that build? Of all the wealthy lords she had encountered—and she had picked the pockets of quite a few of them—not one had muscles like this one did. Most of the rich gents she had robbed had pointy noses, fat limbs, and pale, ghostlike faces. They certainly weren't built like a mountain with bronzed skin and mesmerizing onyx eyes, thick, nearly shoulder-length hair, wide shoulders, and tapered waist.

And that backside . . .

Sweet Mary, his buttocks looked as hard and as strong as the rock of Gibraltar.

That observation brought every thought to a screeching halt.

He's speaking to you, ninny!

Guilty, Kate's gaze shot to his. Oh, Lord, she had been caught gaping! "Wot did y' say?"

"I asked if you wanted a drink." Alec raised his glass, noting the flush on the girl's cheek. "You're old enough to drink, aren't you?" It seemed an easy enough way to get an important question answered.

She frowned. "I'm bloody well old enough t' do anythin' I please."

That didn't answer his question.

"I'm sure you are," Alec placated. "But what kind of person would I be if I got a child drunk?" *Or lusted after a child, for that matter.*

Good God, what was the matter with him? He had been too long without a woman and it was beginning to dull his senses.

Still, there was nothing wrong with wanting to know her age.

Then, why not just ask her?

Because it would be impolite, that's why.

But a child wouldn't care.

Alec silenced his inner voice and waited for her response. Again, he was thwarted when Kate shrugged and replied, "Well, don't worry yerself over it. I don't drink anyway, never liked the taste of the stuff." She made a face to emphasize her point.

Swirling the liquid in his glass, Alec walked to the chair across from her, trying to think of another angle to get her to divulge her age.

"So you don't drink? Well, that's rather commendable, I must say. I don't drink much myself, but I do like an occasional glass of whiskey as you can see. I had my first drink when I was about sixteen, I think. How about you?"

Kate frowned. What did it matter when she had her first drink? It had only been the one time, and she had practically gagged on the poisonous stuff, promptly deciding that that was the first and last experiment she would have with liquor.

Was this the typical conversation the blue-bloods had with one another? Well, for one night she could play along.

"I had a mug of bitters once, about four years past." She grimaced. "I barely got it down m' throat before it came rushin' back up again."

It took Kate a moment to realize how that sounded. Did she actually just tell the man that alcohol made her heave? She had never paid attention to small details like that. But suddenly, and in this man's presence, she felt minutely conscious of such *details*.

"It's an acquired taste," Alec remarked. *How old are you?*

"I guess," Kate returned. *Next subject!*

Alec crossed his legs, giving the appearance of casual indifference. "Maybe you were just too young to appreciate the taste—not that I don't agree with you. I don't like, er, bitters myself. But sometimes things taste differently from one year to the next." *Liar.*

What a corker! Kate thought. Brussels sprouts still tasted like brussels sprouts no matter what her age. She had hated them at the orphanage, and she imagined if she had to eat one at that moment, she would still hate them.

"If y' say so," she replied, deciding to agree not to disagree.

Alec gritted his teeth. *Just ask her how old she is and bloody well get it over with!*

"You know, this brings me to a question—"

"Wot's your name?"

Alec blinked. "My name?" *It's not a hard question.* "Yes, my name. How remiss of me. You did tell me yours, after all. Well, it's Alec."

Hoping to move on to more important subjects, he opened his mouth, but a knock at the door halted him.

Frustrated, he called out curtly, "What is it?" *Bloody hell. So close.* "I mean, come in."

It was Holmes. "Dinner is served, my lord."

"We'll be right there." Stifling his curiosity for the time being, Alec stood up and moved toward the girl. Staring down at her impish face, he held out his hand for her. "Shall we?"

His guest looked at his proffered hand, a frown pleating her smooth brow as she glanced up at him. "Shall we wot?"

Alec couldn't help himself; he grinned. "Shall we go to dinner."

"Oh!" She sprang from the chair, completely ignoring his offer of assistance. "Hell's bells, why didn't y' just say so?" She cocked her head back, stared at him . . . and smiled in return.

Alec was truly bewitched. Those lush, glorious lips turned up in a smile, how they transformed her face. She was already quite lovely, but her smile thoroughly captivated him. Her mouth was unbelievably full for such a petite face. He had the most incredible urge to kiss her. In fact, his head slowly bent toward hers without realizing he was doing so.

Two things happened at that moment: First, his butler, who Alec was really beginning to think deserved a sound thrashing, loudly cleared his throat. Secondly, the firebrand, whose eyes got wider and wider the closer he got, inciting his senses even more by unconsciously licking her lips, chose that moment to speak.

"I could eat me a horse."

Alec chuckled softly. With some reluctance, he straightened and placed her hand in the crook of his arm. "I could eat one, as well."

Chapter Seven

Dinner was a disaster.

Kate stared down at the array of forks next to her plate and wondered why on earth anyone needed more than one. *Leave it to rich folks to make a big deal out of something so simple,* she thought dismally, her nerves taut.

She slid a glance at the man sitting at the head of the table. He smiled, and its warmth touched her like the last rays of an autumn sun. She had to look away for fear he would see she wasn't as brave-hearted as she would have him believe. She was a fool to think this would be easy.

Her cheeks burned with embarrassment for a solid hour. Although she didn't get a single reprimand from her dinner partner, Kate still knew she was clumsy. She had never felt so unknowledgeable or unworldly in her entire life. She always mastered what she set out to do and never gave up until she got it right. Now she was getting tripped up on things like which fork to use and putting the fancy, linen napkin on her lap, which she knew to do only because she saw his lordship do it first.

The worst thing was her humiliation had to be witnessed by Holmes the Hateful, who seemed to lurk around every corner. Kate would look up to find him raising a dubious eyebrow at something she was doing or shaking his head. He would move a dish, passing her chair and muttering, *Use the fork,* when she went to pick up her meat with her hands. Or he would refill his lordship's wineglass—after the man had taken only three sips—making a point to pass her chair again, grumbling, *Good Lord, take human bites, will you?*

Kate wished Falcon were there with her. Falcon would know exactly how to handle Holmes without getting upset over it. Unflappable, that was Falcon.

They were two of a kind, she and Falcon. They had a special bond, one only death could sever. Kate didn't consider Falcon one of the lads, but more an extension of herself. Whatever Kate lacked, Falcon made up for, and vice versa. They were alike in every way but one, and that one thing was insignificant.

Holmes and his baiting were momentarily forgotten when one of the kitchen maids placed a batch of fat rolls next to Alec. Heat rose off their crusty tops. Normally, Kate hated bread; she ate so much of it. But the soft balls of warmth in the basket looked so delicious. Certainly they couldn't be anything like the three-day-old loaves she usually ate.

"Guv'ner," she said, addressing Alec. When he cocked a single bemused eyebrow at her, she hastily revised, "I mean, Alec."

He chuckled. "Yes, Kate?"

She thought to ask him for a roll, but realized she could reach them herself. "Never mind."

Standing up, Kate leaned across the table in front of him and snatched a roll out of the basket. She heard a gurgling noise and turned to find the butler swaying as if he was about to faint. A hard, leaden knot settled in her stomach as she sat back down with her treat.

What now?

Clearly unable to hold his tongue any longer, Holmes said brusquely, *"Miss* Kate"—miss sounded like *mizz,* he put such emphasis on the word—"you are speaking to an earl. You *never* call him by his first name."

Trying to sound just as haughty as Holmes, Kate returned, "Well then, how am I supposed t' get him t' pass the bloody rolls or give me that brown stuff over there?"

"That *brown stuff,* as you so eloquently refer to it, is called gravy. And we do not ask his lordship to pass it to us. That is why there are servants. If you would but take a moment to look around, perhaps you would see them."

Kate did look, and they were there all right—boy, were they ever. Since when were so many people needed to help two people eat? Especially when those two people had full use of their limbs? But the answer to that question was unimportant in light of the embarrassment caused her by old prune face. Oh, how she would love to clout the man! But she would stuff the napkin in her mouth before she let on that he had hit a nerve.

"So I have t' ask someone t' get the brown stuff when I can reach it m'self?" she asked in a saucy tone of voice. "Is that wot yer sayin'?"

"Indeed," was the butler's crisp reply.

Indeed, she mouthed, mimicking him.

"Y' mean t' say that I can't just get up"—she stood up—"reach over here"—she leaned across the table—"and grab these fluffy-looking, mashed-up potatoes"—she did that, as well—"and help m'self?" Bowl in hand, she promptly plopped back down and hoped her expression thoroughly conveyed what she hoped he would do: drop dead. "That is wot I'm not supposed t' do?"

Alec leaned back in his chair and muffled a laugh as he watched the byplay between Holmes and Kate. He would be damned if the girl didn't hold her own against his staunch, suddenly prodding butler. She really was something to behold, a genuine firebrand.

He tried to figure out why he was so drawn to her. It was probably because in all his well-mannered and—what did she call it? Oh, yes—*blue-blooded* days, he had to do everything by the book. There were rules upon rules, plenty of them. Everything from how to address people of different social statuses, to the proper way to speak, to eat, to dress. And, of course, there was that lauded stiff upper lip. It was never good to show too much emotion. Yes, everything was done just so. God forbid a person exhibited an ounce of spirit or enjoyed being impromptu. Those things were definitely frowned upon.

It was ironic really, especially since there were those who thought wealth brought freedom when all it truly did was mire one down in a vast array of dos and don'ts. There were no gray areas.

The distinct sound of Holmes's teeth gnashing brought Alec's gaze back to him. His butler was effectively turning blue from their guest's unrepentant behavior. Alec thought he might have to get up and rap the man on his back since he appeared to be choking. Briefly, Alec wondered what Holmes would do if his lordship did what Kate had just done. Most likely the butler would collapse— in a dignified manner, of course—and then Alec would be forced to resuscitate the man. The idea was less than pleasing, so he decided not to tempt the Fates.

Alec looked to the other party involved in the fracas. Kate's glance swung from the bowl of potatoes to Holmes and back again. An unholy gleam lit her indigo eyes. She gripped the bowl tightly, testing its weight in her hands. He nearly choked on his wine. She wouldn't! Surely the girl wasn't contemplating throwing the bowl at Holmes's head?

Leaning toward her, he put his hands on top of hers. "He can be a bit stiff at times," he said only loud enough for her to hear as he gently guided her hands, and the bowl, back to the table.

"A bit?" Her expression was dubious.

"All right, I'll concede that he can be more than a bit. But he's not always like this."

"Wot y' mean t' say is that he's only behavin' like a sod 'cause I'm here. Right?"

The girl was quite intuitive. "He's just feeling out of his element," he told her, deciding the whole truth was not necessary. "He isn't so bad when you get to know him."

Kate gave him an unladylike snort of disbelief.

"Don't let him get to you. Holmes will lose interest if he no longer has a captive audience." And Alec hoped that was the truth. He should probably just order his butler to cease and desist, and he might do that if the situation went too far. But for the time being, Kate was holding her own and doing quite an admirable job. He sensed she enjoyed the verbal tête-à-tête. Oddly enough, he was beginning to believe his butler did as well.

She sat back, her face mutinous as she crossed her arms over her chest. "It'll be a bloody cold day in hell afore that prissy nabob gives over." She shot Holmes a glare. "I wager he won't be happy until he sees me backside."

"Well, let us endeavor to forget about the unpleasantness for a moment and instead concentrate on enjoying dessert."

Apparently that did the trick. His vivacious guest quickly relegated the problem with Holmes to a distant, unpleasant memory at the word *dessert*. She sat up straighter in her chair and watched wide-eyed as two servants came through the door with silver trays loaded down with various treats.

Alec made his decision quickly, pointing to a slice of pumpkin pie. As for his guest, it appeared the decision was a much more difficult one.

Her hand moved from one dessert to the next, hesitating, pondering, her face a mask of serious deliberation. Her obvious dilemma made her a joy to watch.

To him, dessert was just another part of the meal, his favorite part if truth be told. Nevertheless, he had never hashed over each treat the way Kate was now doing. But then again, he had always known he could have seconds, or even thirds if he was so inclined. He simply had to ring a bell, roll off a list of his desires, and within a short space of time, the items requested were laid out quite decoratively in front of him. For Kate, it must appear like a king's ransom.

"Maggie," he said to the serving girl, "why don't you just leave the tray here? Perhaps Miss Kate would like to sample several of Cook's wonderful treats."

The way Kate now looked at him made Alec wish. . . . He didn't want to look too closely at what he wished for when it came to this delightful sprite. Such small things made her happy. If only everyone could be so easily satisfied. Certainly the world would be a much better place, one in which he would enjoy living every day.

He almost laughed out loud as she snatched her treat from the tray. It was a veritable mountain of chocolate in a spongy cake with gobs of chocolate syrup and a cloud of whipped topping with a juicy, red cherry on top. She dug into the cake with relish.

For such a slip of a girl, she ate like three big men. In between mouthfuls, she plucked at a piece of blueberry pie on the tray, seemingly oblivious to the fact anyone else was in the room.

"Mmm, this is . . . so good," Kate said with her mouth full.

"I'm glad you like it," Alec returned, amusement tingeing his voice. Kate had caused him to laugh and smile more in the past few hours than he had in ages. Perhaps that was a part of the fascination she held for him, her reckless charm, making him want to get closer. "Would you like something else?" he asked as she scraped the last crumb from her plate. She didn't answer, but instead, leaned back heavily in her chair, her expression content and drowsy-eyed. Obviously, she was replete—at long last.

There was a tiny smudge of chocolate icing on the supple curve of her bottom lip that made him want to kiss it away. The impulse was so strong that he sat perfectly still, willing his self-control to kick in.

Slowly, her eyelids drooped, then closed altogether. Alec wondered if he should rouse her. But he didn't have the heart to do so. Besides, he was having a good time just listening to her muttering in her semiconscious state. She behaved in the manner of someone who'd had too much to drink. However, she wasn't talking incoherently about wanting another glass of rum like most drunks would do. Instead, she went on about pies, cakes and cookies as if they circled her head. Then she rested her hands on her stomach and muttered something about a plump Christmas bird and its trimmings.

He chuckled.

Wearing a slight smile, her head tipped sideways. A few

minutes later, her chest rose and fell in the measured rhythm of sleep. She snored quite delicately. Alec was content just to look at her.

His solitary contentment didn't last long as Holmes returned from the kitchen bearing a tray with cups, saucers and a pot of hot tea. He stopped dead in his tracks when he saw Kate slumped in the chair. The expression on his face was priceless.

"Don't say a word," Alec warned in a hushed voice as his butler opened his mouth with the obvious intent of making some kind of stinging commentary.

Standing, Alec moved to the side of the table. He stared down at Kate's inky black tresses, the urge to take a silky strand between his fingers nearly overwhelming.

Bending over, he put his arms underneath her knees and neck and gently lifted her. Straightening, he asked, "Is the guest bedroom clean and ready for company, by any chance?"

With the sigh of a man carrying heavy burdens, Holmes replied, "Yes, my lord. It was aired today, and fresh linens were put on the bed."

Alec nodded. "Good."

He headed out of the dining room and up the lengthy staircase, then down the hallway to the end. The guest bedroom was the last door on the right, directly across from his.

Using his booted foot to push open the door, Alec stepped into the darkened room and moved by memory toward the bed, laying Kate down as gently as he would a rare piece of porcelain. He then lit the wick of the lamp on the bedside table and gazed down at the delicate beauty highlighted by its glow.

He reached out his hand, wanting to touch her, remembering how soft her skin had felt beneath his knuckles when he had touched her in the hallway. He halted a hairsbreadth from her cheek, appalled at his sudden lack of control.

What was he thinking? The girl trusted him. And for the moment, she was under his roof and his protection. He would not act the lecher.

Reluctantly, he moved away from the bed and stepped over to the fireplace. Hunkering down in front of the cold hearth, Alec was glad to see a few chunks of wood stacked neatly to the side. Within a few moments, he had a fire blazing, and the relative chilliness of the room quickly dissipated.

For long moments, he stared into the orange and blue flames, thinking about nothing in particular, just enjoying a sense of contentment that was strange, yet satisfying. It dawned on him that he hadn't thought about his work all night.

Slowly, he turned to look at the angel-faced pickpocket who had succeeded in accomplishing such a feat.

He stood and moved toward the bed, as if propelled by a force beyond his control. He gazed down at Kate's sleeping mien with a sense of wonder.

What was it about her? She was different, *very different*, from the women he knew, but he didn't consider it a negative.

His mother, whom Alec loved despite her continual nagging, would tell him during one of her lectures on life that he needed to find the *right kind* of woman. She had to be of a certain social standard with a particular demeanor. Which, translated, meant the poor girl he chose to be his wife had to be a malleable creature whom his mother could completely dominate. That could be the very reason he had not yet entered into matrimonial bliss. That, and the fact he hadn't met a woman who incited his senses.

Regardless, his work kept him very busy. It also required him to spend a considerable amount of time in London—away from his mother and her machinations.

His sister, Jane, was not so lucky. She was subjected to their mother day in and day out. To Alec's dismay, Jane had become quite timid and relatively introverted. She didn't dare form an opinion their mother didn't give her. It was really a shame. His sister was quite pretty and very smart. If she could only get out from underneath their mother's thumb, she might be able to come out of her shell.

Alec had thought a great deal about having Jane come to London for the Season. She had already had her come out the year before, unfortunately without much success. Alec felt partially responsible for that. Perhaps if he had spent some time socializing with the vacuous and terminally boring members of Polite Society—a laughable term for a bunch of pompous gossipmongers—he would have been able to pave the way for a better entrance for Jane. But sidling up to a group of people who had the power to cut Jane to the quick if they were so inclined didn't sit well with him. He had wanted to handle it his own way, but he had mucked it up royally. Jane had accused him of scaring off any interested man by glaring at them as if marking them for future reference. Alec couldn't help it. The men were all self-indulgent fops, only interested in his sister for her dowry, which was considerable.

Still, Jane needed to meet more people her own age and spread her wings before she became a bitter, old spinster—which living far out in the country had a tendency to lend itself to. But to have Jane come to London meant his mother would come as well. A knot formed in the back of Alec's neck just thinking about it. As much as he loved his sister, he wasn't sure he could tolerate that much time in close proximity with his mother.

His musings were interrupted as Kate made a soft sound, snuggling farther into the pillow. It was a rather rewarding feeling to know he had saved her from the streets, at least for one night. He wasn't sure she actually wanted to be saved, but she was here and, for the moment, content.

Alec debated putting her underneath the covers, but decided it was warm enough in the room to use the quilt at the end of the bed.

Carefully, he removed her scruffy, mud-caked boots and deposited them on the floor, making a mental note to have them cleaned. Pulling the quilt up over her, he tucked it gently around her shoulders, which brought his face in close proximity to hers.

Her skin was bathed in the golden glow of firelight, and her long lashes made shadows on her cheeks. A lock of hair had fallen over her face. He knew an urge to sweep it away.

Why did she move him in such a fashion? They had nothing in common. Their worlds would have never touched had it not been for Anthony's interference. Maybe that would have been better—for both of them. What could he do for her, after all? What difference would one night make in a life such as hers? And what was she doing to his life? She roused feelings in him he hadn't known he possessed. It was as if she had awakened something long dormant inside him. He didn't trust himself to touch her, and that realization had him straightening up and stepping away from the bed.

Turning on his heel, he quietly exited the room.

Chapter Eight

Kate rolled over onto her back, hugging a fluffy pillow and purring like a fat, lazy and very contented cat.

What a wonderful dream she was having. She imagined she slept in an enormous bed of tender, downy feathers she wasn't required to share with three other orphans. No, she had it all to her little, old self.

She couldn't believe her brain had the capacity to conjure up anything so wonderful. Ah, the mind was a wondrous thing to allow her the freedom of deception. She really believed she was warm and cozy as she burrowed deeper into the pillow beneath her head and smoothed her hand over cool sheets, a clean, yet subtle fragrance tickling her noise.

Her eyes flew open.

Where was she? What was going on?

Disoriented, she sat bolt upright in bed, her heart racing. Looking down, she discovered she *was* sleeping in a magnificent bed with mounds of coverings to snuggle under and sheer silk drapes surrounding her in a soft cocoon of gentle color.

A flood of remembered events came rushing back to her.

Her dream had been reality. And currently, she found herself in a lush palace with a rather lush host.

Well, would you look at that? The evening hadn't turned out so bad after its rocky and somewhat frightening beginning. Who could have guessed she would meet an aristocrat, a bloody lord, she would actually, well, *like?* The lads would certainly have a laugh if they heard that. In the world she lived in, it was her and the lads against the wealthy blue bloods.

This blue blood, however, was rather unique, Kate thought as she shook off the last remnants of sleep and climbed out of bed. She flushed with embarrassment as she realized she must have fallen asleep at the dinner table.

Who had carried her to bed? She knew for a fact it hadn't been the butler. He would have deposited her outside the front door—and none too gingerly, she was sure. No, it had been his lordship. *Alec.* She knew those brawny arms could carry her without fail. Oh, how she wished she hadn't been oblivious at the time!

Heat flooded her cheeks, and she decided it was time to quit thinking about the man.

It was still dark out. Using the faint light from the embers in the hearth to guide her, she found the lamp. Fumbling with the sulfur matches, she finally managed to light the wick. Carefully, she replaced the delicate globe that held the light within its embrace.

With the gentle kiss of light illuminating her surroundings, Kate took a moment to glance around. Again, her imagination didn't do the place justice.

The room was done up in shades of mauve and gold. The bed, although not as huge as his lordship's, was quite large all the same. She curled her toes in the plush carpeting beneath her.

In the corner of the room, she noticed a beautiful rocking chair. It seemed incongruous with the rest of the luxurious surroundings. But it was what was draped over the chair that had her walking toward it.

Kate stopped in front of the chair and stared down at the lovely silk robe. The soft glow of light in the room brought out the fire in the burgundy color. It appeared almost liquid the way it flowed along the contours on the chair. Certainly it couldn't be there for her use. But why was it there if not for her to wear?

She gnawed her lip, admiring it for a long moment before hesitantly picking it up. Deciding there was no harm in trying it on, she slipped her arms into the sleeves. She pulled the robe close about her, sighing as she rubbed her cheek against the smooth silk.

Suddenly, she decided she wanted to feel the material against her bare flesh. If she had only this one opportunity to enjoy the luxury afforded her then she wanted to grasp it with both hands.

Taking off the robe, Kate laid it down gently upon the bed. Then she peeled off her grimy shirt. When her breeches were discarded and lay in a heap at her feet, she reached for the robe.

A glimmer of something caught the corner of her eye. Turning toward it, she saw her reflection in the mirror above the scroll-legged bureau. She couldn't recall having ever seen her full reflection before. Oh, she had found discarded, cracked mirrors and seen a portion of her face at angles, but never her whole face at once and most definitely never her body.

She stared at her image long and hard, almost turning away in disgust a few times. But some evil voice prodded her to keep looking, to catalogue the ashen, thin face with the two large, hollow eyes staring back at her, the sunken cheeks, the waist-length, black hair that hung limply about her small shoulders. She didn't want to look farther, but she did. She was compelled.

She eyed her dull skin. Her breasts—if she could call them that—were no bigger than the peaches Weasel often filched from the corner stand. Her frame was relatively straight, no curves to speak of. Her figure, or what there was of it, was boyish—at least in her opinion. She was an adult now and should have a woman's figure. Sadly, she realized that what she saw in the mirror was most likely the best she was going to get.

Finally, Kate forced herself to look away. Slipping into the robe, she let it take away her self-consciousness and soothe her troubled spirit. The few curves she did have seemed accentuated in the silky material.

She moved to the window, intent on getting a breath of fresh air, and nearly tripped on the hem of the robe. That was the only downfall of the beautiful garment. Obviously it had been made for someone much taller than she. As well, it had a strange but not unpleasant smell to it. In fact, the longer she smelled it, the more she liked it. A memory tickled the back of her mind. But she couldn't catch hold of it.

Kate drew back the sheer, ivory-colored drapes in front of the window, undid the latch and pushed the window open. A blast of cold air hit her. She shivered slightly, the silky robe no match for the evening chill. She could almost hear Rat saying it would soon be cold enough to freeze a brass monkey. And that was true. Before she and the lads knew it, winter would be upon them. And then their daily struggle for survival would increase tenfold.

Kate wondered how one night in his lordship's house could have made her forget how frosty the nights could be. It wasn't as if she had been off the streets for weeks. She hadn't even been off them for one full day. But Lord, at that moment, she didn't miss it at all. It was so nice to know she could close the window and curl up in a warm bed. She was about to do just that when she caught a movement by the shrubbery running along the side of the house.

At first, Kate thought her eyes were playing tricks on her. But when she saw a flash of something, or rather *someone*, she knew her eyes had not deceived her and that her sight was, as usual, quite keen.

"Who's there?" she called down in as loud a voice as she dared. She didn't want to wake any of the occupants of the house. Namely, his lordship.

Then a voice, equally hushed but which carried nonetheless, returned, "That you, Fox?"

"Weasel?"

"Yeah, it's me."

She leaned farther out the window, squinting her eyes to see into the darkness. A body came into view under a shaft of moonlight, then two, then three. "Wot are y' doin' skulkin' around out there?"

"Well, that's a fine bit o' thanks we get fer riskin' our bloomin' necks comin' here all ready t' save yer sorry self," Weasel returned sourly.

Kate's entire upper body hung out the window as she said in a fierce whisper, "Keep it down, will y'? Yer loud enough t' wake the dead!"

The lads muttered amongst themselves, obviously not

pleased to have been reprimanded when they were on a noble mission.

Weasel, who had always been in competition with her for the head spot as leader, fixed her with a hard stare, the rays of the moon glinting off his silvery gray eyes.

"So wot's goin' on?" he asked with a knowing expression. "Yer lookin' awfully cozy from where I'm standin'."

Kate fixed Weasel with her own glare, one that told him she knew what she was doing, and she wasn't going to take any guff from him. "Well, cozy ain't such a bad thing in the house of a rich lord, now is it?"

She was just trying to bluff her way along, to make it look as though she were cooking up a plan; when in fact, she had no intention of doing anything. Sure the place was ripe for the picking, but his lordship had been too nice to her for her to do something so low as to steal from him. She wasn't going to think about the fact her conscience normally didn't bother her about such things. Thievery was her life, after all.

This was different, however.

Still, for the sake of saving face, she would probably have to take a trinket. The lads would think something was up if she left without a single pilfered item. She would just have to make sure whatever she ended up taking wasn't too valuable or treasured. She wasn't sure how she was going to figure out if the chosen item was treasured or not, but she would do her best. Besides, she only needed to take a token. And perhaps she would even return it afterward. That was a good idea—if not a first in her book.

But his lordship was the first person she could remember who had treated her like a human being and not some street scum he looked down his nose at. He had let her sit at his fancy table and eat off his beautiful, gold-rimmed plates with silverware that would bring her a pretty fortune on the street. He had fed her his best foods, and when she had so rudely fallen asleep, he hadn't ranted or raved. No. He had carried her with care up to a beautiful room so she could sleep. And he had done all that knowing she was a criminal. In her book, that meant she owed him something. And if all that something could be was to leave his home the way she found it, well, so be it.

Her musings were interrupted as she heard Rat say, "So are y' comin' out or wot?"

The question caught Kate off guard. She hesitated, gnawing her lower lip. Was she going to leave? She knew without testing the door it wasn't locked. She wasn't a prisoner, nor apparently under supervision, which was surprising given her predilection—although she couldn't be positive Holmes wasn't standing outside the door like a bloody sentinel. Yet somehow she didn't think his lordship would allow that. How she knew that to be the case, she couldn't say. Call it her finely honed ability to read people. Call it a guess. The fact remained that she had only been invited to have dinner, and would probably already be back out on the streets with the lads had she not inadvertently fallen asleep.

But she *had* fallen asleep.

So, did she want to leave right at that moment with the lads? Did she want to give up the comfort of her solitary splendor, no matter how temporary it may be?

No. And no, again.

"I think I'm goin' t' stick around for a while an' see wot I can discover," she finally replied.

The lads mumbled amongst themselves for a moment; then Weasel peeked up at her. "Well, don't go gettin' too cozy in there."

"Or forgettin' about us out here," Rat added to Weasel's sentiment.

Kate felt a twinge of guilt. She really was quite comfortable and couldn't help feeling glad she wasn't outside with the lads huddling in the streets, trying to sleep on the cold, hard ground in some dirty, bug-infested alley.

"I'll milk this thing for all I can," she told them, trying to put their minds at ease about where her loyalty lay. "I'll probably only be given t' the mornin', and then I'll be sent packin'."

More low-voiced conversation ensued between the lads, and then Weasel said, "All right, we'll leave y' be. Y' know where y' can find us tomorrow."

Weasel and Rat scuffled away, their heads bent together. One person, however, remained standing at the spot below her window.

"Are y' sure yer all right?" Falcon asked her in a voice laced with concern. "That lord ain't holdin' y' hostage up there, is he?"

A gentle smile filtered across Kate's lips as she gazed down at the one person she knew was as close to a friend as she would have in this world.

"Don't worry. I'm fine. Now go on and catch up with the lads. I'll see y' tomorrow."

Falcon stood there for few more moments before turning and walking away. Kate breathed a sigh of relief. Of all the gang, Falcon was the one who would run headlong into the fray for her regardless of the consequences.

Although Kate felt somewhat confident that his lordship wouldn't do anything to the lads should he find them on his property—even if they did look decidedly suspicious— she still didn't want to take the chance. Perhaps he wouldn't treat trespassers with the same generosity of spirit he had shown her.

Taking one last deep breath of the crisp evening air,

Kate pulled in her head. She felt good, better than she had in a long time, in fact.

Feeling rather blissful and at peace, she swiveled slowly around on the balls of her feet. Her spirits were so buoyed she actually twirled more than swiveled, as if she was a woodland sprite dancing in a magical forest.

As she swung around, her breath caught in her throat. Her gaze met and locked with a pair of intense ebony eyes. Startled, she fell back against the window, her buttocks smacking down on the sill.

Her hand flew to her mouth as she gasped, "Holy mother in heaven! Y' scared me!"

"I'm sorry. I should have announced my presence," Alec said, his voice quiet as he leaned his massive bulk against the doorjamb. "I thought I heard something, and since I couldn't sleep, I came to investigate. I didn't want to knock in case you were asleep," he explained.

There was something disquieting about the way he looked at her. Had he heard her conversation with the lads? Was he purposely not saying anything to see if she cracked and said something to him first?

She imagined that if he wanted to, he could appear quite fierce, as if his size alone wasn't enough to intimidate those who were not stout of heart. Oddly enough, he didn't intimidate her.

She shook off her nervousness and replied, "I guess I was knackered. Been busier than a blue-arsed fly, I have." She didn't feel it necessary to tell him what she had been busy doing. She figured he already knew.

He chuckled, and she wondered what she had said that was so funny.

"I see," he murmured. "Well, when I came in and saw that you were so far out the window, I thought if I said anything it would startle you right over the edge." His smile was gentle as he added, "And that was the last thing I wanted to do."

Kate's cheeks warmed. "Oh," was all she could say, her heart still beating rapidly, but for an entirely different reason.

"You weren't thinking of jumping, were you?"

It was only a joke, but she took it seriously, shaking her head vehemently. "No! I was just . . . gettin' some fresh air," she rushed out, hoping he hadn't overheard her conversation with the lads. "I couldn't sleep either," she added with a shrug.

"Are you all right?" he asked, the concern evident in his voice.

Kate remembered how she had moments before thought that Falcon was her only friend in the world. She wondered if it would be presumptuous of her to consider his lordship sort of a friend as well. It was really too early to tell.

"R-right as rain," she returned, stammering slightly and wondering at it. "How long were y' standin' there?"

Long enough to get thoroughly distracted by the enticing, softly rounded backside that had been presented to him upon his entering the room, Alec silently answered. And Kate thought *she* had been startled? It was nothing compared to the eye-opener he had received seeing her dressed in nothing more than a skimpy, silk robe—*his* silk robe as a matter of fact. Its long length cascaded far past her slim calves. Small, delicate feet peeked out from underneath the hem.

As she had stood at the window, he had been mesmerized, his gaze following that glorious derriere as it wiggled left and right when she shifted her feet. He knew she had been talking to someone, probably one of the lads from her gang. He, she or they were below in the shrubbery.

Alec hadn't heard what had passed between them, but he could only imagine what it was. Perhaps he should be concerned, but he wasn't.

He suddenly realized he was staring at her while she waited for an answer to her question. He shook his head to clear it—which didn't help.

"I'm sorry, what did you say?" God, she looked just as sexy from the front as she did from the back. She was so petite, tiny really.

Sweet Jesus, was he thinking licentious thoughts about a child? Just how old was she? He was plagued by that one blasted, unanswered question.

"I asked y' how long y' were, er, standin' there."

He paused before answering. "Only a moment. Why?"

She shrugged, her fingers twisting the belt of the robe. "Just curious."

Curiosity was a commodity Alec had in surplus at that moment. He told himself to leave, but his feet were rooted to the spot.

His gaze, which should have remained focused on Kate's pixie face, instead moved slowly down the length of her scantily clad figure. She probably didn't know that the robe had parted quite considerably up top. He wondered if he should tell her.

Well, it is not as if you can see anything.

True, but I'm fairly certain she wouldn't want to show that much skin.

Smooth, creamy skin, at that. Don't tell me you didn't notice?

I noticed all right. But I have to stop noticing.

Why? You're a hot-blooded male.

I'm a gentleman first.

"Bloody hell," he muttered out loud.

Kate stared at him quizzically. "Wot was that?"

"Nothing," Alec murmured, pushing away from the

door and stepping farther into the room. Some demon made him say, "I must admit you look rather fetching in my robe."

Her eyes widened. "This is . . . yers?"

He nodded. "I thought you might want it if you decided to take a bath. It was the smallest one I had. Not small enough, I see."

Kate's cheeks flamed at his perusal, which immediately made her disgusted with herself. She did not blush! She was tough, fearless, a leader.

So what caused her to forget that whenever this man came near?

A kind word . . . a sweet smile . . . and deep, dark eyes, that was what.

She realized the scent she had noticed earlier on the robe was his. It made her feel sinfully delicious wearing it. Added to that was the very real possibility it had last lain against his flesh. Or had another woman worn it? The thought shouldn't bother her.

But it did.

"Thanks fer lettin' me use it," she said awkwardly.

The look he gave her made her stomach do a little flip-flop. "You're welcome." It seemed as if they stood there for an eternity before he spoke again. "I was heading to the kitchen for something to eat and perhaps a cup of warm milk to help relieve this bout of sleeplessness I'm having."

Kate wondered why he stared at her as if she might understand the reason he couldn't sleep.

"Since we're both up, would you care to join me?"

Kate's brow puckered. "Milk? Wot will that do?"

"Well, if the tale holds true, then it should help us both get to sleep."

Kate couldn't figure out the correlation between milk and sleep, but she had a proven way to help the man get to sleep if that was all he wanted.

Coming to a decision, she boldly took him by the hand. "Follow me."

Alec readily obliged, although her tiny hand taking his caught him by surprise. His hand held hers loosely, worrying that he might crush her delicate bones within a grip used to clasping hearty men and pummeling Whitfield in the ring.

He followed without question as she led him to a chair that sat in the corner of the room. She asked him to sit, which he did—all too eagerly. Curiosity began to get the better of him. What was the little minx up to?

He waited, tension making his muscles tauten and his heart slow to a heavy, painful thud within his chest. He realized he was gripping the arms of the chair and forced himself to release his hold before he snapped the wood.

God, he wanted her to touch him.

She stood before him, staring down at him with those startling bluer-than-blue eyes, biting the inside of her lush lip, making him want to pull her down into his lap and take that lip between his own.

The air felt charged and thick. She gave him a halting smile . . . and stepped back. He nearly groaned out loud. It appeared she had only meant for him to relax in the chair. The fact that he felt deflated with the knowledge and that his body ached with need disgusted him. He was acting like a randy, green lad. He had come to check on her. That was all.

Still, he had been so certain there was more to her request.

And quite suddenly, he discovered there *was* more, as she knelt down between his thighs.

Could she mean to . . . ?

No, not possible. But that didn't keep the mental picture from entering his head. A bolt of desire shot through him, so swift it was startling and so strong he prayed the evidence wasn't showing.

Where is your touted restraint? Get a grip, man!

"What are you . . . ?" Alec began, only to be silenced when she put a finger to his lips.

"Ssh," she softly whispered. "Just close yer eyes and try t' relax."

"If you insist," he murmured, gazing down at her, wondering if he should resist. But resist what? The question was shrouded in mystery. Suddenly he was a man who loved a mystery.

"I insist," she softly replied.

For a moment, she appeared uncertain, her eyes widening like a frightened doe's. Just as quickly she straightened her shoulders, and the uncertainty was gone. Then she raised her hands, reaching for him. Alec closed his eyes and waited, his nerves strung tighter than a bow.

Good Lord, he silently groaned as gentle fingertips pressed at his temples, massaging in small circles at first, then becoming firmer. He wasn't sure exactly what he had been expecting.

Yes, you were, you dirty-minded—

Alec cut himself off. No matter what he might have been expecting, he was still content. Oddly enough, he was glad his fantasies hadn't materialized. Somehow it wouldn't have been right.

Inch by inch, his body began to relax. "God, that feels good," he murmured.

A tingle of pleasure ran through Kate—and it wasn't

merely from his words. Her body was hot and cold in turn, and her mouth was suddenly dry. She didn't understand the sensations coursing through her body, and she certainly hadn't expected she would feel such things when she had made her offer.

Many was the time she had given Falcon the same treatment, a remedy for headaches and the sleepless nights that plagued all of them on a regular basis. They weren't the healthiest lot. That called for someone who could do a bit of doctoring.

Kate wasn't sure where she had come up with this particular remedy of massage. Perhaps she had seen a bona fide doctor perform it. Although, realistically speaking, she didn't think she had ever known any bona fide doctors, only swindlers who didn't care about their patients, but were merely hoping to fill their pockets with blunt.

Most likely, she had made up her remedy, like so many other things she did—and said. However it came about, it obviously worked—at least from the blissful look on his lordship's face.

"Is that helpin'?" she asked, thinking he might already be asleep. She knew she was good. Falcon told her so often enough.

"Yes, that's helping more than you know." His voice was low, husky. "You're quite good at this. Do you do it often?"

"Aye, too often," she answered, keeping up the slow, methodical motion of her fingers.

His eyes slowly opened, and he stared down at her. A look crossed his face. Anger? Pain? Confusion?

Disappointment.

He put his hands over hers; they were so warm and large.

Then he pulled her hands away from his face and stood up, bringing her with him.

"Thank you," he murmured. "I'll see you in the morning." A moment later the door closed behind him.

Kate stared at the door, wondering what she had done, and why she suddenly hurt inside.

Chapter Nine

When Kate awoke in the morning, sun poured in the window, bright and warm. Rolling to her side, she looked at the delicate crystal clock on the bedside table. It was after nine. Glory, she had never slept this late. She and the lads were up before the sun rose. An empty stomach and equally empty pockets didn't afford them the opportunity to lie around all day. That was a luxury left only to the rich.

The rich!

As if on fire, Kate sprang out of bed, feeling awkward because she had overstayed her welcome. No one had said so, of course, and knowing his lordship, no one would. But she knew it was time to go.

She would put her clothes on, scoop up some little trinket for the benefit of the lads, tip her hat and tell his lordship she was much obliged for his hospitality on her way out the door.

She willed her feet to move, but they wouldn't obey.

Just one more moment.

Kate closed her eyes and hugged herself, reveling in the cool glide of material beneath her fingertips. How grand she felt folded within the robe's protective embrace. For a short time, she had been a princess.

And Alec her prince.

She would remember living the fairy tale for many years to come.

So stop mooning and go already!

I'm goin'!

Yer feet need to be movin' if y' plan on leavin'.

All right! Hold yer breeches!

Speaking of breeches . . . where were hers? She had left them right there on the floor, where she had left all her other clothes . . .

Which were gone, as well!

Bloody hell! She had been robbed!

Who would have guessed the thief in the house would be the victim of a robbery?

But wait! This might have been a more heinous crime than merely the theft of her meager belongings. Oh, yes, this was a crime of petty vindictiveness. And Kate knew just who the culprit was.

Holmes.

He hated her. He had probably thrown her clothes out the front door in the hopes she would scurry after them so he could promptly lock the door behind her. *Or* he had gotten rid of them altogether just to spite her.

Ooh, she was going to get the man!

Swiping a quick hand through her wild locks, Kate gave a furious tug on the robe's belt, tightening it so much it fairly took her breath away.

Shoulders squared and head held high, she marched toward the door, flinging it wide in her high dudgeon.

She walked right into her nemesis.

"You!" she hissed.

The butler raised a condescending eyebrow. "La, you don't say."

"Don't play games with me," Kate warned, narrowing her eyes and planting her fists on her hips. "I ain't in the mood. Now, where are they?"

"Wake up on the wrong side of the bed, did we?" Holmes asked derisively, looking down his nose at her. "Oh, but how could I forget? You're probably surprised to have woken up in a bed at all."

"Ha bloody ha, ha," she ground out through clenched teeth. "Ye're a hoot."

"I do my best," Holmes returned dryly. "Are you leaving, then? So soon? I'm all choked up. Well, I will bid you adieu. And Godspeed."

"All right, that's it! I've had all I'm gonna take from y'!"

"Oh? And just what do you propose to do about it, you little ragamuffin?"

"Ragamuffin!" Kate shouted. "Why, I'll—"

"What's all the yelling about up here?"

Sharply, Kate turned her head. Alec had just topped the stairs and was now heading down the hallway toward them. His eyes were on her, making her consciously aware that she wore no more than his silk robe. The look he sent her warmed her from her toes up.

"Well?" Alec prompted as he came to a stop in from of them.

Kate finally found her voice. "He took me clothes!" she piped up before Holmes could get any words out.

Holmes's eyes bulged. "Good Lord, I would never stoop to such a level, nor would I want anything of yours!"

"Y' took me clothes and don't deny it!" Kate railed. "I want 'em back right now!"

Holmes looked at Alec, clearly indignant at having been accused of something so petty. "I have no idea what she's talking about, my lord," he insisted.

"I—" Alec began.

"Y' can lie to him, but y' can't lie t' me!" Kate continued her tirade at Holmes. "I know y' well enough by now, y' bloody bugger! Now, what did y' do with 'em?"

Holmes's face was turning purple. "I'm not going to tell you again—"

"Quiet!" Alec shouted.

Startled, they both turned identical guilty faces in his direction.

Kate grumbled, "He started it."

Holmes muttered in return, "Did not."

"Enough!" Alec's gaze moved from her to Holmes, obviously daring someone to make another rebuttal. Appearing satisfied they would remain quiet, he turned his attention to Kate. "I can understand your thinking, Kate, but Holmes didn't take your clothes."

"He didn't?"

"No, he didn't . . . because I did."

Kate's brows snapped together. "You?" she asked, confused.

"Well, not *me* specifically," he clarified. "I had one of the maids gather up your belongings and, er, wash them for you. I hope you don't mind."

"Y' . . . washed 'em?"

Alec paused, his gaze probing. "I just thought . . . well, I should have asked. I apologize."

Apology accepted. But the heat of shame crept along Kate's cheeks nonetheless as she thought about what had started the problem.

Her clothes.

Such things as dirty clothes had never bothered her before.

But it bothered her now.

Kate slanted a glance at Holmes. Hell could freeze over before she would apologize to the pompous pain-in-the-butt. She turned her eyes back to his lordship, who was looking at her tentatively.

She didn't know what to say. So instead of saying anything, she pivoted on her heel and walked back to her room, holding her head high as she did.

A few minutes later a knock sounded at her door. She had been expecting it. What she hadn't been expecting was the person on the other side.

"Hello," Alec said softly.

"Hello," Kate returned just as quietly.

He held out his arm. Draped over it was a dress. "I thought you might like something to wear while you're waiting for the return of your clothing."

Kate blinked. First, he cleans her clothes. Then he brings her a dress? What made him do such things? Or even give her a second thought for that matter?

She gazed down at the dress, feeling something akin to longing burgeon inside her. She remembered how she had laughed as she had pictured herself wearing a dress, gallivanting through the dirty back alleys with the lads or sneaking along the mean streets of London with criminal intent on her mind.

But she wasn't on the streets now, was she?

Slowly, afraid it might disappear, she reached out to touch the pretty dress with the small pink and blue flowers on it. It looked like the dress on the porcelain figurine that graced the half-moon table in the hallway.

"It belongs to my sister, Jane," Alec said as Kate smoothed her fingers over the material. "She left a few here after her last visit."

Kate's eyes lifted to his. "Will she mind me borrowin' it?"

Alec shook his head. "This is just one of her castoffs," he answered, and then quickly amended, "I mean, she has plenty of dresses and won't miss one."

Kate was amazed anew by his consideration. "Well, if yer sure she won't mind . . ."

"I'm sure." He put the dress in her hands. "Go ahead, try it on. Jane is somewhat taller than you and weighs a bit more, but it shouldn't be too bad a fit."

Kate held the dress reverently. It was as if Alec had read her mind and knew her fondest desires. Borrowed or not, the dress was glorious, and it was hers—at least for a little while.

She wanted to tell him what it meant to her, but suddenly couldn't find the right words. Nothing seemed adequate. It was probably for the best anyway. She would most likely say the wrong thing and end up insulting him.

He looked as if he was going to say something. Kate waited, not realizing she held her breath. A moment passed in silence. Then he pivoted on his heel and walked away.

Kate gnawed her inside lip, her gaze following Alec's retreating form until it disappeared from view.

Slowly, she closed the door and leaned back against it. She sighed as she gazed down at the dress in her hands. Shaking her head, she chuckled at her own silliness.

Laying the dress on the bed, Kate unbelted the silk robe, letting it slide down to puddle at her feet. Picking up the dress, she was suddenly conscious of being too dirty to wear it. She had only slapped some water on her face the night before. She glanced down at her hands; there was dirt underneath her nails.

Her gaze slid to the room with the big, brass tub in it, similar to the one she had seen in Alec's room the night before when he had sprayed her with water. Her cheeks warmed at the thought.

Padding into the little room, Kate picked up one of the pretty, delicate soaps and inhaled deeply. The fragrance was like a bouquet of lilacs. She wanted to rub the soap all over her, imagining how lovely it would be to smell like something other than sweat and grime. She decided if this was to be her one and only chance to pretend she was a regal lady, well, by God, she was going to pretend away.

Turning the spigots as she had seen Alec do the day before, Kate watched in fascination as the water spilled out. She put her hand under the tap. "Blast!" she cried out when the water scalded her. She had received her first lesson on adjusting the knobs to make the water hotter or colder.

Testing it a few minutes later, she sighed, nearly forgetting to turn the water off when it got too close to the rim.

"Ninny," she murmured, laughing to herself.

Sinking into the warm bath, Kate let her worries slip away. She began to make small ripples in the water with her hand. Before she knew it, the ripples became waves, as she slapped the water, sending spray everywhere, heedless of the mess she was making.

Ducking her head beneath the surface, she held her breath for as long as she could. When she came up she was gasping, and laughing so hard she nearly drowned herself. She was behaving like a child. She didn't care.

When her skin felt sufficiently pruned, and goose bumps prickled her flesh, she decided it was time to get out. Ah, the luxuries of the upper crust, Kate mused as she dried herself off. What it must be like to lie in bed all day or soak in a warm, sweet-scented bath whenever the mood struck.

Briskly, Kate dried her hair. Then she sat down at a small table with an oval mirror in front of it. Picking up a silver-handled brush that lay on top, she stroked it through her tresses until they shone, watching in the mirror as her hair glistened with renewed life.

She ran her hand through its crackling length all the way to the tips. Her hair was long, reaching well past her waist. She couldn't remember the last time it had been cut. It must have been right before she left the orphanage. One thing she did remember was telling herself she was going to let it grow to the ground before letting anyone else near her with scissors. The nuns used to cut it short and, for the most part, uneven. She had hated it.

Grabbing up the ribbon she had used the night before, Kate tied her hair back, leaving a few wisps out to frame her face.

Pleased with what she saw, Kate rose and finally donned the dress. His lordship had been right in his assessment of his sister's physical attributes. From the length of the dress, Lady Jane was several inches taller than Kate and more than a few pounds heavier. But as Kate looked at herself in the mirror, she couldn't help but love the dress regardless of those things. She would just have to make sure to lift the skirt when she walked so she wouldn't trip over it.

Glancing down, Kate wriggled her toes beneath the hem. She looked around for her boots, spotting them next to the door. They hadn't been there before she had taken her bath. Obviously, they had gone the way of her clothes because they were now clean—although there wasn't much that could be done for the worn out bottoms and the scuff marks.

Wrinkling her nose, she picked them up and stared at them with a critical eye. She decided some additional buffing would not be remiss, doing so with her discarded towel before putting the boots on.

Kate took one last hard look at her reflection in the mirror, telling herself she was not going to trip or otherwise embarrass herself before taking a deep, fortifying breath and heading toward the door.

Chapter Ten

Alec was sitting at his desk when he heard the familiar sound of Anthony entering the house uninvited.

"Your Grace!" Holmes's voice rang out. "His lordship is not receiving this morning. Please come back here!"

Whitfield's booted feet rang loudly across the marble floor, not even faltering under Holmes's frenzied request.

"As I live and breathe!" Anthony exclaimed in an exaggerated tone as he barged into Alec's office. "You're still here. Thank the merciful heavens! Let me have a good look at you."

Under Whitfield's intense scrutiny, Alec felt like livestock going to the market to be bartered. He sighed and folded his hands on top of the papers he had been perusing.

"What in God's name are you doing?" Alec finally demanded. This seemed to be a common question he asked of Anthony. Recently, every time the man came over, he started down some twisted path of semistatements.

"You realize you're being very hostile."

Sometimes, Alec thought, dealing with Anthony was like psychological warfare. "You have a capacity for understatement," he muttered. "Now, what are you talking about?"

Uninvited, Anthony plopped down in the burgundy leather wing chair situated in front of Alec's desk. "Why, I'm talking about you, of course. I could barely sleep last night with concern over your welfare. It fairly plagued me."

"And why would you be concerned over my welfare? I can't recall your ever having been worried about me before."

"Good Lord, man, it should be obvious."

"It should?"

Anthony waved his hand in his usual dramatic style. "Well, of course! However, now that I have seen with my own two eyes that you have survived, I guess my worry was for naught. Unless you have committed an act of violence—murder perhaps?—of which I am not aware? Although, if that was the case, I don't believe anyone would fault you for it."

Alec heaved an exasperated sigh and briefly closed his eyes. When he opened them, he found Anthony looking at him with one eyebrow raised in that supercilious way that grated on Alec's nerves. Someday, Whitfield was going to push him too far and get his vital organs rotated.

In a controlled voice, Alec said, "Well, I'm glad I have your permission to kill someone. I'll just run right out now and commit the deed. I'm sure that you've cleared my actions with the constable so I'll not be sent to the gallows when I commit this heinous crime?"

"You mock my words? That is the thanks I get for worrying about your miserable hide? Fine! Next time I'll let your mangy carcass rot!"

Whitfield was at his best when he had a cause over which to have histrionics.

"Are we, perchance, discussing my guest?" Alec inquired in a bored tone of voice, not willing to give Anthony cause to further regale him with more mind-boggling accusations of the horrific deeds he was sure to have committed against Kate—or vice versa.

"Oh, the urchin has been lifted to the status of an honored guest, has she? My, my, this is indeed interesting news."

"Not as interesting as I'm sure you'd like to believe."

Anthony put his hand to his heart. "You do me a grave injustice. Although, I must admit to a certain degree of amazement that there were no acts of mayhem on the part of the viper-tongued urchin. Was there no thievery, even?"

"None."

"And are you sure about that? Have you checked all your valuables?"

Alec was quickly losing patience. Taking out his pocket watch, he said, "Shouldn't you be running to your ten o'clock character assassination?"

Anthony gave him an affronted look. "Gads, but you do endeavor to douse every spark of happiness in my day." He shrugged. "But you see, grumpy, I've a vested interest in the doings of the nefarious gel."

"Since when?"

"If you recall, several of said valuables in this household were gifts from me to you."

Alec didn't recall any such *gifts*. "Such as?"

"Like that cuckoo clock I brought you from Bavaria. Handcrafted, it was. And quite a tidy sum I paid for it, I might add."

That cuckoo clock, like its purchaser, drove Alec quite to the brink of insanity. After two days of listening to the blighted thing, he had had Holmes stow it deep within the bowels of the house. And he had added in his instructions that should the thing, say, get mangled in the process, so be it.

"Why do you care so much about the goings-on here? It's not as if *you* have anything to worry about. The girl is not in your house."

"And may I say praise God for that. However, it is patently obvious that I need to remind you the pit viper tried to rob me. I was a victim, Breckridge. So have a little sympathy, will you?"

"Ah, but the operative word here is *tried*. From what you told me, she did not succeed. So in essence you aren't really a victim, are you?"

Anthony shrugged. "That's because I was too quick for the little scrapper. And do not mince words. Had her knee made contact with the body part she'd aimed for, it could have been disastrous for me. She very nearly put an end to my favorite pastime. Needless to say, that would leave many women bereft."

Alec rolled his eyes. "Please refrain from further elucidation on the subject if you don't mind."

Anthony bowed his head. "As you wish, oh benevolent one."

Alec tested the weight of a small, marble statue on his desk, but figured Whitfield's head would only succeed in breaking it.

Unaware of the threat to his person, Anthony went on. "I would like to know how you managed to remain unscathed. The girl was a complete wildcat when last I saw her, *and* may I add, not at all appreciative of the fate I saved her from. So where are your battle scars? I see nary a scratch on you."

"Sorry to disappoint you, but I haven't any to show. Frankly, Kate was quite well-behaved and rather delightful, to boot."

"So sticky-fingers has a name?"

Alec began drumming his fingers on his desk. "You're beginning to annoy me."

"You mean you aren't thoroughly annoyed yet? Good Lord, I must be losing my touch."

"You'll lose more than that if you persist in prodding me."

"Hark, I believe there was a threat in that statement."

Refraining from a sharp retort, Alec said, "As you can see I'm fine."

Anthony nodded, his look clearly saying he was in awe of this spectacular feat. "Indeed you are. Still, I can't help but wonder if we're talking about the same person. She was quite short with black hair hanging down to one of the nicest derrieres I've seen in some time, a vicious temper and epithets that would burn your ears."

The look Alec gave him said it all.

Anthony took a slim, silver case out of his inside jacket pocket. Flipping the latch, he removed a cheroot and then offered one to Alec. Putting the case away, he then removed an equally handsome silver, engraved lighter and put it to the end of Alec's cheroot, remarking as he did, "I still can't believe we're talking about the same girl who wanted to take my head off last night."

Alec took a long draw on his cheroot as he leaned back in his chair. "Could that, perhaps, have been caused by the way you treated her? If you will recall, you were rather rough."

Anthony took umbrage. "You were expecting me to give

her flowers and candy, were you? Perhaps I should have thanked her for trying to rob me?"

"You could have handled the situation differently."

"Oh, well, certainly you're right." Anthony's tone reeked with sarcasm. "I should have let her kick me in the crotch and take off with my wallet. Of course that would have been the better plan. How stupid of me not to think of it."

If memory served, Kate *had* managed to kick him in the crotch. Obviously, Whitfield had a selective memory. Alec decided not to remind him.

"All I'm saying is I don't think you've given her a proper chance. She has been the victim of a tragic life. It isn't as if she planned to become a thief. Obviously it was the only avenue open to her."

"My, but you are gullible. I pity you. Indeed I do. When the chit robs you blind, don't say I didn't warn you."

Alec looked up and caught sight of Kate hovering in the doorway. From the dark frown on her face, it was apparent she had heard Anthony's comment and was none too pleased to see her nemesis. Her expression, however, didn't detract from her loveliness.

Had he thought her only pretty before?

Slowly, he rose from his seat and moved toward her; the fragrance of flowers wafted over to greet him, telling him she had bathed. His mind made a mental picture of her naked form, the delicate soap running over her body as she closed her eyes, enjoying the feel of the warm water enveloping her.

The last remnants of the dirty street urchin were gone. Her silky, black tresses shone. Her skin was like fine porcelain on a face of sculpted perfection.

Alec's devouring gaze did not miss the swell of her breasts beneath the material of the dress. It didn't help to know she probably wore no undergarments beneath it. Those items, even had he remembered she would need them, would have been impossible to scrape up on such short notice. He felt an immediate and painful tightening in his groin and cursed himself for his weakness.

"You look lovely, Kate," he said sincerely, as he took her hand in his, raising it to his lips to place a gentle kiss on it.

Heat flooded Kate's cheeks and then proceeded to warm her neck and chest. Alec's words thrilled her, but the feel of his lips on the tender skin of her hand did something else entirely, something indefinable. She had never felt the way she did at that moment, as though she was precious and completely a woman. It was wonderful.

Alec looped his arm through hers and escorted her to the settee where she sat down with as much decorum as she could muster in her unfamiliar clothing. She peeked up at him through her lashes, feeling suddenly shy. She was nervous and excited and didn't know what to say or do—most unusual for her. His stare was so intense it fairly took her breath away.

The spell was broken as Anthony, whose presence had thus far been ignored, cleared his throat and said, "This cannot be the grimy hellion who tried to filch my belongings last night, can it?"

Kate slowly turned her head to glare at the man. The irritating lout would have to bring that up and humiliate her when she was feeling so good about herself. How she would love to kick him in his backside!

"My, what a little soap and water can do for a body," Anthony continued in a mocking tone. "Who would have imagined a girl lay underneath the soil and male togs? Quite amazing."

Kate held her tongue, but she doubted it would last

long. She wondered how it came to pass that a man as
nice as Alec knew so many rotten people. The blond-haired
man who was now staring smugly at her and the grim-faced
butler were cut from the same cloth. Unfortunately, she
knew more people like those two than men of Alec's character. In fact, other than the lads—and really just Falcon
for the most part—she didn't know anyone who came
close to being as wonderful as his lordship.

And like a knight in shining armor, he came to her
rescue. "Leave off harassing her, Whitfield."

One blond eyebrow shot up into Anthony's forehead.
"What ho! Since when did I become the villain in this
scenario? I seem to recall I was the innocent victim just
last night."

Kate could no longer hold back as she muttered under
her breath, "Innocent victim, me bum."

"What was that, baggage? Speak up!"

Kate's fists clenched in her lap. She opened her mouth
to give a stinging retort, but again Alec interjected on her
behalf. "She said you're not innocent. Now it's over and
done with, so why don't we just move on?"

"Sounds like your loyalty has switched sides, my friend.
Why is that, I wonder?"

"This has nothing to do with loyalty."

Anthony looked skeptical. "So you mean to say nothing
happened here last night?"

Alec narrowed his eyes at his friend. "What are you
getting at?"

Anthony held up his hand and replied with feigned
innocence, "It was merely a simple question. It's just that
things appear very . . . cozy, shall we say?" He looked
askance at Kate and added, "I do believe that dress looks
familiar. Where have I seen it before?"

Kate swore she was not going to let the man rile her. She would come back when he was gone.

Rising from the settee, she glared at Anthony and then pivoted on her heel and headed toward the door.

"Don't leave on my account," Anthony said, chuckling.

"Take a runnin' jump!" she retorted through gritted teeth.

Her biting reply, so eloquently put, had Alec smiling. Anthony, he knew, liked a sporting challenge, and Kate just couldn't seem to hold her tongue. She was easy to rile, and rather thin-skinned. One would have thought a life on the streets would have toughened her up a bit.

"Don't go, Kate," Alec called out.

She turned, a flash of uncertainty crossing her face. Then that spirit he was coming to admire in her returned, and she tilted up her chin in a challenging manner.

Anthony, appearing satisfied that he had accomplished his goal of irritating Kate, stood up. "Well, Breckridge, it has been delightful, as usual. But I have things to do, so I'll be off." He scooped up his jacket and gloves from where he had thrown them and walked to the door. He stopped on the threshold and swiveled around. "I'll still be seeing you this evening, I presume?"

Alec frowned. "This evening?"

Anthony shook his head as he slipped his jacket on. "Don't tell me you've forgotten? Certainly the darling Lady Hampton would be crushed to find herself so easily dismissed from your mind."

Alec groaned inwardly. "Yes, I had forgotten."

Damn! How had he gotten himself embroiled in going to the Rutherford Ball with Lady Marisol Hampton, he grimly wondered. His mother's strong-arm tactics and his sister's pleading were how. He was now committed to an event he had no interest in attending, escorting a woman who held as much appeal for him as watching the hedges grow.

According to Jane, the lady was the Incomparable of the Season, which Alec suspected had a great deal to do with the young woman's mother being the queen matriarch of the *ton*. Jane told him, repeatedly, one absolutely *must* get on her good side if one did not want to become a social pariah, a complete outcast, a laughingstock . . . et cetera.

For himself, Alec could not have cared less. He never concerned himself with what Society thought of him. But his sister was a different story. Everything scandalized her.

He had only met Lady Marisol once, a month earlier, at the annual ball his mother held at Silvertree, their country estate in Northumberland.

His sister, the little minx, had set her trap to get him to ask Lady Hampton to the ball and gone about accomplishing that goal in the best way she knew how—by crying. She knew he couldn't abide a female's tears; it thoroughly routed him. It was an aspect of his character he considered a flaw. Anthony would have simply said, *Cease that detestable boo-hooing*, and walked away. It was probably the only time Alec wished he were more like Whitfield. But there had been no miracles that night. When Jane got that weepy-faced look, he had buckled under like a rotted floorboard under a fat man.

Needless to say the meeting with Lady Marisol had left him cold. For the life of him, he couldn't figure out why his sister would want to associate with her. The woman had nothing of any interest to say and believed the sun rose and set each day solely for her pleasure. At best, she was mildly annoying. At worst, she was *gratingly* annoying.

And he had to spend an entire evening with her.

The thought had the power to darken Alec's mood. And when Anthony asked him again if he still intended to go to the ball, his voice was not much more than a growl. "Yes, damn it!"

Anthony put up his hand. "No need to take my head off. I'm just the messenger," he huffed and then snapped on his last glove. "I'll see you later—and one can only hope your mood will have vastly improved by that time." Then he turned to Kate and gave her a cocky salute. "Always a pleasure, baggage."

Marching briskly from the room, he let himself out the same way he had let himself in, whisking past an irate Holmes, who closed the front door after him none too gently, if the reverberations were any indication.

Chapter Eleven

"Bloody charmin'," Kate muttered as she glared at Anthony's retreating form.

"He's not too bad once you get to know him," Alec commented.

Kate turned to him, noting the wry expression on his face that told a different story than his words. She recalled him giving her the same excuse about the butler. She believed him as much now as she had then.

Her look, she hoped, conveyed what she thought of his friend.

Alec chuckled. "Point taken. He's a bloody satyr who's a boil on the butt of humanity with no end in sight because he has money and time on his hands." He shrugged. "Overall, he's harmless, though. Don't let him bother you."

"He don't bother me," Kate lied.

She had always been quick to anger, and it wasn't in her

nature to remain silent. Silence meant defeat, capitulation. She knew why the Whitfields of the world would probably always grate on her. Every look, word and gesture seemed to say, "Here I be and ain't I grand?" Just because he had money and some fancy title didn't give him the right to treat her as if she were no better than a piece of trash littering the streets. She was a person, just not one who was born with a silver spoon in her mouth.

"Have you had breakfast yet?" Alec inquired.

Kate found herself caught off guard by his glittering, black velvet gaze. It took her a moment to find her voice. "No," she replied a bit hoarsely.

"Well, I haven't either. Would you care to join me for some?" He put out his arm for her.

Kate didn't need to be asked twice.

In contemplative silence, they walked to the breakfast salon. Only after they were seated and piping hot food was piled on a plate in front of them, did Kate say, "So who's Lady Hampton?"

She hadn't known she was going to ask the question until it was out of her mouth. But once it was, she knew a sudden overwhelming desire to hear Alec's answer.

She had started thinking of his lordship as her knight in shining armor. Prior to that moment, she hadn't given it a thought that he may have a close woman friend or a wife for that matter. Did he have children, too? Something inside her deflated at the very thought.

"Lady Hampton is a friend of my sister, Jane," Alec replied matter-of-factly. "I promised Jane I would escort Lady Hampton to the Rutherfords' ball this evening."

Kate hesitated, and then asked, "Is she . . . pretty?"

"To whom are you referring?"

Who did he think? "Yer lady friend."

Alec's fork halted midway to his mouth, his eggs poised.

"She's not my lady friend." His gaze narrowed slightly, and Kate wondered if she had smut on her face. A moment passed before he asked, "What would your description of pretty be, Kate?"

That was easy, Kate thought. Glittering, perfect porcelain dolls. She imagined Lady Hampton was a real lady, too. Kate could picture the woman driving about the swank part of town in a sleek, black carriage, packages piled high from her shopping spree when she already had everything one could want. She would have a closet full of dresses in silks and satins of every color of the rainbow. Everything Kate would never have.

And she was everything Kate would never be.

"Kate?" Alec prompted,

"Silky blond hair and pale blue eyes with perfect skin," she finally replied, a wistful note in her voice.

Alec, his food all but forgotten, leaned back in his chair, a half grin on his face. "And you believe that defines a pretty lady, do you?"

"Well, that an' lovely gowns. They always have lovely gowns. Have y' ever noticed that?"

"Sometimes they do," Alec said with a shrug. "But sometimes it doesn't matter what a lady wears because she would be beautiful in rags."

Kate snorted in disbelief. "Rubbish."

"It's true." He leaned forward, putting his elbows on the table. "I wouldn't lie about something this important. And I'm telling you that if a woman has a beautiful soul, neither clothes nor a pretty face really matters. She could be rich or poor and it wouldn't change that fact."

"It wouldn't?"

He put his hand over his heart. "I swear."

Kate smiled, and it lit up her whole face.

"You have a lovely smile." Alec said his thought out loud.

"I do?" she whispered, her long black lashes sweeping down to flutter on her cheeks.

"You do." And he should damn well stop noticing, for she was still a child. Wasn't she?

Picking up his fork, Alec jammed a bite of eggs grown cold into his mouth. "So how have you liked your stay here in my home?"

Kate had to blink several times before coming back to reality. She sat there pie-eyed, staring like a dolt, as if she had never seen a dark-haired, handsome lord. She had stolen from a few comely blokes. Yet, whether they were pretty or ugly made no difference. One rich bugger was as good as the next. But she hadn't known one of the Quality who was like Alec. Suddenly Kate felt as though she had been deprived in more ways than one. She knew a part of her would feel a loss when the time came for her to go, and that time drew ever nearer.

"I know it hasn't been easy for you," Alec continued. "Perhaps that's putting it too mildly, what with Holmes and Anthony being their sarcastic best. I must confess to a certain degree of surprise—in Holmes's case only. He is usually the epitome of decorum and staid from the roots of his thinning gray hair to the tips of his high, buffed black shoes. I can't recall having ever seen the man crack a smile. I think he believes he will be breaking some lauded rule known only amongst butlers." He shrugged. "I've grown used to him, though, since he has been my family's butler for nearly my entire life. Needless to say, I have ceased trying to devise ways to break the man down. He is completely immune to all outside influences—or so I thought until you came along. I have never seen him so animated."

Kate snorted. "Animated with anger," she said, picking up the muffin from her plate and pulling off a small piece. "I wouldn't hold yer breath that old toad-face is goin' t' change."

Alec chuckled. "I wouldn't underestimate your powers, my girl. Old toad-face is human like the rest of us." In a lowered voice, he added, "You are an interesting article."

She stopped chewing. "Is that a good thing or a bad thing?"

"Definitely a good thing," he returned, his words touching a yearning, empty spot within her. "But back to my question. How do you like it here in general? And don't worry about hurting my feelings. Be honest. I can take it."

Kate doubted there was much a man like Alec couldn't take. Oddly enough, for being such a huge man—a bruiser as Weasel would say—she didn't think he was the type who resorted to violence unless absolutely necessary. She pitied the person who took him on.

But the question remained . . . how did she like being in his home? He had asked for honesty. But how honest did she really care to be?

"It's . . . nice."

To say she was enjoying all the new sights and experiences, that she felt like an entirely different person, and that the thought of going back to her life was becoming a hard and dismal prospect was something Kate could not voice.

"Nice, huh?" Alec gave her that half grin that made her feel like an icicle beginning to melt. "Well, I guess that isn't bad commentary."

Kate felt as if she had been too cheap in her response, as if she owed him, and herself, something more. "Y' have been very kind t' me." She hesitated and then added, "Although I can't understand why."

"Why shouldn't I be?"

"I'm a thief, remember?" Although how he could possibly forget was beyond her. "It's because I was caught nickin' from yer friend that I was brought here. I'm surprised he didn't haul me in front of a firin' squad, he was that put out. So, as y' might figure, I can't see him doin' somethin' nice." She took a sweeping glance around the cavernous room as she added, "If he thought this was gonna be some sort of punishment, he was far off the mark."

"Although Anthony's thinking does tend to be askew—more to the side of sheer delirium than foaming-at-the-mouth madness—I cannot find fault with him this time around."

Kate felt an unbelievable moment of exhilaration at his words. But her smile faded as she remembered the comment the irritating blond so-and-so had made to Alec when she had first arrived.

"I'm not a charity case, y' know."

"I assure you, I don't consider you a charity case. You are a guest, and therefore welcome here. I can only hope you haven't felt otherwise."

She hadn't. Far from it, in fact.

Alec smiled at her, and Kate wanted to smile in return. Before she had the chance to, he pushed his plate away, tossed the linen napkin on the table and stood up. It seemed to Kate that he was suddenly in a hurry to leave.

Well, she thought a bit sourly, he had a big night ahead of him. He would be escorting Lady Hampton to the Rutherford Ball. Certainly that was far more interesting to him than spending time with a pickpocket who had fallen asleep at his table.

Kate wondered at the knot forming in her stomach as she realized her time in Alec's house was coming to an end. She had stayed well beyond her dinner invitation, and he had already explained he didn't expect her to repay a debt to him because of what had happened with Lord Muck.

"Y' barely ate anything," she rushed out, quickly rising to her feet. "A big man like y' can't survive on them few bites y' had. Here, have me muffin. I only took a little piece out of it." She tossed it to him as if it were the only one left when there were at least six sitting on a plate a foot away from him. But she just wanted him to stay awhile longer. For some reason, she did not want it to end yet.

Alec was genuinely touched. "Thank you, Kate." Her gesture, like her compliment, was probably not second nature. "I only regret that I do not have more time to spend with you. Unfortunately a mountain of work awaits me, and if I don't do it, then it won't get done. As much as I am tempted at this moment to throw it to the four winds, other people are involved." But if ever he wanted to say the hell with it, now was the time, especially with the doe-eyed look Kate probably didn't even realize she was giving him. For once, he actually wished someone else were around to take over his responsibilities. The thought occurred to him that he could hire someone to help, a secretary or a bookkeeper. Plenty of his peers had people like that. Whitfield, for example. Wasn't he always boasting about the freedom he enjoyed, escaping from the daily grind because he had someone to take care of the paperwork? Except Alec knew he wouldn't let any person he employed have complete control the way Anthony did.

"Oh," she said in a small voice. "Well . . . I won't keep y', then. I'll get me clothes an' be off in a wink." She looked down at her borrowed dress and smoothed a hand gently over the material. Realizing she was acting foolishly, she raised her head and hoped her eyes didn't show any of the unwelcome longing she felt at that moment. "Thank y' fer loanin' me the dress . . . an' fer dinner. An' fer breakfast, too," she hastened to add lest he think her ungrateful.

He smiled that beautiful, warm smile.

"Well . . ."

"Yes, well . . ." Alec returned, wondering why his feet weren't presently heading toward his office.

He realized with a start that he was reluctant to leave. Work beckoned, but suddenly no one was home to answer the summons.

He had enjoyed himself more in the past day with Kate than he had in a long while. The girl was like sunshine— and he a man long deprived. She was so natural and cared as little about the rules as he did.

Nevertheless, his life was set in stone, had been since the day he was born. He had no room for disruptions, nor did he have time to be a baby-sitter to a charming child with immense blue eyes who had a propensity for stealing. Besides, she probably wouldn't want to stay even if he should lose his mind and ask. And why would he ask? What possible reason could he have?

Charity case. Anthony's words suddenly reverberated in Alec's head. Kate would never allow herself to be that. He figured she would prefer the streets to taking a handout.

On the other hand, he did have the power to help her, to possibly give her another road to take besides that of being a common thief. Without his intervention, she might very well find herself behind the prison walls that Whitfield was so fond of threatening her with. Such a life would wear her down, break her spirit. He didn't want to see that happen. Kate was a diamond in the rough. All she needed was a little polishing. And after all, hadn't he vowed to

Whitfield that he would do his share to help out those less fortunate?

"Goodbye," Kate murmured, trodding slowly toward the door.

"Would you . . . be interested in staying for a while?"

Kate swiveled around on her heels. "Stay? Here?"

Alec nodded. "If you'd like."

She studied his face. His expression was neutral, giving nothing away of what he was thinking. "Why are y' offerin'?"

"Because I like you, Kate," he returned simply and without hesitation.

Kate's heart swelled at his words, and little prickles of sensation tingled along her arms and legs. She wanted to tell him that she liked him, too, but she would be foolish to do so. She doubted he meant it in the same way she did, as if it might mean something to him to be her friend.

She gnawed on her lower lip and then quietly asked, "Aren't y' worried I'll filch somethin'?"

Alec shook his head. "I don't see why you would. I imagine you engaged in thievery because you were trying to get by. Here you would have a roof over your head and three square meals a day. You'd have no reason to take anything. Besides, I trust you."

Kate had never heard those words from anyone before. "Y' do?"

"I do."

She had never had such a longing to be a real lady, the kind a man like Alec would respect and be proud of, than she did at that moment.

But why was he asking her to stay? What could he possibly want with her? She barely knew him, yet somehow she *did* know him. It didn't make sense. It was as if she had found something in him that had been missing all her life.

When he looked at her, she felt liquid inside. And when he smiled, it was as if the sun had cast its rays upon her. And when he laughed . . .

She felt its warmth inside her.

"Are y' sure?" she asked.

"I wouldn't have asked if I wasn't." He softened his statement with a lopsided grin.

"Then . . . I'd like t' stay."

"It's settled then," he said briskly and then strode toward the door. "I'll speak to Mrs. Dearborn this afternoon about the arrangements."

"Arrangements? For wot?"

Turning in the threshold, he replied, "For you to begin your new job, of course."

Chapter Twelve

"Hullo."

Startled, Kate practically jumped out of her skin. "Wot in the name of all that's holy are y' doin' sneakin' up on people like that?"

"Nobody was sneakin'," Rat insisted, as he emerged from the thick covering of bushes, Weasel and Falcon following closely behind him.

Weasel peered at her as if he had never seen her before. "Since when don't y' know yer bein' followed, huh?"

Since she had found something else to occupy her mind, Kate silently answered.

Rat asked, "What are y' doin' out here in the bushes? An' where were y' all day? We thought y'd be back by this mornin'."

"We were worried," Falcon quietly said.

The tension Kate had been feeling ebbed as she looked at Falcon. "I'm sorry t' have worried y'. I didn't mean t'.

It's just that I . . . I got caught up in some things." Piercing, dark eyes, and bronzed skin, for one.

"Wot things?" Weasel wanted to know.

"Yer not in any trouble, are y'?" Falcon asked in a concerned voice.

"Trouble?" Kate paused, wondering about Alec and the way he made her feel, how she could so easily forget who she was when he was near. She remembered the hollow sensation in the pit of her stomach when she had prepared to leave his home, then the joy when he had asked her to stay, and finally, the confusion and touch of hurt when he had offered her a job. Something inside her warned her of trouble, telling her she should get out before it was too late. But somehow she knew it was already too late.

"Fox?" Falcon prompted.

Kate shook her head, noticing three pairs of eyes fastened intently on her. "No," she murmured, "I ain't in any trouble." Their relief was audible.

"So wot happened t' keep y'?" Rat prompted.

"Nothin' happened."

"If nothin' happened, then where y' been?" Then Rat took a close look at her, as if just seeing her. "And why are y' wearin' a dress?"

Kate wondered at the same thing. Her old clothes had been returned to her, cleaned and even mended. She could have changed. Yet she hadn't wanted to. She liked the way she felt in the dress, as if she were truly someone named Kate and not the Fox.

"Bugger me," Weasel said, whistling through his teeth. "The Fox in a dress, as I live and breathe."

Rat crossed his arms over his chest. "Y' meetin' someone?"

Kate scowled at him. "Now, who would I be meetin'?"

"Y' tell me. Yer the one in a dress, which y' got t' admit is passin' strange."

"Not so strange when me own clothes are dirty," Kate tossed back defensively, telling herself she wasn't lying so much as not feeling it necessary to reveal everything.

"They're always dirty," Weasel retorted. "Wot makes now any different?"

"She don't have t' explain herself t' y'," Falcon said, coming to Kate's defense.

Weasel's face looked like a thundercloud. "Wot's got y' so bloody up in arms?"

Kate stepped in, smoothly changing the subject. "Wot are y' doin' here?"

Rat and Weasel exchanged glances. Then Rat said, "When we didn't see y', we thought maybe the blue blood had done y' in or somethin'."

"So we came t' check on y'," Weasel took up where Rat left off. "An' that's when we seen y' headin' down the street. We thought y' were comin' back t' us, but then realized that y' were goin' in the wrong direction."

"Yeah, the wrong direction," Rat echoed.

"We thought somethin' might be goin' on, so we followed y'," Weasel continued.

"Like wot, for example?" Kate asked, folding her arms across her chest.

Weasel looked to Rat and then to Falcon before shrugging. "Well, that's why we followed y', to find out."

Kate was prepared to tell them that they could have simply asked her when a loud burst of laughter had them turning toward the house from which it came.

Standing in a shadowy corner outside the Rutherfords' sumptuous home, the group focused its attention on the men and women inside. Dressed in their finest attire, the party goers danced gaily around a spacious ballroom under a huge crystal chandelier. Servants dressed in black and white hustled about the room, serving drinks and hors d'oeuvres on shining silver salvers.

Kate remembered having once seen a grand-looking music box in a store window that had a dark-haired man dressed in a formal black jacket and trousers. His partner was a beautiful, blond-haired woman wearing a ball gown of cream satin, a matching satin sash around her waist, its ends streaming behind her. The tip of her cream satin slippers peeked out from underneath her skirt. Smiles lit their tiny faces, and when the key was turned, they began to glide in the rhythm of a dance. It was the most wondrous thing Kate had ever seen.

She had stood at that shop window for the longest time with her nose pressed to the glass watching the couple dancing, imagining herself as the woman, laughing flirtatiously at her handsome partner.

When Kate had caught a glimpse of her reflection in the glass, she turned away. She had never looked in that store window again.

Seeing Alec in his finery as he had stood in the vestibule preparing to leave for the Rutherfords' ball had brought the memory back. He was dressed like the man on the music box, all in black except for the pristine white of his shirt and cravat. A stunning jewel, which Kate was sure was a diamond, winked out from the folds of his cravat. His shoulder-length dark hair had been tied back in a queue. He was the most attractive man she had ever seen, and she had wanted to tell him how wonderful he looked. But she hid from view at the corner of the stairs, her voice not wanting to work.

Then he was gone.

And she with him—unbeknownst to him, however.

More foolishness, Kate thought. Just like when her mind had gone all fanciful because Alec had asked her to stay.

She hadn't taken a moment before making her decision to ask herself what she planned to tell the lads. It wasn't so much explaining to them what she would be doing. It was why she was doing it. That was a question she couldn't even answer for herself.

Alec had said he would talk to Mrs. Dearborn about her duties, but the housekeeper had said nothing to Kate about her new job when she had seen her earlier. Nevertheless, Kate knew she had been offered a once in a lifetime opportunity and she should be happy for it.

Then, why wasn't she?

What could she possibly have been thinking? Alec was a lord, different than most, but a lord nonetheless. He certainly didn't need her for companionship, which, for a fleeting moment, was the reason she had thought he had asked her to stay. He had said she was interesting, in a good way, and that he liked her. Obviously, such things didn't mean the same thing to him as they did to her.

Well, at least now Kate knew where she stood in the scheme of things, her situation made crystal clear with his few words. She was a stranger and he had offered her a meal, a civil word, a soft bed, and now a job. The simple truth was, he was just plain nice. And that was the reason for his actions. She need not look for any deeper motivation.

So why had she followed him, then?

Kate had found out from Mrs. Dearborn where the Rutherfords lived—indirectly, of course. Not knowing what Kate had planned, the older woman practically drew her a map. Soon after his lordship left, she faked a big yawn and claimed fatigue. The housekeeper prepared her bed and very nearly tucked her in, asking if she wanted some warm cocoa, which Kate ever-so-sleepily declined. Then the woman was off, shutting the door quietly behind her. Mrs. Dearborn obviously knew nothing about where Kate came from. Kate wondered if she should inform Mrs. Dearborn that she had never had a room to herself, or a bed for that matter, and that she would count herself lucky if she wasn't woken up at least five times a night because of brawling drunks or because an uninvited guest of the rodent variety had decided to sleep with her. But Kate figured the less the woman knew the better. Besides, she had more important things on her mind.

The need to see for herself the kind of world Alec lived in, up close, compelled her into action. She didn't want to admit she also wanted to glimpse Lady Hampton, because to acknowledge that would mean it was more than just curiosity that had brought her to this place.

As three bodies moved in beside her, Kate remembered she was no longer alone. The lads stood there open-mouthed as they stared in at the opulent surroundings.

"Gawd, would y' look at all the sparklers on them women," Weasel spoke up as the glaze finally lifted from his eyes.

"An' the men I'm sure are loaded down with plenty of blunt," Rat added to the conversation. "Ruddy Nora, we'd be set fer life if we had some of that in our hands."

"Well, forget it," Kate said before she could stop herself. She quickly added, "I mean, it's, er, too risky."

"Geez, I hadn't planned t' just walk right in and tell 'em t' hand everythin' over," Rat returned in a disgruntled tone of voice. "I'm not dumb, y'know."

Weasel narrowed his eyes at her. "Yer actin' awfully jittery, Fox. Wot's the matter?"

"Nothin'," Kate hastily denied.

Of all the things she had not wanted to happen, this was certainly it. To be found spying on his lordship by the lads was the last thing she had expected. But it always ended up that when she desperately wanted something *not* to happen that was when it did.

"Y' never did tell us wot yer doin' here," Rat reminded her.

Kate groaned inwardly. She had hoped they would forget she had yet to answer that question, at least until she could think of a plausible response. Leave it to Rat to bring it up again. He was like a bear with a thorn in his paw. He would keep plucking at it until he got it out.

Pointing a finger toward the Rutherfords' house, Kate said, "The only reason I'm out here is t' keep an eye on his bloody lordship who's in there." She didn't like the way the words sounded to her ears, but she couldn't let on to the lads that Alec was anything more than a potential means to an end.

"I don't get it," Rat said, scratching his dirty reddish brown hair. "If the pigeon's in there, then why aren't y' at his house loadin' up the silverware an' the like? Don't seem like a better opportunity, if y' ask me."

Had her motive been robbery, Kate thought, then Rat was exactly right. "Are y' forgettin' he's got a houseful of servants?"

"Since when can't y' get past a bunch of pasty-faced servants?" Weasel chimed in.

"I can get past them if I want. But I got other things on me mind."

"Other things? Wot other things?" Rat asked, his muddy brown eyes suddenly taking on an avaricious gleam.

"Bigger things," she answered evasively.

"Are y' sayin' his high-muckety-muck ain't booted yer bum t' the curb yet?"

"Not yet."

Weasel and Rat grinned broadly. Falcon, on the other hand, looked at her speculatively.

"So how did y' pull that off?" Weasel wanted to know.

Kate shrugged with an indifference she was far from feeling. "I let him think I was just another sad orphan wot's had a bad life and that I hadn't planned on bein' a thief, but wot else could a poor, hungry lass do?" And for the most part, that was a true story. Except she could have stayed at the orphanage instead of taking her chances on the streets. "It were a bloomin' tragic tale I told the larder. I believe he shed a few tears, I was that convincin'. Anyway, can y' believe the mug felt so sorry for me that he offered me a job?"

"A job?" Rat was incredulous. "In his house?"

Weasel cuffed Rat across top of his head. "Of course in his house, y' nit."

Disgruntled, Rat rubbed his head and mumbled under his breath about people waking up on the wrong side of the pallet.

Kate ignored them both while trying to appear thoroughly smug over her contrived accomplishment. "I told y' I was a bloody good actress. I had the bloke believin' I was just misunderstood."

"I couldn't have done better meself," Rat commented.

"Y' couldn't have done it at all," Weasel cuttingly put in.

"I bloody well could have!" Rat angrily insisted.

"Wot kind of job is it?" Falcon asked, peering at Kate in a way that made her think Falcon could see right through her deception.

"Well, I don't know yet," Kate answered, feeling uncomfortable under Falcon's close scrutiny and wondering if she should tell at least one person the whole truth. If anyone deserved it, it was Falcon. But what was the *whole* truth?

Rat scratched his head. "He offered y' a job an' y' don't know wot it is? Did I miss something, 'cause I don't get it."

"Y' wouldn't, blockhead," Weasel said sarcastically, always ready for a brawl.

"Who y' callin' blockhead?" Rat fairly shouted.

Kate sighed. For some reason, Weasel and Rat's carrying on suddenly bothered her more than usual. She felt . . . tired of it. Perhaps she had just been listening to it for too long.

They had all lived at the same orphanage. Together, they had decided to leave, to be free as they called it, with the hopes of striking it rich someday. All of them were dreamers of a sort. But they had stuck it out, and in the natural, or perhaps unnatural, procession of things, Kate had found herself as leader. Certainly hers was the only gang with a female as leader. Weasel was tough enough, but he didn't have the necessary decisiveness or the calm rationale also required.

She hadn't asked for the job; in some ways she hadn't wanted it. What she *had* wanted, however, was to stay alive. And if staying alive meant leading the group, then so be it. More than a few times she had wished they could find respectable work. Her dreams weren't particularly grand, but they were grounded in reality for the most part.

"When are y' comin' back?" Falcon quietly asked while Weasel and Rat bickered amongst themselves.

Kate sighed. "I guess it will depend on how long his lordship wants me around." Realizing how her words sounded, she quickly amended, "I mean, it depends on how long I can tolerate me job, whatever it may be. Who knows? Perhaps I won't be gone long at all. The stuffy atmosphere will probably send me runnin' for the nearest door after a few days." But for some reason she doubted she would feel that way. "Besides, his high-and-mighty has this irritatin' butler who looks down his nose at me an' acts like he's the bloody Bishop of York. I'm sure I won't be able t' stand him for long."

Kate wanted to reassure Falcon that she wasn't leaving for good, since she doubted she was. Either his lordship would grow tired of her, or she would mess something up and get the boot—or lose her temper one day and clobber Holmes but good. Something, Kate was sure, would happen. Perhaps she would even grow tired of looking at Alec's chiseled profile or those rich, dark eyes. It could happen.

And maybe pigs could fly.

Falcon nodded. "Watch out for yerself."

"I will," Kate promised, knowing she had to protect herself in more ways than one.

"I'll miss y'," Falcon then added in a low voice.

Kate's throat closed.

God, did she know what she was doing? she asked herself for what seemed the hundredth time. Perhaps she was making a mistake. She didn't really know his lordship. She had made a lot of assumptions about him, ones that could prove far from correct.

An emotion she had fought to keep buried deep inside her suddenly overwhelmed her.

Fear.

Fear of the unknown. Fear of the future. Fear of her life spinning out of control and she would be unable to stop it.

"I'll miss y', too," Kate murmured in return. "But I won't be far away, an' it's not as if I won't come 'round. Like I said, it probably won't last."

Then Falcon said something Kate knew she would never

forget. "If this is yer way out, a chance at a better life, I want y' to take it. Y' deserve it. So don't concern yerself with me. I'll be just fine."

Kate's heart compressed tightly within her chest. Everything inside her screamed that she had made the wrong choice, that she should stay with Falcon and the lads. Panic fairly overwhelmed her.

As if reading her mind, Falcon said, "Don't be afraid. Y' know wot yer doin'."

"I—" Kate began, only to be rudely interrupted by Weasel.

"Wot are y' two whisperin' about?"

Before Kate could reply, a voice rang out through the darkness.

"Who's out there?"

They had all been so distracted they hadn't noticed the man now moving toward them.

Weasel and Rat looked at each other, then took off on winged feet.

"Go on," Kate urged Falcon, who hung back waiting for her. "I'll go the other way an' distract him."

"But—" Falcon began.

"No buts! Now go!"

Falcon took one last look at her before fading into the shadows.

Kate watched the man lumber toward her. She stood rooted to the spot before shaking herself into action.

Weaving in and out of the shrubbery, she tried to lose the burly man. But she wasn't in her breeches, making movement restricted. Like a clumsy fool, she tripped over the hem of her skirt and went down hard. The wind was knocked out of her in a whoosh, and it took a long second before she regained her breath. That time cost her dearly as the man was almost upon her.

Tossing her hair off her face, Kate jumped up, but her crowning glory worked against her as the man grabbed her by it, yanking her back.

She turned into a hissing cat, swinging wildly, raking his skin with her nails.

"You little bitch!" the man howled. His hand connected with her cheek with a resounding crack. The blow sent her reeling to the ground.

Kate shook her head, seeing stars. She tasted coppery blood in her mouth. Her tongue darted out to touch her lip, wincing as it ran over the cut.

He reached a meaty paw for her. She reacted, her foot meeting solidly with his shin. He bellowed and grabbed his aching leg.

Kate leapt to her feet. She had barely taken three steps when his fingers wrapped around her skirt; the material ripped. She cried out, knowing her beautiful, borrowed dress had been ruined.

He pulled her to the ground. She struggled as he pressed his bulk over her. "Get off me, y' swine!" Her stomach turned as his hot, foul-smelling breath poured over her face.

"Oh, no you don't! You aren't getting away again!" He pinned her arms to her sides. "I was hired by the Rutherfords to make sure riffraff like you stay away from their home and their guests. Now, what are you doing skulking around out here? Planning on doing some mischief, are you?"

"None of yer blasted business, y' fat cow!" Kate spat, trying to push the man off, but he was too heavy. His grip grew punishing, and she whimpered in pain.

"I can break your scrawny neck," he threatened, his expression menacing. "Now, I want some answers!"

"I have no idea wot yer talkin' about!" She would never

give up her friends. "Now get off of me before I make y' sorry!"

The sweaty brute guffawed. "And just what do you think you are going to do?"

Her bluff had been called. She couldn't move; his body pinned her down completely.

Out of the corner of her eye, she caught a movement. A dark form loomed over her captor. Kate caught a glimpse of what looked to be a very large rock before it came crashing down on top of the brute's head. The man groaned and immediately slumped forward, his fat, greasy head landing on her chest.

Kate heaved his loathsome mass off her and quickly scooted away. A thin sliver of moonlight shone down upon him, illuminating the bloody spot on the back of his head. He was utterly still. A jolt of panic ran up her spine. Was he dead?

"Are y' all right?"

Kate turned to the speaker, shock and anger battling within her. "I thought I told y' to leave?"

Falcon shrugged. "Y' did. I just didn't listen."

"I was handlin' the situation." But they both knew that for the lie it was. "Besides, y' could have gotten hurt."

Falcon appeared unconcerned with what may have happened. "Y've helped me out enough over the years, so I thought I'd return the favor for once."

Kate couldn't stay angry. She knew that had it not been for Falcon, things could have gotten a lot uglier.

Looking back at the still body of her attacker, Kate jabbed his arm with the tip of her boot. He didn't move.

"Is he . . . dead?" Falcon asked in a whisper.

Kate shifted to her knees. Tentatively, she put her ear next to his mouth. "No, he's still alive."

Falcon let out an audible sigh of relief.

Kate stood. "Now, I want y' t' go. An' don't mention this t' anyone, not even Weasel or Rat. Do y' understand?"

Falcon nodded. "Aye."

"Good. Now, go on. I will see y' soon. I promise," she said in a reassuring voice when Falcon hesitated.

"Take care of yerself."

Kate smiled tenderly. "I will," she vowed.

And then Falcon was gone, faded into the night once more.

Glancing down at the unconscious man, Kate prayed, "Let him be all right."

And then like Falcon, she, too, let the blackness of the night swallow her.

Chapter Thirteen

Alec breathed a heartfelt sigh of relief when he was finally able to bid Lord and Lady Rutherford good night. He promptly deposited Lady Hampton back where she belonged—which was anywhere that was away from him—and headed home.

"Welcome back, my lord," Holmes said as he opened the door and took Alec's coat and gloves. "How was your evening?"

"Long." But whereas Alec had felt tired only moments before, he now felt strangely invigorated. "How have things been here tonight? You haven't had any rows with our guest, I hope."

"No, my lord. All has been amazingly quiet. May I say that I am, indeed, surprised."

Alec was mildly surprised himself. He had thought for sure that when he returned he would find broken objects strewn all over the floor and Holmes getting his ears boxed by Kate. But as Alec looked around, everything appeared normal.

"Where is Kate?" he inquired, his gaze lifting to the stairs, picturing the impish face of his new houseguest, as he had been doing all night.

"I imagine she is in her room, my lord." Holmes's tone clearly conveyed that he wished it otherwise. "Shall I send Jeffries to you?" he then asked, referring to Alec's valet.

"No. I will manage fine on my own," Alec said distractedly as he headed up the stairs. "Good night, Holmes."

Reaching his room, Alec paused, listening carefully for any noise, something that would tell him Kate was still awake. After all the jaded women who had attended the Rutherfords' ball and Lady Hampton's inane chatter, he found he needed a breath of fresh air.

And Kate was that fresh air.

Alec decided to check on her. He had no intentions of waking her if she was asleep. He wanted only to see her, make sure everything was all right. He refused to look deeper into his motivation.

At her door, he hesitated. Perhaps she would resent his intrusion at this late hour. He had no real reason to check on her—at least no justifiable reason.

While he deliberated, he thought he heard a faint noise coming from inside Kate's room. Whether real or imagined, that was all he needed. Without a second thought, he opened the door and entered.

"Kate?" he softly called out.

At first, he didn't see her in the shadowy darkness of the room, but then a slight movement drew his gaze to her. She was sitting on the bed, her back to him. He knew at once something was wrong.

"Kate, what's the matter?"

When he got no response, he crossed to her.

Her head was bowed, and her hands were fisted in her lap, her fingers wrapped tightly around the material of her dress.

Alec knelt down beside the bed. Her cheek was smudged with dirt, her hair wild. What had happened? A lump formed in the middle of his chest.

"Kate," he said in a low voice, keeping his manner calm and unthreatening. "What's going on? What's happened?" Gently, he cupped her chin. She resisted when he tried to turn her to face him. "Please, Kate, don't shut me out."

A few minutes passed before Alec saw some of the tension leave her. Again, he coaxed her, wanting to see her face, to look into her eyes. She hesitated and then finally complied.

Air hissed between his teeth when he saw her face. There was an angry red welt by her left eye, and her bottom lip was swollen and cut.

Tenderly he touched a finger to her lip. She winced and turned away. "Don't," she whispered.

"For God's sake, Kate, tell me what happened," Alec begged, feeling at a loss.

Her gaze returned to her lap. "I fell, that's all."

Alec didn't believe her, but refrained from commenting. He would get his answers, but he wasn't going to force her.

Standing, he moved to the bureau where a pitcher of water and a bowl sat. He poured some water into the bowl, grabbed the small towel laying next to it and soaked it in the water. He rung it out and then walked back to the bed.

"Press this against your face," he told her in a quiet yet firm voice, handing her the cloth. "It will help take down some of the swelling."

Kate took the cloth with trembling fingers.

At length, she said softly, "I really did fall." Alec wondered who she was trying to convince. Him? Or herself? "I guess I'm just clumsy. I wasn't payin' attention t' where I was goin'."

Clumsy? That wasn't a word Alec would use to describe Kate. She had a certain poise about her that most women worked years to achieve. Unlike those women, however, Kate came from the streets, which belied the likelihood that she hurt herself, especially to such an extent.

Had she gone out without Holmes knowing it? If so, why? Did she have a run-in with someone?

"How are you feeling?" Alec gently inquired, resisting the urge to brush the hair from her face.

Kate put the cloth aside. "Better," she murmured, but she wasn't, not really. Yet it wasn't her wounds that pained her.

Her fingers ached from clutching the material of the dress so tightly, but she had to hold together the huge, jagged tear her rash actions had caused. The dress was ruined, and it was all her fault.

What kind of insanity could have possessed her to chase after Alec?

After all he had done for her, she owed him an explanation. She just couldn't bring herself to tell him the truth. He would look at her in disgust if he heard how she had spent her evening; following him like a besotted schoolgirl, and then Falcon clobbering that horrible brute who had come after her. Perhaps the brute deserved it, but the authorities wouldn't believe her or Falcon. They were nobodies.

Something inside Kate rebelled at having Alec look at her any other way than he was at that moment, with compassion and something else which had the power to liquefy her entire being.

Suddenly she felt overwhelmed. Tears trickled slowly down her cheeks, the warm droplets splashing onto her hands. She never cried. It just wasn't done. She had an image to uphold, but she couldn't seem to help herself. The tears had started, and they wouldn't stop.

Alec took her hand in his. "Don't cry, Kate."

"I ain't cryin'," she denied even as another tear rolled down her cheek.

"Whatever is wrong, we can fix it," Alec promised.

Kate shook her head, the tears rolling faster. "It can never be fixed."

Alec sat down next to her on the bed. "I'll fix it. Just tell me what it is, Kate."

Hesitantly, Kate looked at him. She could feel the heat from where his hand held hers. It spread up and out like a slow-burning fire before finally settling in the pit of her belly. She was frightened, not understanding the reactions of her body whenever Alec was near. She wished . . . what did she wish? That a man like his lordship would like her, perhaps even care for her? That she could be the kind of woman he would respect? The type that would interest him? Wealthy. Beautiful. Refined.

Aristocratic.

Qualities Kate knew she would never possess as much as she may wish otherwise.

"I'm sorry," she whispered.

"Sorry? For what?"

Kate slowly removed her hands from her skirt. "I've ruined yer sister's dress. I'm sorry . . . I didn't mean t' do it. I swear. It was an accident."

"You're upset over the dress?" Alec asked in disbelief. "That's what all this is about?"

"I can't fix it," she replied in the most heart-wrenching voice Alec had ever heard.

"You don't have to fix it, Kate. The dress is not important."

"It ain't?"

"No."

"But it belongs t' yer sister. Won't she be mad that it's been ruined?"

Jane, Alec knew, wouldn't even miss the dress. She had a closet full of others, more beautiful and far more costly than the one he had lent to Kate.

"No, Jane won't be upset," he tried to reassure her. He smiled and added, "Besides, we just won't tell her."

"We won't?"

A tear glistened on her lashes and then fell on her cheek. Alec could no longer resist. His thumb gently swept it away, and then lingered on her smooth skin. Kate stared at him with luminous eyes, the blue the most vivid he had ever seen.

"No . . . we won't."

A long moment passed before Kate said in a small voice, "I wish I knew how t' sew. Then maybe I could mend it."

"I'll teach you how to sew if you want to learn," Alec heard himself offer, wondering what possessed him to do so.

He shrugged. What the hell? He could give it a shot. At worst, he would look like a fool. At best, he would be a hero. And for the latter, it was worth it.

A quick knock sounded at the door.

"Come," Alec called out before realizing he was in Kate's room, not his own.

"My lord?" came the querying voice of Mrs. Dearborn, her gray head appearing around the edge of the door. Before Alec could ask what she was doing up at such an hour, she told him. "I'm sorry to disturb you, but Holmes woke me and said you were in here with Miss Kate and that there may be a problem."

Bloody Holmes, Alec thought. He must have seen him come into Kate's room.

"Everything is fine, Mrs. Dearborn."

Alec wasn't about to tell his housekeeper the problem with Kate, mostly because he didn't want Kate to be embarrassed. She felt badly enough as it was. Unfortunately, the taper Mrs. Dearborn held in her hand cast a long beam of light into the room, directly onto Kate's dress and the rip that was now exposed.

"Oh, my child, what has happened?" Mrs. Dearborn bustled into the room. Alec could tell she was more concerned about Kate's appearance than the dress.

Mrs. Dearborn put the taper down on the bedside table and began clucking over her charge. To Alec's surprise, Kate let her.

After checking the scrapes and bruises and determining there wasn't much that could be done, Mrs. Dearborn turned her attention to the dress. "It can be fixed," she said resolutely.

Kate made no reply, just shook her head sadly.

"I remember how long it took my poor mother to teach me how to sew," Mrs. Dearborn began, gently cleaning the dirt off Kate's face. "I was the most dreadful student when it came to using needle and thread. I was certain I would never learn how to do it right. Either my thread would break or I'd get knot after knot. With much practice, I finally got it right."

Alec could see what his housekeeper was trying to do. No wonder he was quite fond of her.

"Mrs. Dearborn learned quite well, Kate," he said with a grin. "I've seen her handiwork. She's the one who taught me."

Kate looked at him as if she thought he was kidding. "I can't believe y' know how t' sew," she said.

Alec shrugged. "Well, it's true. And I'm pretty darn good, if you ask me."

"But y' have people t' do that for y'. Why would y' possibly do it yerself?"

"Why shouldn't I? I believe it's important to learn how to do things for yourself." Although his mother had nearly swooned when she found out. Young lords, she had said imperiously, did not sew nor did they press their own clothes or buff their own shoes. That was what servants were for. It didn't stop him, however.

When Kate looked at him as though she still didn't understand, he pressed on. "What if I were lost in the desert and the buttons of my shirt popped off, what would I do?"

"There ain't no desert around here."

"Use your imagination."

"Wot would y' be doin' in the desert?"

"I'm on holiday."

"Yer boshin' me. Why would y' go there? It's hot."

"Let's just say I like hot weather."

"Well then, y' wouldn't need yer shirt, I wager."

Alec raised an eyebrow. "So I guess you would go without your shirt, then?"

Kate gave him a glimmer of a smile. "All right. I take that back. But I still can't figure why y'd get lost."

"It's not important."

"Y' asked me t' use me imagination, and in me head I can't picture a man like you gettin' lost."

A man like him? Alec wondered exactly what she meant by that. Instead of asking, as he might have if they didn't have an audience, he said, "Just take my word for it."

"Where would Holmes be? Or Jeffries?"

"They stayed home."

"Why?"

"They were sick."

"With wot?"

The imp, Alec thought. "With a cold." That seemed to momentarily satisfy her. "Anyway, I'm in the desert, my shirt has lost all its buttons, and there is no one around to fix it. So I must do it myself."

"Where would y' get needle an' thread?"

"I just happened to have them." She raised her brow at that. "I am well-equipped when I travel to the desert," he added in answer to her silent question. "So now I can fix my own shirt, and when I am rescued I shall not be ill-prepared."

"Can y' really sew?"

Alec waved a hand at his housekeeper. "Ask Mrs. Dearborn if you don't believe me."

Mrs. Dearborn nodded. "He can sew, miss. And quite admirably at that."

"See? You heard it straight from the teacher. I was a sewing prodigy. How many men can claim that distinction?"

"Nobody'd admit it, I wager."

"Well, now that we've got that settled," Mrs. Dearborn said crisply. "I will see you bright and early in the morning, Miss Kate."

Kate furrowed her brow. "Wot for?"

"So I can teach you how to sew just like I taught his lordship." And on that note, the housekeeper turned on her heel and quit the room.

Kate shook her head in disbelief, yet she felt oddly excited by the prospect of learning how to sew. And as she glanced down at the rip in the dress, she thought that maybe, just maybe, she would be able to fix it well enough so that Alec's sister wouldn't be angry if she found out what had happened.

And just maybe Alec would admire her accomplishment.

But another thought caused Kate to frown. "Wot about me job?"

An odd expression crossed Alec's face. "What about it?"

"Well . . . do y' still want me after wot I done?" Kate quietly asked.

Alec's face was cast in semishadow, his eyes glittering disks of velvet and onyx. He was so close that the heat of him enveloped her. When his lip curved up slightly, she knew the urge to trace a finger along its smooth contour.

"What exactly have you done, Kate?" His voice had a low, rich quality about it, swirling warm tendrils of languor around her. How she wanted to lean her head against his shoulder and draw in the strength and smell of him.

Unconsciously, Kate edged closer to him. Her fingers brushed against his hand, the slight contact causing her blood to warm and her body to shiver, like when she had touched her fingers to his forehead; only it was much stronger this time.

He shifted one finger, laying it on top of hers. She thought it a mistake, that he didn't know he touched her. But when his finger began to gently stroke over hers, she knew it had been no mistake. That small gesture made her heart sing. Inside, something she couldn't name began to unfurl. Something no one else had ever touched in her before.

"What have you done, Kate?" he asked again, his face seeming closer than it had been just moments before. His words confused her, making her wonder if they were still talking about the dress.

"I've ruined yer sister's dress," she murmured in reply, wondering at the breathless quality of her voice.

"Should I call out the queen's army over it?"

For a moment, his words made Kate recall the man Falcon had clouted over the head. Would the brute remember their faces? Or Kate's, at least, since he hadn't seen Falcon? Would he go to the constable? Would they find her?

Would they hurt Alec because of her?

"Kate?" Alec softly prompted.

"Hmm."

"Don't worry about the dress. Material possessions can be replaced. I'm just glad you're all right."

"Y' are?" she breathed, her body wanting to sway toward him.

"I am." His words were a caress. "When you're ready, perhaps you'll tell me about what happened."

Kate knew he was leaving an open door for her to confide in him. Did he see the lie for what it was? Did he now think her a thief *and* a liar? Her heart pained her with the thought. She wanted Alec to see her as someone good and worthwhile. She vowed to try harder.

"It's late," Alec said at length. "You need to get some rest."

Kate didn't want him to leave. The realization that she wanted to be around him—a bloody lord, no less—struck her squarely in the chest. The way he looked at her made her want something else she didn't quite understand. Her lips began to tingle as he stared at them.

Abruptly, he stood up. For a long moment, he gazed at her with unreadable eyes before murmuring, "Good night, Kate."

When the door closed softly after him, Kate realized they still hadn't discussed her job. But as she grabbed up a pillow and hugged it tightly to her, she knew it didn't matter.

As long as she was with Alec.

Chapter Fourteen

True to her word, Mrs. Dearborn came by the next morning and began teaching Kate how to sew—or attempted to teach her, that was.

Disgusted, Kate glared at the mangled piece of material in her hands. Who would have thought that the Fox— known far and wide for her nimble fingers—would be at sixes and sevens over something as thin as a piece of thread and as small as a needle? Damn and blast if she didn't poke herself with that needle at least a dozen times during her first attempt to sew a straight line! Not only didn't she get the bloody stitch straight, but the lousy thread became knotted over and over again.

The one thing she did learn that morning was that she lacked patience and could be quite testy. She had found herself snapping at poor Mrs. Dearborn. The woman would probably refuse to continue Kate's instruction after the way she had been treated. Who could blame her?

The only good thing that came from Kate's foray into the pits of sewing hell was that Mrs. Dearborn was a fount of information about his lordship, regaling Kate with tales of a mischievous youth.

"Oh, Lord Alec was a handful," the housekeeper said cheerfully as she sewed up the seams of a lovely, decorative pillow. "He was a scamp to the very marrow of his bones."

Kate tried to remain indifferent, not wanting to give the housekeeper the wrong impression. She knew Alec would never think of her as anything other than an employee of a job she had yet to hear further about. She should count herself lucky to have a job. She knew better than to mistake his kindness as something else, something different.

Still, she couldn't help but ask, "Wot kind of things did he do?"

"What didn't he do is the question! The lad just couldn't keep out of trouble."

Kate laid the piece of material she had been effectively mutilating down in her lap and glanced up at the jovial, plump woman. "Are we talkin' about the same person?" she asked, incredulous. "His lordship used t' get in trouble?" That was an idea she had a hard time swallowing. The man she met was proper and forthright with an undeniable air of respectability shrouding him. She figured he had been born that way. He was a blue blood, after all. She could more easily picture him as a lad dressed impeccably from head to toe, sporting that same diamond that winked at her from the folds of his perfectly tied cravat, than as a hellion, a rabble-rouser—which was the image Mrs. Dearborn would have her believe.

"He used to get in trouble all the time," the housekeeper eagerly replied, her head bobbing merrily. Her salt-and-pepper hair was done up perfectly on top of her head, not a single strand out of place. Kate wondered what the woman did to keep it from moving. Even the wind from the open window she sat next to didn't seem to affect it. "Don't let that cool, unruffled exterior fool you, my dear. The man is still a boy at heart."

Kate remembered the too brief episode she and Alec had shared in the bathing room, when he had splashed her. It was rather small in the scheme of things, but it did reveal a slightly different side of Alec, one that had surprised and delighted her, even if she had scowled at him for doing it.

"So wot did he do t' earn such a reputation? Not eat his beef an' puddin's? Or were his shoes not properly shined?"

"Scoff if you will, my girl, but his lordship was fairly on his way to a military academy. He was a terror, leaving toads in his sister's bed and worms in her bureau." Mrs. Dearborn chuckled, her round tummy jiggling with mirth. "Another one of his favorite pastimes was hiding underneath the dining room table when Lord and Lady Somerset were having company. The lad had a fake spider. He would pick a victim, whoever struck his fancy, and very cautiously he would place the thing on someone's leg or set it beside their plate, just waiting for the howls to begin."

"He didn't!" Kate cried in disbelief.

"Yes, he did!" Mrs. Dearborn parried. "And poor Holmes, he had more than one run-in with his lordship. One of the lad's favorite tricks was filling Holmes's slippers with pudding. I'm sure you can imagine what happened the next morning when the butler unknowingly put his feet into them."

Kate's eyes widened. "Puddin'?" she choked out. Oh, now she knew she liked his lordship. *Poor, old Holmes,* her bloody behind! How she would have loved to see the expression on the face of old misery-guts when he sunk his feet into the cold, gloppy pudding!

"God bless Lord Edward," Mrs. Dearborn went on with a wistful sigh. "Lord Alec's father was a sainted fellow. He never quite knew what to do with his young son. He found it difficult to discipline the lad. He said he didn't want to crush the boy's spirit, that he was merely going through growing pains, and someday he would become a fine young man. And indeed he has," she finished with a nod of her head.

Kate silently agreed with Mrs. Dearborn's assessment. Out loud, she said, "He ain't too bad, I s'pose.

The housekeeper went on as if Kate hadn't spoken. "Lord Edward had a keen understanding of people and was much loved."

Kate put down her sewing. "Was?"

"Lord Edward died some time ago." The housekeeper shook her head sadly. "At a young age, Lord Alec found himself thrust into great deal of responsibility. But the lad rallied forth. Indeed, he did. He straightened right up and took over as if he had been doing it all along. I never had any doubt hc would," she said with a great deal of pride in her voice. "Lord Alec was his father's son in every way."

Kate thought about all the weight pressed on Alec's shoulders. Certainly they were very broad, well-defined, and undeniably strong shoulders, but the man should have been able to enjoy more of his youth, which was a strange thought coming from her, a girl who had had no childhood. But she couldn't say she hadn't had her good times. There was Falcon to keep her laughing.

Mrs. Dearborn rose stiffly from her chair and put a hand to her back. "Well, that will be all for this morning, my girl." She came over to see what Kate had wrought, studying it very closely with not a single look of disgust marring her face. "It's coming along," she murmured, patting Kate on the shoulder. Kate thought her lie was very kind. "Tomorrow we shall try some cross-stitches." She held out the intricate and beautiful pillow she had made. "This is for you, my dear."

"For me?" Kate gazed at the pillow and then up at the housekeeper. "It ain't."

Mrs. Dearborn nodded. "It is. Unless you don't want it."

"No!" Kate practically shouted. Shaking her head, she quickly amended, "I mean, yes, I want it." Reverently, she took the pillow, softly adding, "Thank y', mum."

Mrs. Dearborn smiled warmly. "You're welcome, my dear. And my name is Dorothy. My friends call me Dotty."

"Am I . . . ?"

"You are."

Kate flushed with pleasure. "Thank y' . . . Dotty."

The housekeeper turned to go. Kate gnawed on her lip, debating the wisdom of what she was about to ask.

When Mrs. Dearborn was at the door, Kate called out, "Wait."

"Yes, Kate?"

Now that her new friend's attention was focused on her again, Kate felt at a loss for words. But remembering her vow of last night, where she had sworn to try to improve herself, Kate screwed up her courage and asked, "Will y' teach me how t' read an' write? Y' speak so nice an' yer not a highborn lady. Just someone like meself." Thinking she had probably just insulted her new friend, Kate quickly added, "I mean—"

"I know what you mean, my dear." Mrs. Dearborn's tone was kindly and understanding.

Feeling stupid and embarrassed, Kate shook her head

and looked down at her feet. "Forget it. I don't know wot I was thinkin'."

"I think it's a splendid idea, Kate."

Kate's gaze flew to the housekeeper, whose silver-gray eyes twinkled with delight. "Y' do?"

"Indeed."

Kate bowed her head, running a finger over the crooked stitches in the material she had been working on. "I shouldn't have asked. Y' probably got more important things t' do than t' be teachin' me vowels an' the like."

"I'm honored you asked me, Kate." And then in a brisk voice of authority, Mrs. Dearborn said, "We shall begin this evening after dinner."

"But—"

"No buts, my girl. Be ready to work when I return." With a wink and a smile, Dotty Dearborn was gone.

The next morning, Kate recited her vowels and practiced her pronunciation as she stood before her mirror.

"The little lad is in the larder," she said over and over again, not quite understanding how saying such a sentence would help her. But the way Dotty said the words sounded different than how Kate said them. So Kate repeated them until she hated the lad and his larder as well as Becky's beau who had a bushel of baked beans.

In the excitement of the day, Kate had completely forgotten to ask Dotty about her job. Oh, well, Dotty would probably tell her today.

A knock sounded at her door. A moment later, the door opened a crack. "Can I come in, Kate?" Dotty asked tentatively.

Kate smiled. "Y' know yer always welcome. I don't know why y' even ask."

"Because it's the polite thing to do, my dear," her friend replied as she stepped into the room.

Kate made a mental note, adding this newest information to the list she had begun to compile since her instructions with Dotty had begun the night before.

Kate noticed her dress draped over Dotty's arm. "Oh, y' fixed it!"

"I did." Dotty beamed as she handed the dress over for Kate's inspection.

"Y' can't even tell it was torn."

"I did my best."

Kate then noticed the other items Dotty had brought with her. "Wot are those?"

"It would appear they are dresses, my girl," Dotty answered, humor adding further wrinkles to the lines around her eyes.

"Who are they for?" Kate asked, not looking at her friend but at the two dresses. One was cornflower blue with white lace rimming the bodice and hem, the other a delicate pink with tiny red rosebuds.

Dotty held them up to herself. The material barely covered her ample chest and hips. "I don't believe they'll be fitting me any time soon. So, I imagine they are for you."

Kate blinked. "For me? I don't understand."

A secret smile curved Dotty's lips. "There's nothing to understand. His lordship said you were to have them. And here they are."

"Alec—I mean, his lordship—gave these t' me? They're all mine?"

Dotty nodded. "He did. And they are. Now, let's try them on and see how lovely you look."

Kate put on first one dress then another, pirouetting in front of Dotty, who claimed she looked delightful in every outfit. Kate was overjoyed to find that each dress fit her to perfection. Dotty had taken up the hems and nipped in the sides.

Then the big decision came. Which one to wear that day? Kate mulled over her choices as if she had an extensive wardrobe, discarding at will and then changing her mind. She chuckled to herself, thinking she was behaving positively ridiculous.

Finally, she made her choice, donning the pink dress, which Dotty said brought out the rosy flush in her cheeks and the sparkle in her blue eyes.

With an excitement that was hard to contain, Kate sat down for another sewing lesson. Her teacher was very patient and didn't take her to task when she accidentally sewed part of her project onto the pillow she had placed in her lap. Well, at least her stitches were getting a bit straighter, she consoled herself.

Kate was more than ready for breakfast when the time came, and went down the steps with a certain lightness of spirit. She heard Alec's voice, and her heart beat a bit faster. She pinched her cheeks as Dotty had showed her, then squared her shoulders and breezed into the room.

"Good mornin', Alec," she said cheerily, waiting for him to notice her.

To her dismay, Alec barely glanced her way. "Good morning," he mumbled.

Holmes, ever present, passed behind her, hissing, "It's *my lord.*"

Kate threw over her shoulder, "Don't y' have somethin' t' polish?" She walked away before she heard his muttered reply.

Hurt by Alec's disregard, Kate plunked herself down in a seat to his right, not waiting for the footman who rushed forward and pulled out a chair at the opposite end of the table. How did the man think they could communicate with her being all the way down there?

Picking up her fork, Kate jabbed aimlessly at the plate of food placed before her. Alec continued to read his paper as if she wasn't there.

"Anythin' interestin' in there?" she asked with the hopes of some conversation.

Slowly, Alec lowered the paper and peered at her in a way that unnerved her. "No."

Kate fidgeted under his close scrutiny. "Ye're lookin' awful serious. Did someone die?" she nervously joked. Alec obviously didn't get the humor. "Wot's that thing say?" She pointed to the paper, anything to keep from being the sole focus of his intense regard. Still, he made no reply.

What, did a cat have his bloomin' tongue?

Fine. If he didn't want to speak, then he could listen.

Picking up her toast, Kate slathered jam on it and said conversationally, "A hawker at the corner stand read a paper t' me an' the lads once. He had a voice that sounded like he was speakin' out his nose. Annoyin', it was. We didn't even get through the first page before we left. But it weren't because of his voice that we hied off. It was 'cause he made the lads uncomfortable." She paused, gauging his mood, before asking, "Y' wanna know why?"

A moment passed before Alec nodded his head.

Leaning forward, the toast clutched in one hand, a knife in the other, she said only loud enough for him to hear, "The bloke were bent as a nine bob note." When Alec merely raised an eyebrow, she added, "Y' know, he was camp as a row o' tents." The eyebrow inched up. "A nancy boy." Nothing. "A shirtlifter." Frustrated at his lack of understanding, she practically shouted, "Blimey, luv, he was queer!" Which caused everyone in earshot to gasp collectively. Behind her came the sound of breaking glass and Holmes muttering apologies.

Kate didn't care about them. She watched Alec. She thought she saw a weakening of his rigid bearing, perhaps even a slight smile on his lips.

"I understood you the first time," he drawled.

Kate's nervousness began to ease. She wondered if she had only imagined that he didn't seem pleased to see her.

Relieved, she smiled at him.

In return, he frowned at her.

The next moment he rose from the table, bid her good day and excused himself, his boots ringing loudly on the parquet floor.

Kate's usual voracious appetite dissipated. Pushing her plate away, she got up from the table, leaving the room with a heavier tread than the one with which she had entered.

For more than a fortnight, she received the same treatment from Alec. He was not so much cold as he was distant, polite, reserved. For the life of her, she couldn't figure out what had caused the change in him. What had she done?

Kate contemplated leaving. But that was as far as she got. For reasons unknown, she looked forward to the few minutes she spent with Alec at breakfast and supper. But damn and blast if the man didn't up and leave just when things were warming up. Inevitably he would clam up and claim a pressing engagement or a mountain of work, and poof, he would be gone with the wind.

It was boredom making her meaner than a cornered rat, Kate told herself. She lacked for anything to do to keep herself and her wandering, unproductive thoughts from going off half-cocked. Alec had said he would find her a job, but what he said and what he did were two entirely different things. He hadn't mentioned the job again since that first morning. So she spent her time twiddling her thumbs or glaring at his closed office door when she passed it, which was often. There were times when she wanted to do something wild just to get his attention.

She missed him.

Chapter Fifteen

"Planning my demise, are you?" said a voice laced with warmth and contrition instead of cool politeness.

Shocked, Kate's head whipped in the speaker's direction.

Alec.

Her heart skipped several beats at the sight of him, drinking him in as if he were a glass of water after being in the desert for three long days. The man had no right to look so incredibly handsome, especially when she was angry with him.

But why was he back? He had left the house ten minutes ago, telling Holmes he wouldn't be home until late.

Kate hadn't heard him return because she had been in the midst of planning something to get his attention. Oddly enough, his question struck her as rather apropos, considering where her thoughts had so recently been.

"Are y' sure y' want t' know?"

"I guess I deserve that." Alec's grin was boyish and charming. "I've been . . . preoccupied of late. Forgive me."

Forgive me. Two small words took away the bite of pain Kate had been feeling at his desertion. She tried to remain angry with him for ignoring her, but couldn't.

"I was hoping you would go riding with me," he then said.

Kate wouldn't have been more surprised had a big circle of wind sucked her up into the sky.

She blinked. "Ridin'?"

"Yes. As in you, me, and two horses."

Horses? Kate groaned inwardly.

She wanted to do something with him, but why couldn't it be a game of cards? She was quite handy with a deck, knew all sorts of tricks, mostly illegal. If he was set on involving animals, then why not a cat or a bird? Small. Fury. *Harmless.* Did it have to be a four-legged behemoth with an attitude? She didn't know how to ride a horse— and didn't want to know. But that was a confession the devil couldn't have dragged out of her at that moment.

"If y' want," she replied with a shrug, proud that her voice sounded even-toned.

Alec gave her a roguish smile. "I want."

A half hour later, Kate wished the devil *had* made her tell Alec the truth as she held on to the reins of the chestnut mare with a death grip that made her knuckles look as if they would pop through her skin at any moment.

"This is hopeless, I tell y'," Kate muttered, glaring at the back of the horse's head as if this would make the animal obey her. She was sure the horse, called Lady— who in her opinion was misnamed—knew of her displeasure. The bloody beast was purposely trying to annoy her. "Blast y', horse! I said t' go forward!"

Alec watched Kate with a great deal of amusement as

she held on to the horse's reins for dear life. Their horses were ambling. If they went any slower, they would be at a dead stop.

She wore her boy's togs and had insisted on sitting astride, refusing the sidesaddle—or *that blasted contraption*, as she had referred to it. She had told him quite plainly, "I ain't givin' the blighted nag the chance t' toss me on me bum." He thought it best not to tell her the *blighted nag* could toss her on her bum whether she sat astride or not.

Alec told himself the only reason he hadn't gone to Hyde Park to ride was because there would be too many people he might run into who would ask too many questions about Kate. Questions to which he didn't have answers.

Instead, he had gone to a more secluded spot with fewer distractions. It wasn't just to be alone with Kate, although the idea had merit.

At that point, Alec had to remind himself he was now responsible for Kate—in a way. He had offered her employment, and when he found the right job for her, one that suited her skills. . . .

But what were her skills? Besides thievery—which he didn't think he could utilize in a legal fashion and which would obviously negate the whole point behind his offer of employment.

And what was the right job? Maid? Kitchen help? He already had more people than he needed. Besides, he wasn't immune to the grumbling going on around his house. Even if he were oblivious, Holmes would fill him in. His butler made a point of reiterating everything he heard, in detail—just in case.

It seemed the staff liked Kate, but didn't want to work with her. She was a thief, and therefore not to be trusted.

It made the situation very touchy and might cause problems he didn't have the time for. It also might hurt Kate. Why that should bother him, Alec wasn't quite sure. He had never concerned himself with any of his other employees getting adjusted. Either they did or they didn't. Besides, Kate was tough, wasn't she?

A vision of a tear-streaked face rose up in front of him, pain and sorrow battling within the depths of her blue eyes because she had torn her dress. Something had changed inside him after that, something indefinable, making him want to keep Kate near, yet keep her at a distance at the same time.

Nevertheless, Alec had committed himself to helping her. He wouldn't shirk his responsibilities, even though he already had a full plate of things demanding his time, things that had kept him from coming to any decision on what to do about Kate.

But if he should find an ideal spot for her, then what?

Then he would have done his good deed. That was what this was all about, wasn't it? To do something worthwhile for Society? To better his fellow man—or woman, as the case may be?

But Kate wasn't a woman. She was a child.

Wasn't she?

Alec wished he could stop asking himself that question. He was becoming quite batty about the bloody subject. However, the thought did cross his mind that he had never had a more opportune time to ask. But would knowing make any difference? Could he allow it to make any difference? He wanted to believe his actions in regards to Kate's welfare were motivated by concern for another human being and nothing more. Even if she wasn't a child, she was his charge and deserved to be left unmolested, untouched, pure. And if he kept repeating those words, then maybe they would sink in.

"Y' cursed mule!" Kate hissed at the ornery horse. "I'll see that yer made into glue, just see if I don't!"

The horse, as if sensing she was being yelled at, turned her head to look at Kate through one huge, brown eye. "That's right, I'm talkin' about you, y' lazy beast! Don't y' dare glare at me!" The horse's muzzle inched toward her leg, showing teeth. "Don't even think about it, buster! I'll bite y' right back!"

Kate didn't realize how crazy she sounded. She was having a fight with a horse, which was obviously one-sided since the horse could not argue back. But she had built up some frustration that she had yet to vent, and the horse seemed as if it was looking for a fight. She was more than happy to oblige.

She was caught up short by Alec's roar of laughter.

"An' just wot's so funny?" she asked tightly, turning her glare from the horse to the horse's owner.

"You are," he answered, sobering. "You do realize that Lady doesn't have a clue as to what you are going on about, don't you?"

"Are y' takin' the horse's side?"

"I'm taking no one's side," Alec calmly replied. "I am merely stating a fact."

"This horse is purposely annoyin' me!" Kate insisted with a pout.

"Have you stopped to think that maybe *you* are annoying Lady?"

Kate stared at him mulishly.

Alec shook his head and chuckled. "Lady is not so bad once you get to know her."

Kate snorted in disbelief. "That's wot—what—y' said

about the blond-haired lout and old toad-face," she returned.

"In normal circumstances both of them are relatively good-natured."

Kate was ready to take issue on such a blatantly false claim. "Good-natured compared to wot? An angry bull? A nest of bees?"

"If you give Lady a nudge behind the girth, that should get her moving."

Nothin' like speakin' plain English, Kate thought sourly. *A nudge behind the girth? Where the blinkin' heck is the girth?*

She cocked an eyebrow at him. "And where might that girth be?" she dryly inquired.

"Well, the girth is the strap that holds the saddle onto the horse," he explained, pointing to the part in question. "Just give her a gentle kick with your heels and you should be on your way." He gave a demonstration with his black stallion, who promptly obeyed.

"Y' want me t' kick her?" The very idea appalled Kate. The blasted mule would probably just kick her right back.

Alec nodded. "Just remember what I told you about holding the reins, gentle but firm."

Kate's eyes crossed. Gentle but firm? How did one go about being gentle and firm in relation to holding the thin straps called reins? Was he purposely trying to drive her mad?

"Y' want me t' be gentle and firm?"

"Yes. Be relaxed but in command."

Kate was going to scream. "So which is it? Gentle an' firm or relaxed but in command?"

"Both."

"Yer balmy," Kate muttered, feeling irritated by everything. "An' I'm not kickin' this horse! I will not be a party t' animal abuse!'' Threats were one thing; getting physical was entirely different.

"It's not animal abuse," Alec calmly returned. "It's merely a form of conditioning, a signal if you will. Lady understands when you tap her behind her girth that you are asking her to move forward. That is just the way it is done, and I assure you it doesn't hurt the animal.''

"I still say it's abuse," Kate grumbled. "Why can't y' just ask the horse t' go forward?''

"Lady would not understand such a command," Alec replied without inflection, although Kate felt sure he was silently laughing at her.

"How would y' know unless y' tried?''

Alec regarded her closely. "What's really the matter here, Kate? I don't believe this has anything to do with the horse.''

"Yes, it does," she stubbornly maintained. "This horse don't—doesn't—like me an' . . . she's ignorin' me.'' She looked Alec straight in the eye as she added, "I don't like t' be ignored.''

"I can see that.''

"I tried t' be nice," she rushed out. "I tried t' do what I was told an' act like a lady, an' not put me elbows on the table, or swear, or chew the inside of me mouth, or use me fingers t' eat when I'm supposed t' use the fork, or drop water on the hallway floor when Holmes is walkin' down it, or stick me tongue out at him when he's bein' a rotter—an' that was bloody difficult, I vow.''

Alec felt like dirt. He had been avoiding Kate, and she was hurt by it. He had never behaved in such a way. What she made him feel, well, it was new and bloody annoying. His body reacted to her whenever she was near.

He had told himself more than once to end this incredi- ble, yet strange fascination he had with the young and beautiful thief. But he couldn't seem to bring himself to do anything about it. So he had made himself a prisoner in his office, thinking far too often about her smile and effervescence while simultaneously beating himself up over his licentious thoughts. One would have thought he would know better than to invite her out for a ride. But common sense was lacking in his life recently.

"An' I really try not t' swagger like a man," she added to her list with a big sigh.

"Who says you swagger like a man?" That one astonished Alec. It was as far from the truth as one could possibly get. Kate had a sensuous derriere that swayed so enticingly he had found himself distracted more than once—or ten times.

"Holmes," she practically spat the word.

Alec should have guessed. "Holmes is just having himself a grand time pecking at you. Frankly, I think he's feeling a bit territorial."

"Like a dog, y' mean?"

Alec didn't think Holmes would appreciate the comparison.

"In a way," he replied. "Holmes has been with me for a long time. He acts like a mother hen sometimes. I think he still believes me a green lad."

Alec found himself the recipient of a rather appraising look from Kate. "Blimey O' Reilly," she said with a low whistle. "I ain't—have—never seen any lad wot looks like you, an' that's a God-given fact." Her eyes widened, and she slapped her hand over her mouth.

Alec grinned. "I do believe that's a compliment."

A rosy blush crept along Kate's cheeks. "Wot I meant t' say was that you're too tall t' be a lad an' . . . y' have whiskers growin'. So only a blind person would think you're anything but a man full grown."

"I see. Well, that makes sense. Thank you for clarifying things. I was rather confused as to where exactly I ranked in the scheme of things."

"You're makin' fun of me!"

Alec smiled. "I guess I am."

Kate crossed her arms mutinously in front of her. "Well, I don't appreciate it."

Obviously his attempt at getting back into Kate's good graces had fallen short of the mark. She was miffed. But how could he explain to her that he had just been trying to keep a respectable distance, which was damnably hard in light of a freshness he found nearly irresistible.

A light mist of rain suddenly started. Alec took Lady's reins and moved toward the wide, protective cover of a white oak.

Turning to look at Kate, Alec found her eyes closed and her head tilted back as if she hoped to feel the rain on her face. His breath locked in his throat.

Slowly, she opened her eyes and peered curiously at him. "Have y' ever smelled the rain before a thunderstorm?" she asked.

"No, I don't believe I have."

"Have y' ever felt the bite of cold in the air when autumn turns to winter?"

Alec shook his head.

"Well, have y' ever tasted the rain?"

Again, he shook his head. The look Kate gave him made him feel as if he had been deprived. All the things that lay right outside his door, things that were free to every human being, he had never truly experienced. But Kate had experienced them, and he suddenly found himself envying that.

Since he had met her, there were things he wanted to do, to see. He had all the possessions one could want, but not the important things—things no amount of money could buy. Alec knew Anthony would laugh his ass off if he heard him say that. Whitfield believed everything had a price.

Alec sobered as he gazed upon Kate's defiant beauty. He longed to kiss her. "You don't swagger, by the way," he said quietly, leaning toward her.

"I don't?"

Kate was breathless as Alec stared at her with a suspended look in his eyes. She followed his gaze as it touched upon her hair, the contour of her mouth, the curve of her body. She stirred restlessly as his gaze returned once more to her mouth. Her tongue darted out to moisten her suddenly dry lips. A sweet tension stole over her, holding her still. She felt that if she breathed too deeply or inclined her body even a fraction of an inch toward him, she would be in his arms.

Suddenly, Kate realized that was what she wanted, needed, from the first moment she had laid eyes on Alec. But she hadn't understood her frustration having never experienced the thrumming of blood rushing through her veins making every part of her sensitive and aching.

"Please," she heard herself beg in a husky whisper, not recognizing her own voice.

That one word severed Alec's control. "Damn," he murmured right before his mouth captured hers.

The press of his lips had Kate reeling from the sensuous feelings. It was a kiss of such gentle sweetness, such reverence, it touched her to the heart.

Alec pulled her from her saddle onto his lap. His tongue teased the corners of her mouth, then brushed over the swell of her lips, scrambling all thought.

His mouth settled over hers, probing, parting, growing more demanding with each passing moment. Sensations blossomed inside her, fire and passion and need. She knew a yearning as hot as it was haunting.

He groaned her name; it was a ragged, incoherent sound seemingly torn from some deep place inside him, bringing an answering response in Kate.

Her hands clung to his forearms, feeling the strength beneath her palms. Her fingers skimmed upward along arms that could crush her if they were so inclined, arms that could bend her to his will if that was his intention. Yet they were arms that gently embraced her, made her feel protected, cared for. She curled her hands around his neck and dug her fingers into his thick mane of ebony hair.

Kate clung to him as his tongue plunged deeper into her mouth. She was sure he could hear her heart, it beat so loud. Her entire being was more alive than it had ever been. She heard Alec groan, and it was the most wonderful sound ever.

Suddenly, the horse shifted and whickered beneath her. Alec broke away, a look of self-loathing in his eyes.

"God, Kate, I'm so sorry," he murmured. "I promise that won't ever happen again."

Kate was devastated.

Chapter Sixteen

For the rest of the day, Kate stayed in her room, staring out the window at nothing in particular, wondering what had made Alec pull away from her—and not liking the reasons her mind produced.

She heaved a sigh as a knock sounded at her door. For a moment, she felt too lethargic to answer, but thinking it might be Alec, she said, "Come in."

"Supper's on the table, miss," said Nora, one of the maids. "Mrs. Dearborn sent me tae fetch ye." She paused, her light green eyes assessing. "Are ye feeling well?"

No, Kate wanted to reply, but then she would have to explain what was the matter, especially since her appetite was renowned. Considering there wasn't anything physically wrong with her, what could she say? That she was acting pitiful and mooning around because of a kiss, one she had practically begged for? The thought had the power to bring heat to her cheeks.

Forcing a smile, she replied, "I'm fit as a fiddle an' ready t' eat." And eat she would, every bloody morsel put in front of her if she had to choke on it to do so.

With a sluggish gait, Kate quit the bedroom and began the trek down the seemingly endless hallway.

Standing at the top of the staircase, she was about to descend when she heard a voice that stopped her in her tracks.

Alec.

Her heart began to beat like a trip hammer as she thought about seeing him again, eating dinner with him, perhaps. . . .

She shook her head. *Go down the stairs, ninny!*

Kate had only taken one step when she heard Alec say, "Is the carriage ready, Holmes?"

"Yes, my lord," came Holmes's raspy voice.

"Good. I will be dining with Whitfield and shall not be home until quite late. Don't wait up."

"As you wish, my lord."

Kate heard the hollow sound of boots ringing across the marble foyer. Then a touch of cool night air swept up the staircase as the door opened before the decided click of it being shut.

Alec was gone.

Kate couldn't recall what she ate for dinner, but she felt sick from it as she mounted the stairs, her thoughts as heavy as her tread.

She knew she should leave, and decided to do so, knowing she was too uncomfortable to stay. She was sure Alec just didn't know how to ask her to go.

Why had he offered her the job, then?

Did it really matter anymore? He had obviously changed

his mind and decided he didn't want a thief working in his house.

It seemed no one else wanted her there either, Kate painfully discovered, watching one of the scullery maids as she came down the hallway hugging the wall, a wary expression on her pale, timid face.

I'm not some sort of disease, Kate wanted to shout. But it was not the first such look she had received. Well, what could she expect? Open arms?

Foolish, foolish dreams.

Reaching the safe haven of her bedroom, Kate closed the door and leaned back against it. She stayed that way for a long time before stirring herself from her lethargy.

She moved to the closet. Slipping out of her dress, she hung it up, looking at it for a long moment before closing the door. Then she donned her shirt and breeches. The street urchin once more.

Glancing around, Kate felt as if she had forgotten something. She shook her head. She hadn't had anything to begin with. Nothing. Except the clothes on her back. That was all that belonged to her and all she would take.

Picking up the pillow Mrs. Dearborn had made her, Kate traced the delicate embroidered pattern, the stitches so fine, so perfectly done.

Reluctantly, she placed it back in the center of the bed. It belonged there. She was the only thing that didn't belong. She would leave the pillow and the dresses behind, along with the fond memories she had begun to build in the home of a dark-eyed lord.

It was time to go.

Kate had the doorknob in her hand when she heard a sound. She stopped, holding her breath, her ears attuned to any noise.

The noise came again. Clack ... clack ... clack. Something was being thrown at her window.

Whirling around, Kate moved to the window, pushing back the drapes and throwing open the sash.

"Who's there?" she called out into the darkness.

"It's me," a familiar voice returned.

"Weasel?"

"Yeah"

"Is it just you down there?"

"Yeah."

"Has somethin' happened?"

"Yeah."

Kate gritted her teeth. "Well?" Weasel had always been a man of few words. Unfortunately, those few words were never enlightening. "Well, wot is it?"

"It's Falcon."

A chill settled over Kate. "Stay right there. I'm comin' down."

Kate eased out of her room, down the back stairway and out of the house. "Weasel?" she called in a hushed voice when her eyes met nothing but the blackness of the night.

"I'm here." Weasel materialized from behind a tall shrub.

Kate rushed over to him. Now, up close, she could see the fear written plainly on his face. Something terrible had happened. A snap of cold dread crawled along her spine.

"Where's Falcon?"

The whites of Weasel's eyes showed clearly in the darkness. "Falcon's been nabbed by Drake."

"Drake!" Kate's limbs weakened hearing the name.

Drake was the most hated, the most feared, of all the criminals in London. Not only was he a thief, but a murderer as well.

Drake had declared himself the undisputed king of the

underworld, and all who wanted to remain in *his* town had to pay homage, which meant that half the spoils went to him along with anything else he demanded. Those who didn't comply were meted out some form of retribution or met with an untimely and usually painful death.

Thus far, Kate and the lads had managed to steer clear of him. They stole only enough to get by, which made them far from a threat. And if ever there was a time when the thought of having Drake to contend with wasn't enough of a deterrent, there was always the looming possibility of spending time locked behind the dank walls of Newgate. There was nothing worth stealing that would doom her and the lads to either of those fates.

Why was Drake suddenly involving himself in their lives? She posed that question to Weasel.

"He found out that y'd taken up with a bloody lord," he answered succinctly. "He weren't none too happy about the fact that y' didn't let him know."

"Let him know? It wasn't any of his business!" Kate retorted angrily.

Weasel's expression told her he didn't share her opinion. "Have y' already forgotten that the man thinks everythin' is his business? Y' haven't been away that long."

No, she hadn't been away long at all. "But why take Falcon? I don't understand."

Weasel shrugged. "Guess he couldn't get t' you wot with y' bein' all locked up in that friggin' palace with yer new friends." There was a bitter note in his voice.

"They aren't—ain't—me friends." God, her brain was muddled from Mrs. Dearborn's grammar lessons.

"Woulda fooled me since we barely seen y'."

"I've been busy."

"Yeah? Doin' wot?"

"Work."

Weasel eyed her. "Wot kinda work? Y' never did tell us."

Kate flashed him an annoyed look. "This isn't the time t' be discussin' it." Before Weasel could respond, she went on. "Wot I want t' know is why Drake didn't just have you or Rat come and get me."

"If I could read the man's mind, d' ya think I'd be here?"

Kate ignored his sarcasm. "He knows I woulda come."

"Would y'?" Weasel's expression held a shade of doubt.

"Of course!"

"Well, maybe he thought y' needed t' be reminded who yer friends are an' where y' rightly belong."

Kate gritted her teeth. "I never forgot." Still, guilt swamped her. Had she forgotten her friends? Had she not allowed her silly dreams to carry her away, Drake would have left her and the lads alone. "Why Falcon?" she murmured, speaking more to herself than Weasel.

"As opposed t' me or Rat, y' mean?"

Kate's gaze collided with his. "No! Sweet Mary, wot's gotten into y'?"

"Yer askin' why, why, why," he said in an exasperated tone. "Have y' not heard a thing I've said to y'? Can y' really not figure it out?" He threw up his hands. "Yer livin' in the house of a *wealthy* lord. Drake thinks y've been holdin' out on him, keepin' the loot t' yerself."

"What loot? I haven't taken a bloody thing."

Weasel's eyes widened in disbelief. "Y' haven't? Well, wot the churnin' hell have y' been doin' with yerself all this time? Sippin' tea and eatin' cakes?"

"I never said I was goin' t' take anything!" Kate fired back, even though she had given just that impression.

"Are y' crazy?" Weasel's expression said he thought so.

"Ye're in the house of a rich nabob an' y' don't take nothin'? Wot kinda thief are y'?"

Kate knew she should be indignant over his comment. There was a time when she took great pride in being a thief who had never gotten caught, who could pinch the bread right off your plate and no one would be the wiser. But she could think of nothing but Falcon.

"Where did Drake take Falcon?" she asked, her nerves frayed to the bitter edge.

"T' the warehouse."

Kate groaned. The warehouse was just that, a big pit, old and falling down in places. Drake ran his business out of it. It was his own little empire. And like the rulers of most empires, he had made the place as impenetrable as a fortress, every possible entrance or exit monitored and all windows covered and reinforced. Trying to get inside undetected would be as futile as throwing a pebble at the walls of Jericho and expecting them to come tumbling down.

"We have t' get Falcon back."

"Easier said than done," Weasel muttered.

"We can figure somethin' out if we put our heads together." She hoped she sounded more convincing than she felt. "We've been in tight situations before an' have always come out all right."

"But we ain't never been in this kind of situation," Weasel pointed out. "This is Drake we're dealin' with. Besides, there's only the two of us against a lot of them."

Kate narrowed her gaze at him. "Two of us? Wot about Rat? Has somethin' happened t' him?"

Weasel's pointed look implied she was missing something. "I shouldn't need t' remind y', of all people, that Rat don't have a brain in his noggin. He'll just get our gullets cut that much quicker if we include him on any plan.''

Kate knew Weasel was right. Rat had never been able to follow a plan to the letter. There was always something he forgot to do.

"I guess it's just the two of us, then," she said, trying to keep the despair from her voice. "We'll have t' find a way t' get into the warehouse."

"Have y' completely lost yer mind? Only a blinkin' fool would break into Drake's domain! I don't fancy gettin' seven shades of crap kicked out of me for tryin'.''

"Well, wot do y' suggest we do? I don't hear y' makin' any suggestions.''

Weasel frowned. "Y' don't need t' rain holy hell down on me. I ain't the one who took Falcon. If y' want me advice, I think y' outta do what Drake wants.''

"An' wot does Drake want?" Kate asked, dreading the answer.

Weasel shrugged. "It ain't so much.''

"Well, tell me already!''

Falcon's lips twisted. "He wants y' to pinch a few trinkets from the cove.''

Kate groaned inwardly, her heart constricting at the very idea of taking anything from Alec. But she couldn't say she was surprised by Drake's *request*. As soon as Weasel had mentioned Drake, Kate had known trouble was around the next bend. She didn't need to ask what would happen to Falcon if she said no.

Then Weasel said, "Drake wants the first thing in his hands by tomorrow night.''

"Wot do y' mean *the first thing?*''

"Crikey, where's yer head?" Weasel asked in an exasperated tone. "Do y' think Drake's gonna want one small thing an' that's the end?''

Of course not.

Kate tried to clear her foggy brain. She needed a moment to think of her options. Surely there was a way around her predicament. Somehow she could save Falcon and leave Alec out of it.

But how? That was the question.

Kate shook her head. "Drake's balmy. How does he think I can keep nickin' things without no one bein' the wiser?"

"Don't think he cares, I wager."

"Aye. He don't care if he sends me t' the three-legged horse is wot yer sayin'." But Kate knew she would be in her own personal hell long before that fate came to pass. "Just how long is this supposed t' go on?"

Weasel shrugged. "I guess until he thinks ye've delivered the goods."

That's not an answer, Kate wanted to scream, the weight of the world suddenly pressing in on her. "An' how am I t' know if I've delivered the goods?"

Weasel heaved an irritated sigh. "Y' keep askin' me questions I have no way of answerin'. For Falcon's sake, just get what y' can get—an' quick. Drake ain't the type t' sit around waitin'."

"Y' don't have t' tell me that! I bloody well know he won't wait." Panic was starting to make Kate unravel. She had to regain her composure, to remain calm. Falcon was depending on her. "Look, I'll do wot I have t' do. Meet me here at the same time tomorrow night an' we'll go see Drake together."

Weasel nodded, his expression grim. Kate watched him disappear into the darkness.

Never before had she felt so alone.

Chapter Seventeen

Kate spent many hours wandering the streets after Weasel's departure, contemplating the mess she found herself in and wondering how she would resolve it.

When a distant clock tolled the midnight hour, she knew that whether she wanted to or not, she had to return to Alec's house and plan her next move from there.

Gazing upward into the light of a single shaft of the moon, she prayed hard that an answer would come to her and that she wouldn't have to use Alec as the instrument to gain Falcon's release. She hoped God was listening.

Kate breathed a quick sigh of relief finding the servants' entry still unlocked. She wouldn't have liked to knock on the front door and explain to Holmes why she was outside the house rather than inside. Most likely if he knew it was her, he would play deaf anyway.

There was only one taper's dim light to guide her up the back stairs to her room. The semidarkness suited her mood and allowed her to retreat once more to her thoughts.

I'll do wot I have t' do.

Those words reverberated in her head as Kate slowly mounted the steps, no longer feeling inclined to boast about her skills as the premiere pickpocket in London. At that moment, she wished to be anything but a thief.

But she was a thief; that was a reality of which there was no denying. And she had to use whatever cunning was necessary to save Falcon. Drake was evil; even the most stouthearted folded under the man's menacing gaze.

Again, the question of what she planned to do rose in her mind. Options, she reminded herself, there must be one or two.

She rehashed the possibility of offering her services to Drake. As much as the man repulsed her, she would pledge her loyalty to him if he would let Falcon go.

But would Falcon or the lads ever be truly safe from that moment forward? They had always been independent, living under no one's thumb. Once in Drake's sight, they were in his clutches for good. The point of no return. And any resistance to that fate would be met with severe consequences.

Kate made her first decision. Once she had Falcon back, they would leave London as quickly as they could—and never return. It was the only thing to do if they ever wanted to be free of Drake.

Distracted, Kate made her way down the hallway to her room, struggling with one possible solution after the next.

"Oh!" she gasped as she walked straight into a solid wall of muscle—warm, welcoming, and thoroughly masculine. Steel bands encircled her waist, and Alec's darkly handsome face loomed before her "I'm . . . I'm sorry." She cursed her overwrought nerves and averted her gaze, trying to collect her wits. "I didn't see y'."

"Is everything all right?" Alec asked, his voice washing over her like a summer rain. For a moment, Kate felt the strongest desire to tell him everything, to be honest and perhaps ask for his help. He was a powerful man with powerful friends. Certainly he would know what to do.

But what was she thinking? Her problem was not Alec's problem. She didn't want him to get hurt. This was Drake she was dealing with. He wasn't one to sit back should someone, anyone, interfere in his business.

"I'm fine," Kate lied, thinking her voice sounded unnaturally loud in the quiet stillness of the hallway.

"Where are you coming from?"

Staring down at the carpet, she replied, "Nowhere in particular. I was . . . havin' trouble sleepin', so I thought I'd take a walk."

A few moments ticked past. When Alec didn't say anything, Kate peered up at him. His eyes probed the very depths of her, making her want to look away again. But that action would be far too telling.

Holding her breath, she waited for him to challenge her explanation. He appeared as if he might.

Finally, he said, "I was having trouble sleeping, as well."

Kate wrinkled her brow, now noticing that he wasn't wearing his evening clothes, but a navy silk dressing gown instead. He had said he was going out with Anthony and wouldn't be back until quite late. When had he gotten home?

Kate wondered if his inability to sleep had been the reason he was standing in front of her bedroom door. Had he hesitated on her threshold, wondering if she might be awake as well? And if she had been, would he have suggested his warm milk remedy for sleeplessness? Would he perhaps have gone so far as to ask her to join him in a glass as he had once before? And would she have agreed, knowing how she felt about him and knowing what she had to do?

Alec gazed down at Kate, realizing how dangerous it had been to come to see her. He knew he couldn't trust himself around her. He should have stayed away, but common sense had deserted him somewhere between dinner that first night and her story about the hawker from the corner stand who was—how had she referred to him?—ah, yes, *camp as a row of tents.*

Perhaps that was why he asked, "How old are you?" Knowing the answer had suddenly become paramount.

Kate looked at him quizzically. "I'm almost eighteen. Why?"

Eighteen? Alec nearly choked. He hoped his stunned expression didn't show. God's teeth, it was a weight off his shoulders to know he hadn't been having indecent thoughts about a child. He had begun to believe he had turned into a pervert. Although at eighteen Kate wasn't far out of childhood. On the other hand, she was old enough. But for what? It was a question he was afraid to answer.

"What does my age have t' do with anything?"

Instead of answering, Alec said, "I was thinking about getting some brandy. Would you care to join me in a glass?"

What the bloody hell was the matter with him? He should say good night and walk away as fast as his feet would carry him, instead of heading toward certain trouble with a lass who did something to his peace of mind. Part of him hoped Kate would refuse his offer. An even bigger part prayed she wouldn't.

Kate studied him for a moment. "No milk?"

Alec chuckled softly. "No milk."

They stood there for another long moment, uncertainty and something else flickering in Kate's eyes. Finally, she shrugged. "Why not?"

Alec was almost tempted to tell her why not. She was too innocent by half. But she was walking away, heading in the wrong direction. Forgotten was any possible intention he had of setting things straight.

"The brandy is in my room."

His room? The words were like a cannon shot, stopping Kate in her tracks.

She hadn't been in there since that first day, but she hadn't forgotten a single thing. Her mind had stored even the most minute detail.

As if in a trance, she turned around. Words eluded her as she proceeded Alec, heading toward his door—his room.

His bed.

Once inside, her gaze focused on the closet she had snooped in when she had clutched Alec's shirt to her and breathed in his scent. She flushed, remembering the embarrassment she had felt getting caught red-handed. Yet despite that, she would most likely do it again if alone at that very moment.

But she wasn't alone.

The door clicked shut behind her, effectively trapping her. But if she were honest with herself, she would admit she wanted to be trapped. She had experienced many things in her life, some pleasant, most not. But what took place between a man and a woman behind closed doors was a mystery to her, and something she longed to experience. But not with just anyone.

Only Alec.

She was letting herself get carried away. Alec had done nothing more than to ask her for a drink, even if it did happen to be in his bedroom. Besides, hadn't he said to her just that afternoon he was sorry he had kissed her? That it wouldn't happen again?

Yet she couldn't lie to herself. She had dreamed of him, of them together, for only in her dreams could anything so wonderful and so completely impossible have ever transpired.

Lifting the brandy snifter off the round table near the bookshelf, Alec poured two glasses. He had brought the bottle up when he had come in earlier. Instead of grabbing one glass, he had grabbed two. At the time, he hadn't acknowledged his actions as anything other than wanting a drink for both hands. His intention had been to drink until his head was heavy, his sight dim and his mind numb. Somewhere along the way that plan had changed.

He watched Kate covertly, his eyes slowly moving over her profile. Even with her humble background, there was nothing average about her. From the exotic tilt of her eyes to her small feet, she was unique.

Her hair was held off her face by a single ribbon, and the boy's togs she had reverted to wearing fit her snugly enough to be a complete distraction. Her skin glowed in the soft lamplight. When she moistened her lips, his groin tightened painfully.

He probably would have stood there drinking her in for an eternity had she not turned to look at him, a flicker of uncertainty and another intangible emotion showing in her eyes.

"Is that for me?" he heard her softly ask, which finally got him moving.

Walking over to where she stood, Alec handed her the drink. Their fingers briefly met, then their eyes.

Kate took the glass from him, hurriedly putting it to her lips to down some of the potent liquid. Alec watched as her eyes widened. She coughed delicately, putting a hand to her mouth.

"Are you all right?" He laid his hand on her back, rubbing in slow circles.

"Aye." She swallowed hard. "I think . . . I like it."

"I have found it has quite a warming effect." Alec gently took hold of her wrist as she put the glass to her lips again. "I wouldn't drink it so fast." She glanced at his hand and then at him as if he were an alien creature come to life. He released her. "It can be rather potent, especially for those not used to it."

Putting the glass to her mouth, Kate took another taste, and another, until only a sip's worth remained. Alec's gaze followed her tongue as it traced the contours of her lips tasting the residual liquor left like the dew on a rose petal. He, too, wanted a taste. The thought had his gut clenching.

He could do no more than blink when she breathed in a husky voice, "More . . . please."

Dear God, he had to snap out of it.

Kate held out her glass, and Alec hoped his hand would remain steady as he poured another draught. "It appears you've acquired a taste rather quickly."

"Hmm," she purred, sticking the tip of her finger in the glass and then putting it into her mouth, gently sucking. Alec felt any resistance on his part wither and die. "I like the way it makes me feel . . . inside."

"And how does it make you feel?"

"Like I've swallowed warm butterflies," Kate replied languidly.

Her response, so honest, so guileless, brought a smile to Alec's face. "I've heard it described many ways, but never quite so accurately."

He wondered if she even heard him as she began wandering about his room, touching this and that.

At length, she said, "Have y' read all these books?"

"Yes. Would you care to borrow any of them?"

Turning halfway, she looked at him, a flicker of sadness, perhaps even pain, crossing her features. "I . . . don't read so good—well."

Alec cursed himself. How could he have been so careless? She couldn't read. Where and when would she have learned? That moment seemed to delineate the chasm between their backgrounds.

Kate stared down at the floor, and Alec felt like a lout. He told himself to leave off, to pick another topic. Instead, he walked over to stand next to her.

"I can teach you how to read—and to write, if you would like."

Her eyes were luminous as she gazed up at him. So small a thing meant a great deal to her. Suddenly, it meant a great deal to him as well.

"Y' will?" Kate asked in a voice barely above a whisper.

Alec smiled down at her. "I will."

The joy slid from her eyes, and something else he couldn't decipher entered them. Looking away, she murmured, "I can't."

Alec assumed she was saying she couldn't learn how to read and write, that perhaps it would be too hard. But she was smart, and could do anything she set her mind to.

"You can."

Kate slid a glance his way, and he wondered what was going on inside her head. She seemed as if she would protest further. Instead, she said, "Now?"

"Now what?"

"Can we read?"

Before Alec knew what she was about, Kate skirted the small, round table they stood next to and knelt down, pulling out a slim volume sitting on the bottom shelf of the bookcase at the very end. Alec groaned when he saw what she had.

"Kate—"

"Can we start with this one?" she interjected, her face eager.

"Why that one?" When he had hundreds of books.

Kate turned the book over in her hands, a blush staining her cheeks. "It's a pretty color. It stood out." She glanced around at the rows of books and then added, "Besides, it looks like the smallest one ye've got."

Gently, Alec plucked the book out of her hand. "This is not a good one to start with."

Apparently, she didn't like his answer. Her lips pursed. "Why not?"

Alec had hoped she would let him pick out another one without issue. "It's not suitable."

Standing up, Kate put her hands on her hips. Apparently, she didn't like that answer either. "Wot y' mean t' say is that it'd be too hard for someone like me t' read."

"No, that's not what I mean."

Alec looked down at the blasted book covered in a cheerful red. It had been a gag gift from idiotic Whitfield. Even when the man wasn't there, he caused trouble.

"You're positive you want this one?"

"Aye," she answered with a crisp nod of her head.

Alec knew when he was beaten. "Fine."

Kate snatched the book from his hand. "Wot's—What's that say?" she asked, pointing to the title.

Alec moved to stand behind her. "It says . . . *Erotica.*"

Kate glanced over her shoulder at him, a slight frown between her brows. "Erotica? Wot's—What's that?"

At that moment, Alec begged for a shaft of lightning to sever him in two. He had to explain to a woman whose warmth enveloped him, who created a burgeoning need inside him, who made him want to experience the world through her eyes, what erotica was. In short, it was her smile, the way she tilted her head, the sparkle in her eyes . . .

And what it did to him.

"Well?" she prompted impatiently.

Alec took a deep breath. "An exact definition would be literature intended to arouse sexual desire."

She gazed at him blankly for a moment before a dawning realization had her plopping the book down on the table as if she had been scorched. "Oh," she said in a small voice. "May I have another glass of brandy?"

Alec obliged. She stared at him over the rim of the glass. He, in turn, stared at her. Her cheeks were flushed, and he wondered if it was from the brandy or the book.

Kate finished her glass and helped herself to another. Alec thought to protest but decided against it. She seemed slightly frazzled and might need the brandy's relaxing effects. He knew he sure as hell did. He was about to snap in two. The way she looked at him with those doe eyes was really too much.

"This is nice," she murmured at length, her words a little thick. Alec wasn't sure if she was talking about the brandy or their being together.

"This is very nice," he agreed, knowing exactly what he meant.

He told himself that if he were an honorable man he would tell Kate to go, to run to her room and bolt the door behind her. Honor, however, seemed to have up and deserted him. If Kate wasn't such an innocent in the area of men's lust, she might know the thoughts running rampant through his head at that moment. But she didn't. And that only made it far worse for him. And her.

She looked lovely with the rosy flush on her cheeks and

the sparkle in her eyes. Her eyelids were heavy, her body supple and languid.

She moved around the table and out toward the middle of the room. Alec couldn't help himself; he followed.

He knew then that he was going to kiss her. If he were honest with himself, he would admit he had known it when she said yes to having a drink. Had she not agreed, he might have kissed her in the hallway.

One way or the other, he *was* going to kiss her.

Even as he trailed behind her with a measured tread, a small voice still managed to tell him that he wasn't thinking clearly, that he was courting trouble with every step he took, that he didn't need any more conflicts in his life. Kate had once said that he was no lad, but a man full-grown. And she barely eighteen. A child-woman. Then there was a wall called class distinction sitting squarely between them. He had never been one to care about the rules, but Kate. . . .

The vultures of Society would whip away that brave and spirited mantle that enshrouded her and leave her raw. How could he protect her? She would be miserable, and he along with her. They were standing across a great divide, and he didn't know how to breech it.

Still, he took another step and another, the devil on his shoulder telling him it was just a simple kiss, nothing more. And what was the harm in a kiss?

Then he was next to her. Kate turned as if expecting him. He noted the soft flush on her cheeks, the vivid blue of her eyes, the sculpted contour of her jaw, before settling his gaze on her lips. He cupped her cheek, smoothing his thumb over the petal softness of her skin. She trembled as his fingers trailed along the graceful curve of her jaw, down the slender column of her throat, before sliding around to the back of her head to tangle in her mass of inky tresses.

His other arm encircled her waist, pulling her closer. She did not resist. "You're beautiful," he murmured.

Kate blushed and lowered her eyes. "I'm not."

Alec lifted her chin. "You are. You're so lovely it beggars my ability to describe it."

She hesitated, capturing her lush bottom lip between her teeth. "But wot—what about this mornin'? I thought y' were disgusted with yerself for touchin' me?"

"I *was* disgusted, but not with you. Just myself. I didn't ask you to stay here because I wanted to take advantage of you."

"I never thought y' did."

Kate's adamant response moved him.

God, he was a slug.

But just this once he would allow himself to hold her, to feel her warmth, to experience something only Kate possessed.

Just a kiss. . . .

Alec's gaze slid downward, over the soft material of her shirt where it hugged the curves of her breasts. Her chest rose and fell in short bursts, telling him that he affected her. Good. He didn't want to be the only one.

"Why me?" she quietly asked.

That was the only easy question Alec had been asked all night. "You're different, Kate."

"Different from what?"

"Every woman I know," he replied honestly.

She had soul. She was genuine.

And he wanted her.

Bloody good sense be damned.

Chapter Eighteen

Falcon's haunting face rose in front of Kate's eyes as Alec's mouth brushed tentatively against hers. She told herself that all the desire and sensuous feelings Alec was beginning to stir to life in her must be put to the side. It was wrong. *She* was wrong. But how did she stop the flood from coming? His onslaught demanded her full attention; his need, her need, eclipsed all rational thought.

Then she was kissing him back, his heat seductive, his nearness overpowering. His lips were so warm, so sweet, and as heady to her senses as the brandy. Perhaps more so.

His mouth demanded as he pulled her tightly against his body, his tongue caressing hers, velvet and satin combined. She tasted him, explored him, drew his tongue between her lips as she would a sweet length of chocolate.

"Alec," she murmured in a voice she didn't recognize

as her own as his mouth trailed down the sensitive column of her neck, tasting her, testing her will. "I wish . . ."

Alec's hands moved slowly over her back and down to gently cup her derriere, bringing her in close against his arousal. "What, Kate? Tell me what you wish."

"I wish . . . I wish y' would kiss me again."

He obliged. His mouth scorched her, sending tendrils of flame through her body.

In his arms, Kate felt as if she was suddenly transforming, like a long-overdue butterfly emerging from its cocoon. She could feel it in her bones that she was on the verge of something momentous, a road that once taken, there would be no turning back. It was frightening and exciting all at once.

She knew she had no right to ask for anything from him. He had given her far more than she deserved. But she desperately wanted this one last thing. She would have the memory of his touch to sustain her in the dark days and nights and years ahead.

She kissed the side of his neck, savoring the warmth of his skin and the hint of salt. She ran the tip of her tongue along his ear, over the line of his jaw, down his throat to dip into the hollow at the base. She felt wanton, wicked . . . and oh, so much like a woman.

Alec's voice, next to her ear, was a low growl. "I shouldn't be doing this, Kate, but I want you. God only knows that I have tried not to want you. I came up with every reason, every excuse, to keep away. Even when I kissed you the last time I told myself it didn't mean anything."

Kate ran her fingers through his silky hair. "But it meant everything t' me," she whispered against his ear.

Alec placed his palm against her cheek. "Tell me to stop, Kate, and I will," he vowed in a hoarse voice. "I need you to tell me. I don't think I can if you don't say the words. So say them, Kate.''

Kate hesitated, but only for a hairsbreadth. Then she shook her head. "I can't. I don't want y' to stop."

He hesitated, an expression on his face of resolution hard-pressed, defended, and then abandoned.

Reaching around the back of her head, he slowly pulled the ribbon from her hair. He spread her long, curling tresses around her, his gaze soft with appreciation. He cupped her face in the warm strength of his hands, then leaned to touch her lips with his own, testing their sensitive folds before probing the sweetness within.

She met his gentle foray, touching her tongue to his, wanting to taste him, know him, become lost in him.

He took a ragged breath as his hand moved to free the buttons of her shirt. She, in turn, trailed her fingers along the collar of his dressing gown and skimmed its edges before moving her hands underneath to press against the muscled planes of his warm, solid chest.

He drew down one sleeve of her shirt, then the other, murmuring soft words as his lips tasted her neck, feeling the pulse that beat frantically beneath his touch. His hand gently cupped her breast, and she gasped.

Spurred by that small sound, his mouth moved along the ridge of her collarbone before lowering in slow, torturous degrees. When at last his mouth fastened over a taut nipple, she was glad his arms supported her.

Her breasts began to swell and ache, her nipples taut, distended. She arched back, wanting to give him access as passion stretched her on its sweet rack. Heat sluiced through her limbs, dampness pooling between her legs as he gently removed her breeches.

As Alec eased away from her to strip away his clothes, she made a soft, inarticulate protest. She couldn't help watching him, absorbing the virile strength and beauty of his body. When he stood before her gloriously naked, she felt herself drowning in her own unbridled need.

She reached for him. With a groan pulled from low in his throat, he came to her.

She hadn't realized they had moved until she felt something solid at the back of her knees. It was the bed. His bed. Their bed.

In what seemed like slow motion, she was lifted onto the soft mattress. It was cool and solid beneath her suddenly fevered body. Then Alec's big, hard form enveloped her, pressing her down farther into the softness.

Her emotions raged. There were so many things she wanted to say but never would. She would give Alec her body, needed to do so desperately. But she had to try to hold on to her heart.

And her soul.

For giving either of them would surely mean her destruction.

There was no future for them. But there was this one blessed moment, a breathtaking sunrise she would merge with, feeling the heat of its rays scorch her and transform her forever.

Trembling, Kate spread her hands over the powerful muscles of Alec's back, feeling the ripples of tension caused by the restraint he kept on himself.

Every nerve was heightened to acute awareness. Alec's breath was a caress where it whispered over her sensitive skin. His tongue edged along her chin and down her jaw until his lips closed around her earlobe. His tongue traced the outer contours of her ear before dipping inside.

She followed his lead, exploring the cleft in his chin with her mouth as her hands tested the resiliency of his iron-hewn buttocks; even her feet played a part in the sensual exploration as she rubbed them up and down the backs of his firm calves. Whatever he could do, she could do as well. She knew a secret thrill when he moaned.

"What are you doing to me, Kate?"

The deep timbre of his voice sent a shiver racing down her spine. Her nipples hardened painfully as he moved his chest over them. She cried out when his teeth gently closed around one aching bud, arching up off the bed, her fingers tightening in his hair.

"You like this?" was Alec's softly voiced inquiry, stopping for a moment as if waiting to hear her response. Her hands pushing his head back down answered his question. He chuckled. "I guess so," he murmured, before he went back to laving the rosy tip.

Kate learned what true bliss was as Alec's hands moved over her body. He did not neglect a single spot. And where his hands went his lips followed. She never knew how sensitive the backs of her knees where until his mouth and tongue explored the tender underside.

She felt like a bud just beginning to open its petals. She reveled in his touch, marveling at the things he was doing to her body. Magic. Pure magic.

"Alec!" she gasped when he slid down the length of her and settled himself between her thighs.

His tongue and teeth grazed the sensitive flesh of her inner thigh, moving upward until he was at the core of her. His tongue probed the delicate folds, finding the hidden pearl and sucking gently on it. His arms eased underneath her legs, and his hands reached up to cup her breasts, his fingertips plucking at her nipples as his mouth drew her essence. Blood raced through her veins as something uncoiled within her, aching, building.

Alec taunted her mercilessly. And when she thought she could stand no more, his mouth left her. She begged for him. He resisted her pleas. Instead, he trailed kisses over her hips, her stomach, before closing gently over one peak and then the next before poising above her, a question in his searing ebony gaze.

Through the haze of her passion-induced fever, she heard him ask, "Do you know what happens now?"

"More exquisite torture?" she breathed as she reached up to trace his lips.

His chuckle was a low rumble in his chest that vibrated through her body. "Yes," he murmured; then his mouth closed over her finger. Simultaneously, his manhood probed at the heat he had created between her thighs as he settled more firmly on top of her. She gazed into his eyes and couldn't help knowing a moment of fear at the unexpected. She had seen the full satiny length of what had sprang free from his trousers.

He couldn't mean to . . . ?

"It won't fit."

His smile was tender as he kissed the tip of her nose. "It will. You'll see."

Kate didn't think so. But then his mouth was on hers, hot, demanding, taking and giving all at once. Her fears floated away. All she knew or wanted was for Alec to get closer to her and then closer still. She wanted to melt into him, to merge, to become one.

It was instinct, perhaps, that guided her hands between their bodies, finding him, burning for him as she stroked his thick, satiny length from tip to base. His muscles tautened, his arms corded as he held himself slightly away from her, his face a mask of pleasure and pain.

"Dear God," Alec said hoarsely.

"Do you like it?"

"Yes," he groaned. "Too much." With an anguished

look on his face, he eased away from her. "You make me tremble, sweet Kate."

The pounding of Kate's heart made speech too difficult. "It will hurt a little. But I promise you, it will only be momentary."

She wanted him. Now.

Kate pulled him to her with ardent arms. He acquiesced with rampant grace, entering her with one swift stroke. She cried out, but his mouth covered the sound, taking it into him as she took his manhood into her.

Passion blazed and spiraled within her as he rose above her, poised, drawing ecstasy to its outer limits, sweet tension glazing their bodies in sweat.

Her breath quickened; hunger grew as Alec claimed her, possessed her, becoming so much a part of her that she didn't know where she began and he ended. They were one.

Kate felt on the brink of something unnamed. She caught Alec with both hands, pulling him down. He plunged into her, deep, and then deeper still in an onslaught of burning necessity. Faster, stroke by stroke, she reached out for that glimmering place which beckoned her.

Then he filled her, hot and heavy. His roar of surcease mingled with her own explosive, breath-destroying glory.

In the aftermath of their lovemaking, Kate reveled in the feel of Alec, his weight not crushing but comforting.

Lifting his head, he stared down at her. In the darkness, she couldn't make out his expression, but she didn't want to know if it was good or bad. She wanted to forget about tomorrow until it came.

She cupped his face with both her hands, bringing it down close to hers. Slowly, her fingers moved through his thick, dark hair. Her mouth touched his with the barest whisper. "Please . . . again."

His manhood stirred to life inside her.

"Kate . . . we can't. Not yet."

"Why not?" she asked in a quiet voice as her fingertips whispered along his back.

He dropped his head and grunted.

"Why?" she prompted, loving his discomfit.

"You must be sore," he murmured, but his lips were nuzzling her neck.

She, in turn, pressed her lips to the warm column of his throat, murmuring, "Have I worn y' out, then? Can't say as I'm surprised. I mean, y' aren't a young lad anymore, now are y'?"

His powerful muscles shifted, causing heat to rake over her. She caught her lip between her teeth to keep from groaning. The feel of him was sweet seduction.

"Not a young lad anymore, am I?" There was a challenge in his voice.

Kate shrugged with an indifference she was far from feeling. "Everybody gets old. I wouldn't let it bother y'."

"Oh, I won't," he replied in a low, silky voice as he began to move slowly inside her.

Kate was hard-pressed to remain cool as he entered and withdrew with a torturous slowness. In . . . out . . . in . . . Oh, God!

Capturing her wrists in his viselike grip, he brought her arms up over her head. "I'll try not to put you to sleep."

Kate closed her eyes and made her silent confessions.

She had done the unthinkable. What she had vowed she would not do.

She had fallen in love with Alec Breckridge, Lord of the Realm.

And she had done so with all her heart and soul.

Chapter Nineteen

Kate awoke the next morning and stretched languidly, like a cat after a nap. But as the fog cleared from her head, the dawning light of remembrance stole over her. She shot straight up in bed.

But not her bed.

Alec's bed!

Her gaze flew to the French doors. The bright light of day poured in! *Oh, God!* she groaned inwardly. How could Alec leave her in such a precarious position? Didn't he care that anyone could walk in and see her in his bed?

In the shrouded darkness they might be able to pretend that he was not a lord and she a thief, but when the sun rose on a new day, life must return to its normal course.

Sweet Mary, where were her clothes?

A knock sounded at the door. Kate's eyes locked on it. Her heartbeat slowed to a painful thump in her chest.

It was only Alec, she told herself.

But why would he knock? It was his room after all.

Courtesy, that was why. Mrs. Dearborn had told her several times that one knocks before entering a room.

But what if it wasn't Alec?

If it wasn't, then only a mere inch of wood separated her from disastrous discovery.

"My lord?" the voice on the other side queried, kicking Kate's burgeoning worry into full-blown panic. Yet the voice was nearly unrecognizable. It wasn't the usual harsh, spiteful tone she was used to hearing that now called out for entrance, but a relatively pleasant and gratingly polite one instead.

Bloody hell, it was Holmes!

Of all the people she *did not* want seeing her at that moment!

Kate scanned the room, searching out a place to hide. Then she spotted her discarded clothing. She jerked her gaze down to the white satin sheet, all that covered her naked form. As if things weren't bad enough! Now she had to scramble around in the buff!

But she had no time left to think about things she could do nothing about. She had to act. And fast.

She leapt from the bed. Unfortunately, an unexpected soreness from her late night activities had her moving much slower than usual. She barely had time to hoist the sheet off Alec's bed and wrap it around herself before Holmes, the impatient lout, stepped into the room.

"My lo—" he began before he choked on the word, his hazy gray eyes bulging from sockets that were suddenly too small to contain them.

Oh, how she hated the man! The Lord had to be punishing her for her fall from grace. She prayed she didn't look as guilty as she felt, standing there poised in as dignified a manner as a woman in a man's bedroom wearing no more than a thin satin sheet would allow.

She watched in suspended motion as the shock gradually lifted from Holmes's face. Simultaneously, his eyes narrowed by degrees.

"Yes?" she inquired in her most superior tone, raising an eyebrow at him. "Can I help y'?" *Out the door, for example?* she silently added.

Holmes found his voice. "What in God's name do you think you're doing, guttersnipe?"

Kate gritted her teeth. The man had gotten into the habit of calling her by an assortment of derogatory names whenever Alec wasn't around to hear him. And he used these words with vigor and reckless abandon knowing how much it annoyed her.

The hand that held the sheet together clenched. She felt just angry enough at that moment to take a swing at Holmes. Unfortunately, that wasn't an option. Not with her precarious hold on the sheet. So she had to be content just to glare at him.

She opened her mouth to speak, but Holmes forestalled her, saying, "Are you in here stealing something? You are, aren't you?"

"No!" Kate vehemently denied, but just as quickly her anger rose to the fore. "And just who the hell do y' think y' are questionin' me? It's none of yer business wot I'm doin'!"

Holmes's face began to redden. "Oh, yes it is!"

"Says who?" Kate countered.

The expression on his face made her think he had tasted castor oil; his nose wrinkled up to his forehead. "I've been here longer than you!"

As if that was an answer.

Kate waved her hand. "Big deal," she scoffed.

To her delight, the butler's face reddened further. With any luck, he would keel over.

"It will be a big deal when I call the constable," he threatened.

"Yeah? And wot are y' goin' t' tell him when he gets here? That I carried off his lordship's sheet?" She bit her tongue.

Damn and blast, why was she pointing that out? Yet, how blind could he possibly be? Did he really not comprehend why she was in Alec's room, practically naked? Was his shriveled brain not comprehending even though his eyes were beholding? Apparently not.

"Just wait until I tell his lordship you were in here!" Holmes admonished as if they were children about to receive a dreaded scolding from their parents for breaking something.

"Oh, no!" Kate mocked, but inside she didn't know what to expect from Alec. Certainly he didn't owe her anything, and he hadn't promised anything he hadn't delivered in full last night. She blushed to think about it.

"You better not think of leaving this house before you have been thoroughly searched," Holmes went on vigorously. "And then I want you to get out and never darken his lordship's doorway again."

"I don't think that's your decision, Holmes," a deep voice said from behind him.

Holmes spun around to find his employer standing behind him in the doorway. The butler's face, Kate was happy to see, was flushed. But her interest in annoying the man lasted only a second as Alec's larger than life presence loomed in the doorway. His eyes met hers, causing a shiver to run down her spine as every silken caress, every husky, whispered word of the hours spent in heated passion, flooded her thoughts. That one look had the power to melt her to her very toes. She had to remind herself to breathe.

Holmes's grating voice shattered the moment.

"M-my . . . lord . . . I didn't realize you were there," the butler stammered before quickly regaining his professional composure. Snapping his back into ramrod straightness, he went on to say, "I did not see you at breakfast, so I came to find out if aught was amiss. I knocked, of course, and when I did not hear you bid me entrance, I assumed you were not in your room. I turned to leave, but then I heard scuffling and felt it necessary to investigate. Well"— he drew out the word dramatically—"imagine my surprise when I opened the door expecting to see you and found"—he cast a quick, disparaging glance over his shoulder before spitting out— "*her.*"

Kate resisted the urge to slap the snotty-nosed toad across his smug face. She did, however, mutter a few choice words under her breath.

She caught Alec glancing at her with a raised eyebrow as if he had heard what she had said, which was clearly impossible. But Lord if his expression didn't show his barely contained amusement. Among his many other talents, did the man also read lips? That thought had her blushing, especially when she remembered where those lips had last been.

Alec, acknowledging Kate's sudden discomfort—while admiring how absolutely fetching she looked wrapped in his bedsheet—forced himself to turn his attention back to Holmes.

He leaned his shoulder against the doorjamb, wondering when his butler was going to catch on to the fact that things had changed between him and Kate. It should have been glaringly obvious considering Kate's state of dress, or rather, undress—which was deuced hard to ignore.

Now Alec was forced to decide what his next step would be. He had given their new situation a great deal of thought in lieu of conducting any business that morning. He discovered he had no particular inclination to keep his relationship with Kate a secret. It wasn't as if he was ashamed. He couldn't say he knew exactly what Kate thought, but she was realistic.

One of the things he had decided was to set her up in a lovely town house, perhaps with a view of Hyde Park. She would like that. Also, it would keep her close enough to be convenient to see her on a regular basis. And that was something *he* would like.

If she stayed with him, he could offer her all the things she would never have in her own world. He would give her the finest clothes, take her on exotic trips, and shower her with jewels. Something inside him wanted her to experience the things she had been deprived of, to see the joy on her face and to share in every moment. If she would let him, he would give her all the things most women would love to have.

But Kate isn't like most women, is she? In fact, she isn't like anyone you have ever known.

Alec forced his thoughts aside.

He could tell Holmes was waiting for some kind of pat on the back or a word of praise for his sleuthing. "Are you quite finished?" Alec said instead.

Holmes had the good sense to look abashed, apparently realizing his tattling had not been a good thing. However, he didn't know when to quit. "But, my lord, certainly you can see why I was so concerned."

Alec pushed away from the doorjamb. "Frankly, Holmes, I can't." He closed the door behind him. He did not want to set the entire house to gossiping.

"Well . . . she's a professed thief," Holmes marched on. "And she was alone in here."

Alec continued to stare at him.

"I would not be surprised to find your valuables missing. It would be remiss of me not to point this possibility out to you, my lord."

Kate, her patience obviously having worn thin, piped in, "Nothin' is missin', y' old coot!"

"Old coot!" Holmes fairly bellowed, his face turning red.

Alec stepped into the fray, a place he knew all too well. "Have you always been this suspicious of people, Holmes?"

Holmes took umbrage. "Not always, my lord. But I think the situation warrants my concern."

"I appreciate your vigilance. But your fears are unfounded."

Alec couldn't believe his butler actually thought Kate was in his room on some secret mission to raid his drawers, perhaps hie off with his socks or cravat. Holmes knew that he kept nothing of real value in his room. Alec hated to have to point out the obvious, but his butler appeared to be obtuse—or perhaps Holmes was hoping what he was seeing was not what it appeared to be.

"If you haven't noticed, Miss Kate does not have any place to hide stolen booty."

Holmes looked at Kate closely as if seeing her for the first time. Suddenly a dawning awareness came over his face, his eyes widening. If it was possible for a man to blush, Holmes was doing so.

"I . . . well," were the only words the butler could formulate at that moment.

Alec stole a glance at Kate. She was staring daggers at him. What did he do? Was it his comment to Holmes? Good Lord, could she possibly think Holmes would never catch on? His butler merely had a burr up his behind at finding her in his room, most likely thinking he hadn't been diligent in his duties. Whether Alec had said something or not, Holmes's senses would have eventually returned, and sooner rather than later. It was better this way. Holmes was a militant where the other servants were concerned. His butler would squash any gossip that might begin—whether he liked Kate or not. Gossip didn't bother Alec. He had certainly been the brunt of enough. Nevertheless, it might bother Kate.

"Wot are y' starin' at?" Kate angrily demanded when Holmes remained gaping at her as if she were some new kind of creature. "Have y' never seen someone in a sheet before?"

Alec knew that if he didn't act with haste, Holmes would regain his tongue and proceed to make some off-colored remark before he could be stopped.

"That will be all, Holmes. Please tell Cook that I would like him to make something special for dinner tonight."

Holmes nodded, then inquired, "And may I ask what the occasion is, my lord?"

"No, you may not," Alec told him curtly, growing annoyed by Holmes's meddling.

Holmes inclined his head and turned to leave.

"Holmes?"

"Yes, sir?" Holmes asked with a hopeful note in his voice as he looked over his shoulder at Alec.

"Not a word."

Holmes cast Kate a quick look and then headed out the door, closing it quietly behind him.

Alec stood there hesitantly for a moment, wondering what to do next when Kate spoke up.

"Are y' balmy?"

He decided to play innocent. "What do you mean?"

"Y' know exactly what I mean! What could have possibly made y' tell Holmes about . . ." Lowering her voice, she added, "You know."

Alec raised a brow. "You know?" It took every ounce of self-possession he possessed to keep from chuckling at such a description of what had transpired between them. Had Kate not looked as if she wanted to chop him into little pieces, he may have given in to the urge.

"Aye, y' know what I'm talkin' about! So don't give me one of them crooked smiles of yours and think I'll melt into a puddle."

Alec smiled anyway. "You mean you won't?" When all she did was glare at him, he moved to sit down at the end of the bed. "Truthfully, Kate, I'm not so sure what has gotten you upset."

Kate stormed forward, dragging the long, white sheet behind her like the train of a wedding gown. With an angry hand, she yanked the unruly material around to the front as she stood facing him. Holding the thin, clinging sheet with one hand, she used the other to poke him in his chest. "Oh, don't y' play that game with me! Y' know exactly wot—what—has me so upset!"

"I didn't realize that my pointing out the obvious was going to bother you this much."

"Pointin' out the obvious . . . ? Who decided it was obvious? Holmes certainly didn't."

"Perhaps not at the moment I told him," Alec replied. "But he would have figured it out sooner or later. I would rather have it come from me than be bandied about behind my back."

Deep down, Kate knew he was right. What was done, was done. Better to just move forward and try to forget—forget Alec's smile and his laugh and the way he made her feel.

A thought filtered through her mind. . . . Would he have acted differently if she had been a fancy society lady instead of a nobody?

Pain lanced through her at the thought.

Kate stepped away from him. "I ain't—I'm not—mad at y' tellin' Holmes," she lied. "I'm mad that y' make a big deal out of what happened. It ain't—isn't—a big deal. Not t' me. And now you'll have the man thinkin' I care. When I don't."

Slowly, Alec stood up. Kate automatically took a step back. His right eye began to twitch, his lips pressed into a grim, taut line. His presence was positively towering.

"What the hell is bothering you?" Alec snarled. "You had no problems last night. So what has happened today, I damn well want to know."

"Don't bring up last night!"

"And why the hell not?"

"Don't yell at me!"

"I'm not yelling at you!"

"You are!"

"I'm not!" he fired back, and Kate realized they were both yelling loud enough to wake the dead. He took a steadying breath and said in a calmer voice, "I'm just trying to get a handle on what I did wrong. That's all. I never imagined what other people thought of you would bother you this much."

"It doesn't!" Kate denied a bit too vehemently. "I don't care what Holmes or anyone else thinks!" And she didn't, not for herself at least. She just wanted things back to the way they were, before her heart was involved.

Alec cocked an eyebrow at her, his look plainly skeptical. "If you say so."

"I do! But if it means so double-damn much to y' why it bothers me, I'll tell y'. It's nobody's business what you and I were doin'!" Her chest rose and fell as if she had just finished running a race.

She turned away in disgust, not with him as much as with herself. She had known it was going to be hard, that it would hurt. But she was not ready for it to be this bad, for the ache to be so intense. She had not yet had the opportunity to steel herself against Alec, to make herself immune to his handsome face, penetrating eyes, and tender words.

Kate realized she had probably been foolish to think she could ever forget him, that she could erase what had transpired between them and go on as if nothing had happened. But it was too late to change what should never have been. All she had left were the lads, and they depended on her. Beyond that was a girlish dream that could never, would never, become a reality.

"Look, Kate—"

"It shouldn't have happened," she said in a barely audible voice. "It was a mistake."

Alec hadn't known exactly what to expect after making love to Kate, but her telling him it was a mistake hadn't crossed his mind.

He had thought that one night with her would assuage his hunger. Yet something had shifted inside him between last night and the early morning hours which followed, disarming him entirely, making him want her even more. He could no longer deny his attraction. After some thought, he had put the matter into perspective.

He was ready to take the next step . . .

And ask Kate to be his mistress.

He had never had a mistress; he hadn't the interest or

the inclination. But with Kate . . . well, he wanted more of a commitment. As well, she had been a virgin, and he had compromised her. He would make it up to her. She was practical and would understand the way things had to be.

Putting his hands on her shoulders, Alec slowly turned Kate around to face him. Her body was stiff, and she wouldn't look at him.

Placing a finger beneath her chin, he tilted her head up. Her eyes were glassy, as if she wanted to cry but couldn't. That look pierced him to the core.

"What we did, Kate, it wasn't a mistake. I wanted you, and you wanted me. There is nothing wrong in that. And I don't want you to ever feel differently."

"I do feel differently," she said softly. "And what we did *was* a mistake. You and I come from two separate worlds. Y' can't come down to mine, an' I can't reach high enough t' come up t' yours."

"I'd be a fool to say that we have similar backgrounds. I'd be even more foolish if I were to tell you that I understand what your life was like. But that doesn't mean there isn't something undeniable between us. Tell me you don't feel it, Kate."

Kate wanted to say nothing, to deny the passion she felt for Alec and that even seeing him affected her in ways she had never thought possible.

"I feel it," she whispered. "But I have t' stop feelin' it."

"Just enjoy it, Kate. Let's both enjoy it." Alec pulled her close, smoothing stray tendrils from her face. "Life's too damn short to do otherwise. It seems I've only just begun to realize that."

His words clutched at Kate's heart, making her want to run away to keep from feeling the yearning inside her. But suddenly it seemed as if nowhere would be far enough for her to run. And for Falcon's sake, she had to maintain a tight grip on her emotions.

Kate pulled away from him. He hesitated, then released her. "I need t' get dressed," she murmured.

"Certainly," Alec returned, his voice crisp and a bit tight. He headed toward the door, but halted midway and turned around. "I almost forgot. I have something for you."

Kate lowered her lashes, afraid her eyes would reveal how desperately she wanted him to stay, to hold her. God, why couldn't he just be a vicious brute for once? Why couldn't he use his tongue for more than speaking his honeyed words or touching her in a way that made her body sing with delight?

Reaching into his pocket, he pulled out a long, thin blue box. Walking back to her, he picked up her hand and placed the box in her palm. "Open it."

"What . . . what is it?" she breathed as her head rose and blue eyes met brown.

"If you'd open it, you'd find out."

Kate swallowed the lump in her throat, and with slightly shaking hands, she opened the box. The sight that greeted her took her breath away. She could do no more than stare.

"Well? What do you think?" he asked, his gaze expectant.

It never crossed her mind to lie. "It's lovely," she whispered.

Kate's gaze returned to the blue velvet-lined box, awed by the stunning necklace spread out before her. She gently ran a fingertip over the jewels.

"You can take it out, you know," Alec told her.

"What are these?" she asked, pointing to the scores of

brilliant gems lining the necklace and sparkling like a thousand stars.

"The blue stones are sapphires and the others are diamonds," he replied casually, as if describing mere baubles instead of priceless gems.

"I . . . I don't understand. Why are y' showin' this t' me?"

"Try it on," Alec replied in lieu of an answer.

Kate shook her head. But Alec had already taken the necklace out of the box and moved behind her. She shivered as the cool metal touched her skin.

Alec took her hand, leading her to the mirror. "Look."

Kate felt decadent—decadent and wonderful. The gems glistened against her skin. Certainly the whole thing was a dream, magical yet forbidden.

Her eyes met Alec's in the mirror. "It's beautiful."

Alec placed his hands gently on her shoulders. Heat radiated from his body in waves, engulfing her, making her feel as if no clothes separated their bodies. "It's you who are beautiful, Kate," he murmured close to her ear. "They suit you, you know. The sapphires go perfectly with your eyes."

Kate flushed at his compliment. She looked away so he would not see the longing in her eyes. "What's this big stone here in the center?" she asked, running her finger over the faceted surface of the large gem that stood out from the rest.

"It's called the Blue Water diamond," Alec replied, his attention not on the necklace but on the woman who wore it. "It is the only one of its kind."

He wasn't sure what had come over him. He had been sitting in his office thinking about Kate and their situation, and the next thing he knew he was at the safe, wanting to see the diamond. It reminded him of the exact shade of blue in her eyes. The necklace was unique—as was Kate.

Slowly, she turned in his arms. "The only one of its kind?" she breathed. "I don't understand."

"It's simple, really. I thought you would like to wear it tonight."

Kate's expression showed her confusion. "Tonight? What's happenin' tonight?"

Alec shrugged. "Well, possibly nothing. It depends on you."

"What are y' sayin'?"

"I'm saying that I would like to ask you to have supper with me this evening."

"Supper?"

"Yes. Just the two of us. I've taken the liberty of having special arrangements made."

Kate swallowed but couldn't speak. He couldn't do this to her. Not now! She couldn't allow him to be her knight anymore, or fulfill her every dream, or make her love him any more than she already did.

"I thought the green salon would be a cozy place to share some champagne in front of a roaring fire before sitting down to a candlelight dinner with no servants to disturb us. I will serve you . . ." His eyes blazed down into hers. "And then perhaps you would dance with me."

"I can't dance."

"I'll teach you," he murmured in a silky voice.

Kate pictured them together, his body molded against hers, touching her everywhere. "Why are y' doin' this?" she asked, her voice raw with emotion.

"I want to make you smile. So say you'll join me, Kate. Please," he added when she hesitated.

All it took was that one word and Kate was lost, hopelessly and completely. Why it was so, she couldn't say. But oh, how she wanted to do this one last thing with him, to be held tightly in his arms and never let go. And it was with her female heart and not her hardened mind that she replied, "I'll join y'."

And with that, Alec's mouth came down on hers. Kate's hands moved up and over his broad shoulders.

The sheet was forgotten as was the rest of the world.

Chapter Twenty

Hours later, Kate stared at her reflection in the mirror, wondering if it showed that she was now a woman in every sense of the word.

The sheet lay discarded in a heap on the floor at the end of the bed. Alec had spent the rest of the morning making slow, sweet love to her. She shivered in remembrance, hugging herself tightly, loving the feel of Alec's robe against her skin.

She missed him now that he was gone, although they had lingered quite a long time over their parting kiss—several parting kisses actually—which had them close to returning to bed to wile away the afternoon as they had the morning. Reluctantly, Alec had finally departed. After making sure no one was about to detect her, Kate hustled back to her own room, or rather, the guest room. It was not hers, and she had to remember that.

Now, alone, she could think with a clear head at last—
as well as berate herself for her stupidity.

How could she have allowed herself to make love to Alec
again after she swore that last night was the only time she
would? Her conviction was now stronger than ever . . . she
must leave.

The sooner, the better.

Moving to the bureau, Kate removed the top from the
box containing the Blue Water diamond. She glanced
down at the spectacular necklace, unable to believe the
extent of Alec's giving nature. That he should present
her with not only an enormously expensive item, but a
treasured family heirloom as well, without even a flicker
of hesitation, left her speechless.

The gems winked at her, sparkling and magnificent . . .

And tainted with the painful deception she was forced
to play out until the very end.

She knew what Alec had laid in her lap, the bounty of
what she had been given. This one-of-a-kind piece of jew-
elry whose immeasurable value had been placed in her
care would be the item that would free Falcon from Drake's
evil clutches. The Blue Water diamond was the exact bargaining chip she needed. Drake would drool over it. There
would be no need for her to steal anything else to secure
Falcon's release. Alec's gift had served a terrible purpose.
It was indeed a cruel twist of fate.

A knock sounded at the door.

"Come in," Kate called out, hoping the guilt she felt
didn't show on her face—and hoping it wasn't Alec. She
couldn't face him, not when her mind was resolved to a
course of action. She doubted she could carry out her plan
if he was in front of her, smiling that heartbreaking smile
that crinkled the corners of his eyes and brought out the
dimples in his cheeks.

It wasn't Alec.

"I'm sorry tae be botherin' ye, Miss Kate," the little maid, Nora, said, her tone polite, which grated on Kate's nerves. She wanted to tell the girl that she was one of them, not some visiting dignitary. But since the day Kate had arrived, the servants hadn't known what to make of her. Was she the guttersnipe, the charity case, or the master's new lover? What, exactly, was she? It was laughable how these people, who had the same background as she, perhaps even a shade better, steered clear of her. She was an enigma. She had no place among the upper class, but while in Alec's house, she had no place among the working class. Well, what did she expect?

Hesitantly, the red-haired maid moved into the room. "His lordship asked me tae bring this tae ye." She produced a large white box from behind her back.

Kate's heart dropped. It was another gift from Alec. She didn't want it. Any other woman would be ecstatic to have such a generous benefactor. But not her. She dreaded that white box. It was another knife to her heart.

"What is it?" she asked in a low, tentative voice.

"I dunnae know," the maid replied, giving her a puzzled look.

Kate realized the stupidity of her question. Alec wouldn't have made Nora privy to what was in the package.

Dispassionately, Kate watched the maid put the box on the bed. Feeling as if she were somewhere outside her body, she walked slowly over to the bed. She wondered if the box would disappear if she blinked—or better yet, if *she* would disappear.

"Aren't ye goin' tae open it, miss?" Nora prompted.

With a slight tremor in her hands, Kate reached for the box top. She stopped when she realized Nora was watching with rapt fascination over her shoulder. Kate simply stared at the maid, hoping she conveyed the message she wanted to be alone.

It was clear Nora was disappointed; probably her curiosity was at the breaking point, as was the rest of the staff's, Kate was sure. Well, she thought grimly, let no one say she couldn't keep a secret. She was the queen of secrets.

Once Nora had departed, Kate continued to hesitate. Finally, she raised the top of the box. She could do no more than stare at the magnificent gown lying neatly folded inside. She willed herself not to touch it, not to take it out of its tissue-lined cocoon, but her hands were not her own as they wrapped around the stunning midnight blue satin gown and lifted it up in front of her eyes. The satin material glimmered in the candlelight, and the lace delicately rimming the bodice was so fine as to be gossamer.

With infinite care, Kate swept the gown out of the box and held it up to her. The length was perfect, almost as if it had been made for her, which was impossible. Wasn't it? Could Alec have had this made for her? No. It had to be his sister's gown. At that moment, Kate didn't care.

The skirt of the gown fell in rich folds from directly beneath the bodice. The bodice itself was scooped and would display quite a bit of skin, but it would also show off the Blue Water diamond to perfection.

Closing her eyes, Kate allowed herself a moment to picture herself in the gown—and in Alec's strong arms—twirling about within the flicker and flame of the hearth's warming embrace. She would glide about as elegantly as you please, laughing and smiling . . .

And in love.

Her eyes flew open. She could not think that way! Not now, not ever!

Once more, a knock sounded at her door. Before she

could form any words, the door opened and in walked the man of her dreams.

Kate still had the gown pressed to her. The thought that she should put it down on the bed passed briefly through her mind, but she was mesmerized by the eyes locked with hers.

"I see you got my gift," Alec murmured, his words rolling over her as if he had touched her. "I hope you like it."

Kate willed herself to ignore the desire radiating from Alec, even though she knew it mirrored her own. "It's lovely," she said, hating the breathless quality of her voice.

"So will you wear it tonight?" he asked, coming to stand before her.

"Aye." She watched the dawning of a smile on his face that was more magnificent than the sunrise.

Every part of her ached to smile in return, to step into his arms and hold on tightly, to savor the feeling of being protected, cared for. But she could not. She had to steel herself against the feelings he stirred within her.

"I'm a bit tired," she lied, a reliable excuse that had come in handy in a way she was coming to hate. "I think I'll lie down for a while." She didn't want to be alone with him again for fear of losing the battle she was fighting within herself.

"That's a good idea. Get some rest. I wouldn't want you to be too tired to dance with me." He kissed her on her forehead and then turned on his heel, heading for the door. He stopped suddenly. "Oh, I almost forgot something. Stay there." Then he was out the door, but was back within a minute. His grin was positively wicked as from behind his back he produced another white box, similar to the first one that had held the gown. This one was smaller. "This is for you."

"Not another gift," Kate groaned under her breath. Her

eyes widened as she realized she had spoken the words out loud. Thankfully, he hadn't heard her. "Y' really shouldn't keep doin' this, y'know." But her words were mild. She couldn't bring herself to hurt his feelings.

"I want to." He placed the box in her hands. "Open it."

Kate smiled hesitantly, then did as Alec bid.

Inside the box was a beautiful pair of dainty, soft kid slippers that matched the gown perfectly.

With care, she put the gown on the bed and picked up one of the delicate shoes. It looked as if it had been made for a princess.

Alec was making her into that princess.

Kate felt overwhelmed by his generosity. She dropped the shoe as if she had been burned and turned away.

Alec moved behind her and put his hands on her shoulders. "Is everything all right, Kate?" he asked, sounding worried.

Kate sometimes wished he were a little less perceptive—and a lot less of a gentleman. It would make things easier.

"Fine," she replied, wanting to laugh at how far from the truth that was. "What time should I be ready?"

"Eight o'clock." Leaning down, he whispered in her ear, "I can picture you in the gown, Kate . . . your creamy skin enhanced by the color. I will be envious of the way it hugs your body, touches you"—he put his hand at her waist, slowly squeezing, testing her flesh, before skimming her sides, his thumbs teasing the undersides of her breasts—"like I want to be touching you." His warm breath sent tendrils of heat racing through her body.

Kate closed her eyes, praying the stirring within her would cease. She tried to turn and look at him, but he held her firm.

"I can't seem to help myself." His voice was thick with

need. "I want you right now. I can't get enough of you, Kate. You've become a fever in my blood."

Kate felt herself melting. But that little voice she loved to hate reminded her why she could not succumb to the sweet rapture of Alec's words no matter how much she might want him to hold her, touch her, slide into her and then torturously out, inch by agonizing inch until . . . rapture, bliss. Soul-shattering ecstasy.

She squeezed her eyes shut.

Reluctantly, she moved out of his embrace and walked to the window. Staring out at the shifting sky, she wondered when the night had become her enemy. "Eight o'clock, then."

He hesitated, perhaps thinking to say something. She could sense his confusion, but could do nothing to ease it.

She listened to his footfalls as he walked away, thinking, not for the first time, of how quietly he moved for such a big man.

Kate told herself to stand firm, to let him go, but she swung around nevertheless. "Alec," she called out, stopping him in the doorway. His face was so handsome she could barely breathe. His beautiful eyes held no foreknowledge of what she was about to do as he waited patiently for her to speak. Quietly, she murmured, "Thank you . . . for everythin'."

"You're welcome." His grin was positively boyish. It made her think of a rainbow—one she knew she would be foolish to chase.

Then he was gone.

Kate stood for a long time staring at the door, willing her feet to move and urging her unproductive thoughts to leave off. She stayed that way as dusk fell the rest of the way and darkness began to envelop the room.

Her movements were sluggish as she finally stirred herself. Walking to the French windows, she opened them and stepped out onto the balcony. She took a deep breath of the clean night air. The thought struck her then that the air had a different quality to it uptown than it did from her part of town. But then again, everything was better in the posh West End—everything and everyone. She wanted to savor the time she had left so she could carry the memories with her in the long years ahead.

But the end was drawing ever nearer, and she had to get ready.

Chapter
Twenty-One

"Why, my lord, don't you look dashing!" Mrs. Dearborn exclaimed in her usual jovial manner as she met Alec at the top of the staircase.

Alec inclined his head in acknowledgment. "Thank you, Mrs. Dearborn. I do my best."

He was attired from top to bottom in black. The only thing that broke the line was the pristine whiteness of his shirt and the small portion of his emerald green satin vest showing beneath an exquisitely tailored black evening coat. A diamond winked from the folds of his perfectly tied cravat. His shoulder-length dark hair gleamed in the faceted light of the chandelier, completing the picture of a handsome aristocrat.

"I can't wait to see, Miss Kate," his housekeeper went on to say. "I'm sure she will look stunning. She's such a lovely young woman."

"That she is."

A mental image of Kate in the blue satin gown he had had made for her, with the help of his coconspirator, Mrs. Dearborn, popped into Alec's head. He had paid an obscene amount of money to get the gown done on short notice. But he wanted tonight to be special for Kate, and that didn't include giving her his sister's hand-me-downs. He hadn't even contemplated the possibility that she might decline his invitation; that had not been an acceptable option.

"Well, I don't think I can contain my eagerness any longer," the lively older woman said. "I will go check on her." She went to move past Alec, but stopped. Looking him square in the eye, she added, "I really like Miss Kate and I hope you two have a wonderful evening." Her knowing hazel eyes were filled with romantic notions, but her expression was motherly.

Alec shook his head as he watched his longtime housekeeper disappear down the hallway. He chuckled as he turned and descended the stairs. Mrs. Dearborn was unique. He couldn't help but notice the habit he had for surrounding himself with people who weren't like everyone else. They were all special in their own way.

Alec was glad to see Kate had made a friend. Certainly she needed one besides him. She could use a woman's influence in her life.

He remembered what Anthony had told him, that Kate was a charity case. It had been a ludicrous statement then, and it was just as ludicrous now. Kate was no one's charity case.

Alec strode toward the library, intent on enjoying a glass of port, when he heard a shouting voice coming from the upper recesses of the house. Quickly he headed back to the stairs to see Mrs. Dearborn running down the hallway.

"My lord! My lord!"

Seeing her panicked mien, Alec took the stairs two at a the time. He met up with the housekeeper at the top of the stairs. Her face was flushed, and she was out of breath. But it was her eyes he noticed the most; they were filled with an emotion he had never seen reflected there before.

Fear.

"What is it, Mrs. Dearborn?" he demanded, grasping her upper arms to hold her steady. "What has happened?"

"Oh, my lord," she wept.

"Tell me, Mrs. Dearborn! Has something happened to Kate? Has she been hurt?"

Mrs. Dearborn shook her head. "No, my lord. She hasn't been hurt."

"Then, what is it,?"

The housekeeper looked at him sadly, a lone tear rolling down her cheek. "She's gone."

Those two words were like a hammer to his chest. "Are you sure? How do you know she's gone? Maybe she's just out for a walk." She wasn't, he knew. And the pitying look his housekeeper gave him said that she knew as well.

"When I went in to check on Kate, her room was dark. I lit the sconces and found her gown and shoes lying on the bed." Slowly, Mrs. Dearborn lifted her arm and held out a folded cream-colored piece of paper. "I found this as well."

Alec shook his head. "But that's not possible." He would not take the note. "That can't be from Kate. She doesn't know how to write."

Mrs. Dearborn's face was drawn. "Kate had such a thirst for knowledge. It seemed a terrible shame to me that she had been denied an opportunity to learn."

"What are you saying?"

"I've been teaching her how to read and write," she

confessed. "She was doing it for you, to surprise you. At least that's what I thought."

Alec's hand trembled as he took the paper from his housekeeper's grasp. For a long moment, he merely stared at it.

Slowly, he opened the piece of fine parchment paper with its slightly scalloped edges and the Somerset family crest emblazoned at the top. His jaw clenched as he read the words written inside.

When he was finished, he crumpled the note in his tight fist, willing the anger to outweigh the pain of Kate's betrayal.

"My lord?" Mrs. Dearborn asked, concern in her voice and etched on her features. "What has happened? Where has Miss Kate gone? Is she all right?"

"I'm sure she is," Alec replied bitterly. "As to where she has gone, I don't know. Wherever it is, she couldn't get there fast enough."

"You mean . . . she wanted to leave? I thought . . . well, I thought perhaps something had happened and she had to leave. She seemed rather peculiar all day, not like herself."

Alec had noticed that as well, but contributed it to her feeling strange about the new situation in which they had found themselves. He thought perhaps she was confused, maybe even a little scared. God knew, he was.

Bloody fool! She had been playing him like a goddamned harp! She was good at deception. Anthony had seen it. Holmes had seen it. Only he, Alec, had not seen it. She was probably laughing at him right now, thinking him a gullible clod.

But what did he think? That just because he wanted it to be so, she would change? She had lived on the streets and had hoodwinked many people with that guileless face of hers. What made him believe he was any different?

Alec let out a roar of anguish, throwing the crumpled note against the wall before storming down the stairs and disappearing into his study, the door slamming loudly behind him.

Mrs. Dearborn picked up the discarded note, intending to throw it away so that no one else would know his lordship's private business.

She headed down the stairs but had not gone three steps before her worry for her young charge overwhelmed her. Slowly, she uncrumpled the note and read the words:

Yer pretty blue dimond and my blue eyes go so well together that I cudnt resist taking it. Cunsider it paymunt for what u took from me.

* * *

Every step Kate took was heavier than the last. She hated Drake. But more than that, she hated herself. By now Alec had to have read her note, and he was most likely roundly cursing her name.

It was over.

It should never have begun, but that did not soothe the painful ache in her heart.

Falcon.

She had to concentrate on Falcon and nothing else. Tonight would pass, and tomorrow would come just as it did every day regardless of what she wanted—or whom. Enough days would pass and the pain would ease a little more every day. It had to . . .

For living with a broken heart would be more than she could bear.

"Why, my dear Fox, what are you doing skulking about

out here? A person could get hurt, you know. This is a bad section of town.''

Kate froze.

Slowly, she turned around to find Drake standing behind her. For being such a fat man, he could move with an unearthly stealth. She should have been expecting him. She had sent Weasel to tell him to meet her.

''Drake,'' she spat, her demeanor returning to that of the Fox, the criminal, as Kate, the young lady, ebbed away. Her anger at all she had lost because of the ugly man in front of her made her want to say things she knew she couldn't say if she wanted to keep Falcon safe.

Drake eyed her closely. ''Well, I see you haven't changed, street trash.'' The words moved off his tongue as slowly as molasses on a cold day. His weight also made him wheeze after every third word. ''Those blue eyes are as sharp as my dagger. One would have thought that the time you had spent with his lordship would have tempered your disposition.''

''An' one would have thought that y'd have exploded by now,'' Kate retorted fiercely. ''So I guess we're both wrong.'' She cursed herself for her loose tongue.

Drake's already red face mottled even more. ''You know, I never realized how frightened Falcon is of knives,'' he drawled, his words sending a snap of cold dread down Kate's spine. Why had she provoked him? ''I don't think I'll get the chance to gut the lad. He will probably have a heart attack before I lay a finger on him.''

''Leave Falcon alone!''

''I don't think you are in a position to be issuing orders. If you care what happens to your friend, I would suggest you keep your mouth shut. Do we understand one another?''

With narrowed eyes, and a jaw clenched so hard she was sure her teeth would crack, Kate did not utter a sound.

She needed to remain calm. But the hatred and anger wanted to boil right through her skin as she looked at Drake standing there, smug in the knowledge that she would do what he told her.

He wore fancy clothes as he always did. A crook pretending to be a well-to-do gentleman. Yet his clothes weren't even close to the quality worn by the rich aristocrats he so much wanted to be like. No decent tailor would wait on him. So the fabric and cut of his clothing was always a shade inferior, which Kate knew infuriated him.

"You've made a smart choice," Drake said. Then he rubbed his hands together and ambled his bulk toward her. "Now, let me take a good look at you."

"Wot for?" Kate snapped, hard-pressed to control her disgust as she backed away.

Drake moved within inches of her face. "I don't think I like that tone."

Before Kate knew what he was about, Drake's hand swung out and slapped her hard across the face. The blow had her seeing stars. She faltered, barely catching herself before falling to the ground. Sheer will refused to let her crumble. Drake wouldn't have her on her knees. Not if she could help it.

Kate put her hand to her stinging face. She could taste the coppery blood from the cut on her upper lip caused by the ruby ring Drake always wore on his pinky. But the blow did not put fear into her heart, as she knew he wanted. No, it only stiffened her resolve. This was her world. The only one to which she had ever belonged. There were no feather beds or silver spoons.

Or love.

Kate flinched when Drake reached out his fat hand and then produced a handkerchief. She stared him dead in the eye. Fear had no place in her world. To survive, she had to be tough. She would do as he asked, but she would never relinquish her pride. It was all she had left.

"That's better," the fat man drawled as he dabbed at her lip. "Now, if you behave yourself, I promise I will make you forget all about this unnecessary unpleasantness. I'll have you singing in delight, my little dove."

Drake's words hit Kate like another blow.

He knows!

As if reading her mind, he said, "Yes, I know your little secret." He used the handkerchief to wipe at the saliva at the side of his mouth.

Kate's heart lodged in her throat. *Did he also know about . . . ?*

"Did you think you could keep it hidden from me?"

Breathe! Kate ordered herself.

"Yes, I did." She paused. "How—how did y' find out?"

Drake merely smiled; it was pure evil. "You shouldn't stroll around in dresses, my dear. From what I understand from my lackeys, you made quite a fetching sight."

Kate's heart began to thump harder in her chest. "Y' watched his lordship's house?" Oh, God, Alec could have gotten hurt, and it would have been all her fault.

"Did you think I wouldn't? How could I trust a scheming, lying bitch like you to pay me my proper respect? You should be glad you came when you did."

Chills prickled Kate's flesh. "Leave him out of this."

"You're not proposing to tell me what to do, are you?"

"Leave him alone!"

"Is that devotion ringing in your voice?" Drake inquired, an avaricious gleam in his beady eyes.

Kate cursed herself. She had revealed too much. She couldn't allow him to have another sword to hold over her head. "Wot do y' want from me?"

He ignored her question. "Imagine my chagrin to find

such a prize was right under my nose. People who deceive me don't live long enough to talk about it." The veiled threat hung heavy in the air. "However, you will soon soothe my wounded pride with your mouth and your ripe flesh."

"Never!" Kate exclaimed before she could stop herself, her stomach churning at the mere thought of his filthy hands pawing her. She would go to her grave before allowing him to touch her.

"What was that?" Drake raised an eyebrow. "Think of dear Falcon," he reminded her, his black gaze promising retribution.

Kate gritted her teeth.

"Good girl," he murmured, yanking off her cap and wrapping a piece of her hair around his pudgy finger.

Kate's skin crawled; bile rose in her throat. She had never considered herself a violent person, but at that moment, she wished she had a knife.

"Where's Falcon?" she asked through gritted teeth.

Drake's hand stilled, and Kate thought he was going to hit her again. He wanted to be in control of the conversation, but he seemed to be forgetting she held some of the strings as well. She was the possessor of the Blue Water diamond. Drake had something she wanted. But she had something he wanted.

"Where's Falcon?" she asked again, but in a more demanding tone this time.

Drake clenched his jaw. He looked like a volcano ready to explode. Then he surprised her as a grin crossed his ugly face. "Wouldn't you like to know," he taunted, his eyes gleaming. "You know, my little Fox, looking closely at you now, I can see what a pretty wench you are. You have a good deal of potential. With the sweet body that I'm sure lies hidden under those rags, you could make a bundle working for me. You could live like a queen instead of filching purses and pocket watches like a common thief.''

"I would rather be a common thief than a whore," she spat.

"Suddenly you have become a saint? How quaint. Do you think because you whored yourself to the earl that you're suddenly above the rest of us? Just because it was a rich lord who lay between your thighs doesn't make you any less of a tramp. I wouldn't put on airs." He paused studying her. "Or were you perhaps thinking a man like the earl might possibly want someone like you?"

Kate stiffened. It was as if Drake had read her mind. But she would refute his words until her dying day. "Are y' out of yer bloomin' mind? I have no interest in some arrogant blue blood. And he has no interest in me."

"Why do I not believe you?"

"I don't care if y' believe me!" she returned furiously, not realizing that she was giving herself away by her anger.

Drake smirked. "Of course I believe you, little Fox."

"Did y' bring me here t' discuss this rubbish or do y' ever plan on gettin' down t' business?"

"Ah yes, business . . . that really is more important than your schoolgirl crush, isn't it?"

Kate clenched her hands at her sides. "Wot d'ya want?"

Drake stroked his chin. "I want many things, my girl . . . and as you know, I usually get them. But what I want today is to acquire some of those treasures the earl is fond of. I assume you have something for me?"

Kate could feel the heat of the Blue Water diamond searing her where it lay in her pocket, reminding her of her betrayal.

"An' if I don't?" she risked asking, not yet ready to relinquish her last hold to Alec.

Drake's eyes narrowed, his expression menacing. "If you don't, I will clip Falcon's wings. You will find your friend floating facedown in the Thames."

Blood drained from Kate's face. She didn't doubt that Drake would do exactly as he threatened. Why did she have to push him? Getting Falcon back was the only thing that mattered.

"I see you're getting the picture. Good." Drake circled around behind her and said close to her ear, "I would hate to see something happen to our Falcon, but accidents can occur. It would be tragic to have the life of one so young end abruptly. Wouldn't you agree?"

Kate nodded, swallowing the bitter acid rising in her throat as his horrible breath assaulted her, hot and filthy against her neck.

Clamping her eyes shut, she dug her nails into her palms as Drake put his sweaty palm on her buttock and squeezed. She heard him grunt his approval.

"I might be willing to make it easy on you, sweet—if you cooperate."

"Never!"

"Never say never," he told her in a guttural voice, his hand moving up her hip and side, finally clamping on to her breast.

Kate had taken enough pawing. Swinging her elbow back into his gut, she secured her release. She knew a feeling of immense satisfaction as he groaned.

"Bitch!" he swore, doubled over. "Just wait till I get my hands on you."

Kate knew she had to think fast. She couldn't let her mistake cause Falcon to be hurt. "I didn't come here t' be pawed. Y' said y' wanted somethin' from his high-and-mighty in order for me t' get Falcon back. Well, I got somethin'."

"Forget about getting Falcon back, you little whore!" Drake spat as he slowly straightened.

It took all the strength Kate had to still her panic and her racing heart. She had something he wanted. He would change his mind.

She drew the diamond from her pocket and held it up in the white rays of the moon. The gem came to life. The blue diamond appeared liquid, like a shimmering, glossy lake. Its effect was mesmerizing.

"So I guess y' don't want this, then?"

Drake's attention moved from her and pinned to the diamond instead. Relief flooded Kate.

"What is that?" he asked, licking his lips as he reached for the necklace.

Kate pulled it away from his grasping hand. He scowled. Now she held all the cards. No one in their right mind would be able to resist a gem of this magnitude.

Dangling it in front of him like a carrot, she replied, "It's called the Blue Water diamond. It's the only one of its kind."

Again, he reached for it, and again she pulled it away.

"I will exchange this for Falcon," Kate went on. "That's the deal. I've kept my end of the bargain. Now release Falcon."

Drake raised one bushy eyebrow. "To what deal are you referring?"

"Don't play games with me. Y' know wot I'm talkin' about. Y' wanted somethin' valuable from the nabob in return for Falcon. Y' can't get nothin' more valuable than this."

"How do I know it's real?"

Kate was incredulous. "Are y' blind? Anyone can see this is real. Besides, do y' think I'd be so foolish as t' bring y' somethin' fake?"

Drake shrugged. "One never knows." He put out his hand. "Let me see it."

Kate shook her head. "Not until I see Falcon."

"Your bargaining power is slim to none. Now don't press me. Give me the diamond," he ordered.

Kate shook her head. Drake didn't know the meaning of fair play or keeping a deal. She would go to her grave before handing the necklace over. She had given up much by taking the bloody thing, destroying all hope of anything happening between her and Alec. Perhaps there had never been any hope to begin with, but he had been kind and considerate. He had treated her like a lady when no one else ever had. She had repaid him by stealing from him. It was unforgivable. And it had ended whatever might have begun.

"Once I have Falcon back, y' may have this damn diamond with my blessin'."

"Your devotion is touching," Drake said smugly. "But your energy could be put to far better use." He shrugged then. "Obviously you have made your choice. I thought you were smarter, however."

Kate saw him nod toward a spot behind her. Out of the darkness came two of his thugs. She had nowhere to run; Drake had effectively trapped her. She would not give up so easily!

She tried dashing beneath the two men; her only thought was keeping them from taking the necklace. She would lose her one opportunity to get Falcon back if they did.

Kate darted to one side, then the other, just missing the steel bands of the burly men who sought to capture her. She was lighter, quicker; that was her only defense. One of their meaty hands could easily crush her; but she had her wits, and she would use them to the fullest.

"Get her, you bloody idiots!" Drake bellowed, his immense bulk keeping him from joining in the chase.

Kate was sure she was winning and that she would successfully escape. The men lumbered after her, but she stayed just out of their reach.

"I'll kill Falcon."

Kate stopped dead in her tracks. Those three words ended the chase. The men were upon her in moments, each one taking an arm as if she was actually strong enough to break free if she were so inclined.

"Don't just stand there, fools!" Drake bellowed at his men. "Get the diamond!"

"Oh, yeah," one of the men muttered, slipping his hand into her pocket and pulling out the necklace. His eyes widened like saucers, and he gulped. "Geez, wot a rock."

"Give it to me, idiot!" Drake ordered.

"Sorry," the big man mumbled as he put the priceless necklace in his boss's hand.

Drake held up the necklace and viewed it closely, turning it around. "Hmm."

Kate was numb. She had lost. "Ye've got wot y' wanted, Drake. I've kept my side of the bargain. Now where is Falcon?"

"All in good time, my girl."

"Y' can't beat that necklace. No one in the world has one like it."

"So you've said."

Kate tried to jerk her arms free from her huge captors, but it was a fruitless endeavor. They didn't budge.

Glaring at Drake, her chest heaved with frustration and anger. "Wot are y' goin' to do with Falcon? I deserve t' know."

Drake laughed without mirth. "You deserve to know, do you? Unfortunately, we do not see eye to eye on that."

"Damn y'!" Kate exploded.

Drake's hand snaked out, cracking harshly across her face for the second time. "You're trying my patience!"

Kate would have fallen had Drake's thugs not had a hold of her arms. "Wot do y' want?" she whispered, knowing she was beaten.

"I want you to go back to the earl's home and get me more things like this one," he ordered, pointing to the necklace.

Kate's eyes widened. All thoughts ceased.

Go back to Alec? She could not go back. Ever.

"I can't."

"Oh, yes you can. If you ever want to see Falcon again, you will."

"I can't, I tell y'! He has t' know by now the necklace is gone. Y' think he'd be fool enough t' let me back into his house after wot I've done?"

Drake's gaze raked her form. "You underestimate the power of your charm, pet."

"A smile an' a kind word won't make it all better." Kate only wished it could.

"Well then, I guess you've got your work cut out for you, don't you?"

Kate's stomach clenched in a hard, leaden knot. "So y' want me t' get one more thing and then I'll get Falcon back?"

Drake shrugged. "Maybe yes, maybe no. I guess it will depend on what you bring me."

Kate knew then that he would never be satisfied with just one more thing. He would keep demanding she get more and more, if not from Alec, then from someone else. She would end up becoming another one of his mindless pawns to use at his whim.

An ache welled inside Kate's chest.

248   *Melanie George*

"The man will have the law lookin' for me." Although Kate knew in her heart that Alec would not. It just wasn't the way he did things. It was part of what made him so unlike anyone she had ever known.

Drake didn't look at her. Instead, he studied his newest acquisition. "Once again, you're mentioning things I do not care about. The how, when, and why are your responsibility to figure out. You're a smart girl. I'm sure you'll come up with a solution. Just keep thinking about good, old Falcon and how horrible it would be to disappoint me and work from there."

Then Drake nodded, and the two thugs holding Kate's arms released her. She rubbed them to get some of the feeling back, knowing her arms would be black and blue where their meaty fingers had gripped her.

"Can I at least see Falcon?" she asked, needing to make sure everything was all right.

"We'll see." The expression on his face said he relished having control over her. "If you do what you're told, *exactly* the way you're supposed to, I will let you speak to Falcon tomorrow. But I want you back here at the same time and not a moment later. Do we understand one another?"

"Aye," she replied tersely.

Drake's smile had a cruel twist to it. "I know you'll do your best not to disappoint me, won't you?"

Kate gave a curt nod, watching the fat man and his two bodyguards until they disappeared from sight.

Then she broke down and cried.

Chapter
Twenty-Two

The sound of glass shattering against the fireplace echoed throughout the study, yet Alec did not feel the sense of satisfaction he had hoped for.

Razor-edged shards of expensive crystal sprayed in all directions. Nothing hit him. He doubted he would feel anything even if it had.

He was numb.

A quick knock sounded at the door before it opened. "Is everything all right, my lord?" Holmes asked tentatively. "I thought I heard—"

"Get out!" Alec thundered.

When he did not hear the door immediately close, Alec swiveled slowly around to face his butler. He knew, and did not care, that he looked like the criminally insane with his clothing disheveled and his face unshaven. But whether Holmes noticed his state of disarray could not be determined since his butler stood in the threshold like an effigy in wax.

"What part of 'get out' didn't you understand?" Alec snarled, his words slurred.

Holmes blinked while his hand searched behind him for the doorknob. "I . . . apologize, m-my lord."

The next moment he was gone.

Alec growled low and turned back to stare into the fire, seeing only the blackness that was his mood reflected in the flames.

He was drunk.

But he could not get drunk enough to forget.

Kate.

Why had she done it? He'd treated her well. He had given her all he had to give.

God's teeth, man! Stop these infernal thoughts!

Pushing away from the fireplace, Alec stormed to the sideboard. Another drink was looking better and better.

He grabbed a glass, picked up the bottle of Scotch, and turned the bottle over. Nothing came out. He shook it.

Sonofabitch, not one drop left!

The bottle went the same way as the crystal glass.

The door creaked open again. Alec clenched his jaw. Did bloody Holmes not know when to quit? Did the man have a death wish?

Alec didn't turn around. He wasn't in control. He felt volatile and completely unlike himself. "Holmes, you were warned," he growled. "When I turn around, I expect to be alone in this room. Don't make me tell you again."

Alec waited for the door to close and was relieved when he heard it click shut. He put his hands, palms flat, on the sideboard and bowed his head.

"Hello, Alec," murmured a tremulous voice, the sound striking him with the force of a lash across the back.

Alec stiffened.

Was he dreaming? Certainly he had to be. That could not be her voice, the one that tormented his soul.

Slowly he turned around to find Kate standing with her back against the door, her hand holding the knob as if preparing for a quick getaway. His eyes narrowed on her beautiful, treacherous face, the muscle in his jaw working. He damned himself to hell as he realized that he did not loathe the very sight of her as he should for her betrayal. But he did hate himself for the way he felt at that moment, for the relief that welled inside him at seeing she was all right, that no harm had come to her out on the streets. He almost laughed at that last thought; it was truly ludicrous. Kate was a product of the streets.

And at that moment, she was probably safer on the streets than with him.

"I don't have any valuables on me, so you're out of luck." His barb found its target. She flinched.

"I guess I deserved that," she said in a barely audible voice.

"You guess?" Alec exploded, striding angrily toward her. "You bloody well are right you deserved that—and much more." He reached out to grab her arms but stopped himself, clenching his fists at his sides instead. "You're taking a big risk coming here. How do you know I didn't inform the constable about your crime?"

"Because I know you."

Her soft reply, made without hesitation, disarmed him. "I could have," he persisted, but there was no conviction behind his words.

"But you didn't, did you?"

Alec found his anger lessening, and that was the last thing he wanted. He could not allow himself to be fooled again.

"Where's the necklace?" he demanded.

"It's gone."

"Gone? What do you mean *gone*?"

"I mean I don't have it any more."

"You sold it off already? Bloody hell, you move fast." Alec swung on his heel and moved away from her. "I guess Anthony was right about you."

"I guess he was," Kate murmured, closing her eyes.

She had stood outside in the bushes for a good hour before sneaking in, feeling like a fool as she stared at the window of Alec's study. She could see him pacing around, downing one drink after another, anger—and perhaps pain?—etched on his face.

She could imagine how glorious he had looked when he had come down the stairs in his perfectly tailored black suit like the one he had worn to the Rutherfords' ball, waiting to escort her to dinner. She would have given anything to have been on his arm.

Alone in the green salon, Alec would have swept her off her feet. It wouldn't have mattered that she didn't know how to dance; she doubted her feet would have touched the floor. He would have been the enchanter, and she the enchanted.

Now she was the betrayer.

And he the betrayed.

She should have just crept in after dark and done what she had to do. Or she should have picked another victim. There were plenty of rich lords from which to choose. But that would have required planning. And time. Time was something she didn't have.

"I hope ye'll believe me when I say I'm sorry." How insignificant the words sounded, she thought.

Alec growled. "And I hope you'll believe me when I say I don't believe one damn word out of your mouth."

Kate shook her head. What had she been thinking to come back? Alec hated her.

She hated herself.

"I'm sorry," she whispered, and meant it all the way to her soul. "I shouldn't have come." She knew her motives had not been only to steal something else for Drake. "I guess I just wanted to . . ." She stopped, knowing that if she finished what she was about to say, she would be relinquishing the last thing she had left: her pride.

"I'll leave." She would find someone else to steal from. Drake would never know the difference. But hadn't she already known that before she had taken that first step into Alec's house and toward his study?

Yes.

Yet it hadn't stopped her. Her reasons for coming had been cloaked by the lies she allowed herself to believe.

Turning away, Kate pressed her forehead against the cold, hard wood of the door as she tried to push down the emotions rising within her. She ached. The pain seemed worse now than it had when she had first left. Why had she tortured herself like this?

As though reaching for a lifeline, she grasped the door-knob and swung open the door. At the same moment, she felt the heat of Alec's body behind her, planting his large hand against the door and slamming it shut.

"Goddamn you!" he hissed in a low, harsh voice.

Kate didn't move; she couldn't even had she wanted to. Alec was so close. His warm breath whispered against her ear, and the incredible heat rising from his body wrapped about her like a cloak. His chest came in contact with her back, and she could feel every sinewy muscle. How she longed to turn around, touch him, feel his skin beneath her fingertips, know his taste, his texture.

She closed her eyes, remembering how good it had been,

how he had brought her to the height of ecstasy and beyond. He had made her a woman.

More than that, he had made her a human being, one who had feelings and dreams.

One who could feel love.

"I'm sorry," she breathed. "I shouldn't have come."

"Why did you?"

"I-I didn't want to."

"That doesn't answer the question, Kate."

Why did he have to push her to answer the one question she didn't want to? Well, what had she expected? She owed him a pound of flesh, but he wasn't extracting it by berating her. No, he was doing so by demanding the truth.

She shivered when his hands settled on her shoulders. As if in slow motion, he turned her around to face him. She didn't resist. When their eyes met, fire flared between them.

She refused to think about what would happen tomorrow. She had been allowed a taste of heaven and would revel in the bliss for as long as could.

Alec bent his head toward her, and Kate knew he was going to kiss her. A small part of her urged her to push him away, but a much larger part ached for that kiss.

Her eyes fluttered closed, and when his mouth touched hers, a bolt of pure white lightning went through her. She didn't hesitate in her response. She kissed him back with passion, longing. Love. Her hands moved up the hard wall of his chest and then along the smooth, firm contours of his neck to entwine in his silky, dark hair.

Drowning.

She was drowning in the feel of him. She wanted to imprint everything about him in her memory.

"Kate, what are you doing to me?" Alec murmured

against her mouth before taking her lips in a ruthless, drugging kiss.

He pulled her close, then closer still. Kate was barely aware when they slipped to the floor, heedless of the unlocked door. Her need for him was too strong.

"Alec," she breathed as his mouth ran down her neck, his tongue dipping into the hollow at the base of her throat. She shivered as the cool air touched her skin as he undid one button, then the next. When his warm, moist mouth closed around her aching nipple, she moaned in delight—and remorse.

With frantic hands, she tried to take his shirt off, wanting desperately to touch him as she had pictured herself doing while she stood outside watching him. She wanted skin against skin, but he resisted. He alternated between gently sucking her swollen nipple and laving it, trailing his tongue between each valley and peak.

Kate tossed her head back and forth, her hands kneading his muscular shoulders as her breathing quickened. Sweet Lord, what he could do to her body, playing her like a finely tuned instrument. She was at a fevered pitch when finally he removed his mouth from her breast.

Slowly Alec slid upward. His shirt felt like the coarsest linen as it brushed over her tender peaks. She was sinking below the surface and didn't care. She wanted to keep going down, hoping the morning would never come.

At last, her fingers found the buttons of his shirt, undoing them with clumsy, shaking hands. She sighed in contentment as the garment slid off his shoulders and was thrown to the side. Her palms rubbed over his smooth, warm flesh, from his broad shoulders to his muscular chest and along his taut, flat stomach. Her finger whispered along the edge of his waistband. Without removing his lips from hers, he lifted up so that she could have better access.

She took the opportunity given her and undid his trousers. When her fingers brushed along the tip of his manhood, he groaned and she delighted in the wonders of being a woman.

She stroked the satin-textured sheath of his engorged length, reveling in the smooth glide of silk against steel and the knowledge that the tiny acorn can fell the giant oak.

Her power over him lasted only a minute as he took over again, undoing her breeches and slipping them slowly down her thighs. He lifted each foot and kissed her toes before working his way up her calf, then behind her knee.

All thoughts ceased as he moved up her inner thigh, tasting, licking, heading toward the core of her, where the heat he had brought to life throbbed, wet and quivering. She shivered in anticipation.

She cried out as his tongue touched the peak hidden between the swollen flesh at the juncture of her thighs. Liquid fire coursed through her as he loved her, stroke upon stroke, building, urging, until every nerve in her body vibrated.

She hungered, writhed. Fire and light made her blind to all else but Alec. He could create such magic with his mouth. She grasped his shoulders, her fingernails digging into his flesh. She tried to pull him to her.

"Please, Alec," she begged, needing him inside her. But he would not come. He wanted her in a frenzy and would settle for nothing less.

When finally she could take no more, Alec rose above her, settling himself firmly between her thighs. Kate gazed up at him, knowing emotions that she had wanted to keep hidden reflected in her eyes. His dark, glittering gaze showed the extent of his desire—and some other elusive emotion she wanted desperately to reach for.

Their eyes remained locked as she guided his manhood into her waiting warmth, sheathing him completely. With a ragged groan, he plunged into her fully, making her cling to him as he rocked back and forth inside her.

"Kate," Alec said in a low, husky voice as his lips came down, capturing hers in a searing kiss.

Kate was swept into his demand, into the conflagration. Whispered, incoherent words escaped her lips. She called his name; he moaned hers as heat gathered where their bodies were joined.

"Oh . . . yes . . . Alec. . . ."

They reached the summit together, their limbs entwined and their bodies beaded with sweat.

They stayed that way for a long time, neither speaking, neither knowing what to say to ease the pain slowly creeping back in.

Alec rolled off her, but didn't get up. Kate wondered what he was thinking. Was he angry with himself because he had touched her? She couldn't blame him.

Abruptly, she sat up, suddenly ashamed of her behavior, of how she had succumbed to him so easily.

Scooping up her shirt, she hastily donned it, not daring to look at him. She didn't want to see the condemnation in his eyes.

"I shouldn't have come," she whispered into the deafening silence.

"You said that already." His voice was leaden.

"I won't say it again, then."

Kate stood up, thankful her shirt went down past her rear end. She moved behind a wing chair to pull on her pants, realizing that it was silly to hide; Alec had seen everything there was to see.

"What will you say, then, Kate? I haven't heard anything yet . . . not why you left, not why you came back . . . and not why you felt you had to steal the diamond. I just don't understand.'' He sat up; firelight gleamed off his bronzed, sculpted torso, shadowing the rippling muscles of his abdomen. ''Was it the money? You know you could have come to me if you needed something.''

Kate wished it could be that easy. She could have asked him. He would have helped. But she couldn't involve him. She cared too much.

''I don't know what y' want me to say.'' She glanced away, brushing stray tendrils off her face.

''How about the truth for once?''

''I don't know what ye're talking about.''

Alec jumped to his feet, his face a mask of fury. ''You know damn well what I'm talking about!'' he said in a low, harsh voice. ''Why did you come back, Kate? If you were as heartless as your little note made you out to be, I think you would be out congratulating yourself on your victory instead of standing here looking miserable.''

Kate's gaze cut to him. ''I'm not miserable!'' she lied. ''I'm ... I'm ...'' *I'm wretched, an' lost, an' lonely, an' y' shouldn't look at me with that gaze that makes me want t' fall into your arms an' stay there forever.*

Alec paced the room, an Adonis, naked and unabashed, furious and glorious.

Honesty versus her deception. Sunlight to her darkness.

An aristocrat and a thief.

And she was the queen of wishful thinking.

''You're what, Kate?'' Alec demanded. ''Why can't you just talk to me? As much as you may think otherwise, I'm not the enemy.''

''I never thought y' were.''

Alec moved toward her, and time stood still. She watched him. He was a sleek, fierce cat, and she the prey.

He was in front of her. His heat abraded her, cut through

her, wrapped around her like the sun around a spring bud, coaxing her to open.

Fear, pain, and joy tumbled inside Kate as he put his hands on her shoulders, unyielding, yet oddly gentle. "Talk to me, Kate. Tell me what is happening. There has to be a reason you would do this to me."

Kate opened her mouth, greatly tempted to tell all, to confide in him. She knew he could solve this problem for her.

But it wasn't his problem to solve, she reminded herself. And she would never be able to forgive herself if he got hurt because of her.

She tried to move out of his embrace, but he would not let her. "I shouldn't have come." She had to get out, get away. He wanted truth, and truth she couldn't give.

She wanted love . . . and love she would never have.

Alec's hands tightened their grip. "Goddamn it, stop saying that! I'm sick of hearing those blasted words!"

"I've got t' go."

He hesitated, his jaw clenching and unclenching as he stared hard at her. He dropped his hands to his sides and took a step back. He wasn't going to stop her.

Did she want him to?

Yes.

Kate found it hard to breathe as his smoldering dark gaze held hers and pulled her forward as if she were in the grip of something invisible, a bond that couldn't be explained.

She tilted her head back, and he tilted his down. His gaze whispered over her hair, her nose, her cheeks. But when his eyes settled on her lips, they began to tingle. Her tongue slid out to moisten them. She heard his sharp intake of breath and watched as his head slowly, inevitably descended. Her lips parted in anticipation.

Alec kissed her. Bliss, bright and burning, flared behind her closed eyes. He tasted like whiskey, smoke, and sunshine. She could not resist him. She doubted a time would come when she ever could. Her body sighed into his as if it belonged there, as if it had been made only for him.

He pulled slightly away. "Will you come with me?" he asked in a hoarse, yearning voice.

Kate shivered as his warm breath tickled the hair on her neck. All she could do was nod in answer.

He threw on his pants, left the rest behind and took her hand, leading her to the door. She hesitated when he opened it. She didn't want anyone else knowing she was there. She was too humiliated, too ashamed of what she had done. But Alec wouldn't allow her to falter, and so she followed because she could not deny him. She was relieved to find no one about as they headed up the stairs. She knew where they were going.

To Alec's room. To his warm, inviting bed where she had experienced her first bliss-filled hours of lovemaking under his magical tutelage.

Her heart sped as they stepped into the dimly lit recess of his room. She had no time to think, to protest—although she would not.

He turned and pulled her hard against his chest, his lips capturing her in a hot, demanding kiss as soon as he had closed the door behind them. He backed her up against the door, her arms clung to his neck. His hands cupped her buttocks, and he lifted her off the ground. She wrapped her legs around his waist, wanting only to melt into him, to feel the burning desire of his manhood fill her, have him possess her in a way so elemental, so physical, the memory would be branded in her mind forever.

With infinite care, Alec placed her upon the bed, his body following, covering her with a burning heat.

A knock sounded at the door.

"Is everything all right, my lord?" Holmes called out, his tone sounding anxious.

Kate was nearly lost to the heady delight Alec was creating with his mouth, his tongue, his hands. Hearing the butler's voice, she stirred from the sensuous fog of passion.

"Alec, Holmes is at the door."

"Hmm," was his reply as his lips traced the curve of her neck, her shoulder bone, and then down the valley between her breasts.

"Oh, God," Kate groaned when he took one aching, rigid peak into his mouth while a large hand cupped and molded her other breast.

The knock sounded again.

Kate shook her head, putting her hands to his shoulders. It was like trying to move a mountain. "Alec, for God's sake, answer him before he comes in here!"

"Huh?" Alec stared down at her. It took a moment for rational thought to come back, and then he bellowed in an irritated voice, "I'm bloody fine, Holmes! Now go the hell away!"

Holmes was forgotten as Alec's mouth descended, fierce, possessive, dueling with her tongue in a battle she knew she could never win.

He was seduction. He was fire. He was ecstasy.

And he was hers.

For this moment. Just this one brilliant moment. . . .

Many hours later, after Alec had made love to her two more times, Kate lay awake staring up at the ceiling. Alec's gentle breathing told her he slept. Quietly, and very carefully, she slipped out of his embrace and from the bed. She stood there for a long time just staring down at him.

He was glorious—in both body and soul. He deserved someone very special. That person was not her.

She donned her clothes with automatic movements and then crossed to the opposite side of the bed. Her hand reached out to stroke his cheek, but stopped. She could not disturb him.

It was time to leave.

Her steps were leaden as she walked to the door. She took one last look at Alec before heading out into the darkened hallway.

Alec awoke with the sunrise. He reached for Kate, but the bed was empty.

His eyes flew open.

She was gone.

Shortly thereafter, he discovered a priceless Chinese vase had gone with her.

Chapter
Twenty-Three

"I hate to say I told you so," Anthony drawled the next morning as he sat in Alec's office, a gloating look on his face, "but I bloody well did tell you so. That chit was trouble from minute one. You should have let me take her to Newgate as I wanted to. A few days in that rat hole would have straightened her right up."

Alec didn't feel inclined to discuss the matter with Whitfield, but the man's comments were so preposterous, so damn outrageous, that his voice would not be stilled. "You told me so? What the hell are you talking about? You brought her here."

This seemed an unimportant fact to Anthony. "Well, you should have known better than to let me decide such an important thing. *You pick the poison* . . . really, Breckridge."

Alec gritted his teeth and managed to still the hands that longed to pick Anthony up by the scruff of the neck and shake him until his brain's rattled. "Bloody Christ! *You* said that!"

Anthony quirked a thoughtful brow and lay a finger against his chin. "La, so I did." He shrugged dismissively. "It's all the same in the end, isn't it? Disaster."

Alec glared. He didn't need the man rubbing in his stupidity—and Anthony thrived on dissension. "How the hell do you know my business anyway?" he asked, his irritation mounting.

Anthony nodded toward the door. "Yon butler is a fountain of information—when coerced just so. A few threats, manipulation of the conversation, trickery." He shrugged. "Generally, it is a veritable plethora of useless crap—until now, that is. Let me tell you, it feels damn good to finally get something I can sink my teeth into. You are as pious as a monk."

Alec scowled. Bloody Holmes. He should have known. "Do you always listen to servants' gossip, Whitfield?"

Anthony raised an eyebrow, his expression clearly amused. "Only when the servant in question can produce proof of said gossip," he returned. "I don't want to be looking like a fool now, do I?"

"Of course not," Alec drawled, knowing his look said that he thought his friend had already passed the point of no return. "And what exactly is this proof?"

"Why, that empty spot on the table in yonder vestibule is what," Anthony promptly replied. "I really didn't need Holmes to show me; I noticed the vase's absence right off—I am quite the connoisseur of rare antiquities, if you will recall," he boasted.

Connoisseur my bloody behind, Alec almost said out loud. Anthony figured since he was the owner of so many rare antiquities, thanks to his father's discriminating taste, such expertise was translated down through the generations.

Whitfield wouldn't know an antique if it bit him in the arse.

Anthony went on, "But Holmes seemed eager to show me that the vase had acquired legs overnight." He shrugged. "And who am I to complain?"

"Who, indeed," Alec muttered, deciding he was going to kill his butler when he saw him next.

"If you recall, I was there when the lovely Countess of Clydemore gave you that vase," Anthony remarked, obviously feeling it held some relevancy, which practically ensured it did not. "What was the reason for such a lovely gift?" He scratched his head. "Oh, yes! You had supposedly saved her from drowning. Odd, but I understood from some of her acquaintances that she was a superb swimmer."

Alec gritted his teeth, a tic starting in his eye. "Your point is?" he ground out.

Anthony smiled benignly. "No point."

"I didn't think so."

Alec stood up and moved to the fireplace, staring unseeingly at the cold, empty grate. His entire body felt as lifeless as that hearth.

"So where has the thankless jade gone?" Anthony then asked, not knowing when to quit, as usual.

Alec clenched his hand into a fist at his side. "How the hell would I know? It's not as if she has made me privy to her plans."

Swinging on his heel, Alec headed toward the sideboard, his favorite place of late. Even though he was suffering from a severe hangover, that would not be a deterrent. In fact, another binge was beginning to look like sunshine on a cloudy day.

"Are you planning on offering me any of that or are you

going to drink it all yourself?'' Anthony drawled, slumping back in his chair and tipping a pretend glass to his lips.

Alec looked from the bottle of Scotch he held in one hand to the glass he held in the other, which was filled to capacity, and felt the greatest urge to say yes, he would be drinking it all. He was in the mood to drift into oblivion once more, but realized he was beginning to appear rather pathetic.

He had been hoodwinked, so what? He wasn't the first, and he sure as hell wouldn't be the last. Yes, it was bloody hard to fathom Kate's betrayal, not once, but twice. But he had nobody else to blame for his stupidity.

"Well?" he heard Anthony prompt.

Alec grabbed another glass and poured his friend a shot as healthy as his own.

"That's more like it,'' Anthony said, eyeing the drink he was handed with appreciation. He clinked his glass against Alec's. "Here's to getting back to business—and as well you know, I don't mean the actual working kind.'' He winked and put the glass to his lips.

"To getting back to business,'' Alec repeated with little enthusiasm, trying to block out the image of Kate that popped into his head. Damn he was sick of himself!

He put the glass to his lips and downed its entire contents.

Kate remained deep within the shadows of the alley, pressing her back flat against a grimy wall. A strange sensation crawled over her skin. Something was not right. A rat scurried past her feet, its movements seeming rather frantic as if it, too, sensed the strange undercurrent.

She had returned to the same place she had met Drake previously. She held the vase tightly to her body, feeling a disgust that was starting to become a part of her. She had put no thought into her decision on what to take from Alec's house. It didn't really matter because in the scheme of things it was all the same. She couldn't bear to coldly catalogue his possessions, so she just took the vase as she walked out the front door.

How she hated Drake! She had never wished a person dead before, but she could honestly say she wished the man six feet under.

Behind her, she heard a noise, so faint most people would not have noticed. But out on the streets one learned quickly to distinguish the difference between a rat scurrying between piles of garbage and the sound of a person acting clandestine.

The hairs on the back of her neck rose.

Twirling around, Kate squinted into the darkness that was unbroken by even a single shaft of light. It was as if that area was painted black.

"Who's there?" she called down the alley, her body tensing. No response came back, but she knew someone was there. "I've got a knife," she lied. "I know how to use it." Another lie.

"Fox?" came a faint voice, barely discernable.

"Who's there?" Kate repeated.

"It's me," the voice responded, still low.

Kate heard a moan and what sounded like someone falling. Was the person hurt? Should she assist? Or was it just a ploy to pull her deeper into the dark, deserted alley?

She hesitated, and then moved slowly toward where she had heard the voice. She halted midway as the person stumbled forward. She gasped, her eyes widening.

"Help me."

"Oh, my God!" Kate cried as Falcon crumpled to the

ground. She dropped to her knees beside her friend. "Falcon? Falcon!"

Kate put her hand underneath Falcon's head and lifted it into her lap. A cloud shifted, allowing a slim beam of moonlight to illuminate Falcon's face. Her indrawn breath lodged in her throat. She tried to keep her hands steady as she used the edge of her shirt to gently wipe away the blood trickling from a cut on the corner of Falcon's mouth.

Tears welled up in her eyes. Falcon had been abused, and she had not been there to keep it from happening.

Everything was her fault! If only she hadn't made herself cozy with Alec, none of this would have happened!

"Is it really you, Fox?" Falcon asked in a weak voice, looking up with only one eye as the other was nearly swollen shut.

"Aye, it's really me," Kate whispered, trying to hold back tears and be strong as she stroked her fingers gently across Falcon's cheek. "Wot happened? Did Drake do this t' you?"

Falcon nodded, but Kate could tell even that small movement was painful. "He said I was givin' him lip, but I weren't sayin' anything, I swear. I just wanted out of there."

A deep pain constricted Kate's heart. "I know."

"I knew ye'd come for me, so I tried me hardest not t' rile Drake." Falcon shrugged, and then groaned from the pain it caused. "I don't know what happened. Drake—he just went nuts. He started sayin' that y' weren't comin' for me. He was tauntin' me an' tellin' me that y' didn't care about me no more an' that y' said I could rot in hell. He said y' were having too good a time with the earl an' that y' were goin' t' leave me forever."

This time tears did run down Kate's face. She couldn't stop them. "Oh, Falcon, y' know I would never forget you."

"I know, but I was tired of Drake callin' y' names. I just couldn't take it anymore. I'm sorry," Falcon said in a ragged whisper.

"Just try not t' think about it," Kate murmured in a soothing voice. "It's over now. We'll go home."

Home.

What a warm word for a cold alley. They had no real home, and Kate felt that deficiency all the way to her soul. If ever there was a time she needed somewhere to go, now was that time.

Falcon tried to sit up, wild-eyed and agitated. "Y' don't understand, Fox. I can't go with y', not now, not ever."

"Wot do y' mean y' can't go?" Kate asked in a cajoling tone, trying to scoff off Falcon's statement even as strange, frightening feeling began to creep up her spine. "Ye're safe now. I won't let anythin' happen to y'. I swear. We'll leave London an' never come back. We'll go tonight if y' want."

Falcon sat up a little bit more, wincing in pain. "Y' don't understand."

Kate looked into Falcon's eyes and saw anguish reflected within. "Ye're worryin' for naught. Y' need t' rest. Y' aren't yourself right now wot with that lump on the side of your head."

"I don't need t' rest!"

Kate was startled by the vehemence in Falcon's voice, but not deterred. "Aye, y' do. Now, let's go before Drake catches up."

"Aren't y' listenin' t' me? Don't y' know what I'm sayin' to y'?"

Kate did not want to hear any more. Something inside her rebelled at the thought running through her head. "Everythin' will be much better in the mornin'. Ye'll see."

"It won't be better in the bloody mornin'!" Falcon

shouted, pushing Kate away. "I killed him! I killed Drake! Oh, God, wot have I done?"

Kate froze.

"Y' couldn't have," was her low-voiced denial. "I just saw him last night. He was fine."

Falcon swiped away the tears that were beginning to flow. "Well, he ain't fine now!"

"Are you . . . sure?"

Falcon laughed without mirth. "Aye."

"How . . . ?"

"I stabbed him."

Kate winced at Falcon's bluntness. The words had been spoken with no hesitation, no emotion. And the look in Falcon's eyes frightened Kate; they were cold and empty.

Kate remembered how Drake had said he taunted Falcon with a knife. It was a horrible irony that he had fallen victim to it. But she felt no remorse. The world was a better place without the man.

"How did it happen?"

Falcon heaved a weary sigh. "It was an accident. I kept tellin' meself not t' let him get t' me. In me head, I could hear y' sayin' he wasn't worth the trouble, t' let it go. An' I swear I listened for as long as I could."

"Didn't Drake tell y' that I had come for you? Did he show y' the diamond necklace I gave him so that I could get y' back?"

"No, he didn't tell me none of that," Falcon replied. "Did the necklace belong t' that lord?"

Kate nodded. "But I would have taken it from Satan himself if it was the only way I could get y' back."

Falcon's head dropped. "God, I knew all that. Why did I let him rile me?"

"Because he has a way of crawlin' under your skin, that's why." Like a filthy, evil disease. "What else did he say?"

"He said y' didn't care about wot happened t' me an' that y' told him y' wouldn't give him a single pence t' save me."

Kate had never felt angrier in her life. She couldn't bear to see the terror and pain reflected in Falcon's eyes. She knew firsthand what Drake could do to a person. The man was the devil incarnate.

"I didn't believe him," Falcon added.

Kate gave a sad smile. "I know y' didn't," she softly returned. "I don't want you t' worry anymore. I will take care of everything."

Falcon stared at her for a long moment.

"What is it? What's the matter?"

Falcon hesitated and then said, "Drake, he . . ."

"What?" Kate prompted.

"He said . . ." Falcon couldn't meet her eyes.

"What did he say? Tell me, Falcon. He can't hurt us anymore."

Falcon hesitated, but then looked up at her. "He said that y' were not only a lousy thief, but that y' were also a . . ."

"A what?"

"A whore."

Kate should have known the man had filled Falcon's head with lies about her. It was just his style.

"He said y'd leave me for the nabob. That . . . that he pleasured y' an' . . . that y' found yer callin' on yer back with yer legs—"

Kate put up her hand to stop the flow of Falcon's words. Rage glistened inside her like a living, breathing thing.

Kate felt suddenly ashamed of what she and Alec had shared, of how wonderful he had made her feel, the way he could make her forget where she was—and who she was—with a mere look and a tender caress. She knew what had motivated her to do what she had done, but that didn't stop her from feeling like the whore Drake had called her.

She searched Falcon's face. "An' do y' believe I'd do that and leave you?"

"No," Falcon murmured. "Y' wouldn't leave me for no bloody lord."

"Y' an' the lads are the only family I have." And Kate knew she had to treasure them more than she had before. She needed them, and they needed her.

"I know," Falcon replied quietly.

Kate pulled herself together. Now was a time to be strong. "Let's get out of here. The lads are probably worried sick."

"You go."

"We'll both go," Kate said firmly and with a great deal of authority.

"I can't go. If I do, I'll just bring trouble for y' an' the lads."

"We've been through worse."

"We've never been through this," Falcon returned. "People will be after me. Now, please go. An' . . . an' tell the lads that I . . . I love them."

Kate couldn't breathe. Her whole world was falling apart, and she felt helpless to stop it. "I'm not leavin' here without y'. We stick together, remember?"

"I don't want y' to get hurt."

"No one will get hurt." Kate wished she could be so certain. "Now, who saw what happened between you an' Drake?"

"No one saw me. I crawled out an open window in his room. His coach was under the window. It broke me fall. But his men are still goin' t' know it was me who killed him when they find me gone."

Kate's brow wrinkled in thought, and then an idea began

to form. "Drake was holdin' y' at the old warehouse, right?"

Confusion showed on Falcon's face. "Yeah, but so wot? He's dead, an' even you can't change that."

"I don't intend t' try," Kate replied. Picking up the vase she had set beside her, she held it out to Falcon. "Take this, will y'?"

Falcon held the vase at arm's length and looked it over. "Wot is it?"

"It's a vase that I took from . . . his lordship," Kate answered, trying to think of Alec in an impersonal way. It was impossible. "I was gonna give it t' Drake so that I could get y' back."

"But I thought y' said y' gave him a diamond necklace?"

"I did."

"But Drake was greedy, right?"

It was a question that needed no answer. "Look, I want y' to take the vase back t' his lordship for me."

"Me? Why?"

"Because I asked you to." Kate looked away for a moment before adding, "I doubt highly he'd want t' see me anyway."

"I don't understand. Where will y' be?"

"Don't worry. I'll be back before y' know it. Just take the vase for me, all right?"

Falcon hesitated, staring at Kate with probing blue eyes. "All right."

"After that, I want you t' find the lads. Y' know where they usually are." She put her hand on Falcon's shoulder. "If for some reason things—if I'm not back come the mornin', I want y' to go see his lordship. He'll help y' an' the lads."

"I don't understand. Wot's goin' on?"

"Nothing," Kate replied, hoping that would be the

truth, but knowing it was unlikely. "His lordship is a good sort. Decent." Kind, sweet, wonderful, amazing, and a whole host of other things that only succeeded in breaking Kate's heart to think of them.

"Sounds as if ye're interested in this blue blood," Falcon interjected perceptively.

"I'm not." But Kate knew her words lacked conviction. She couldn't explain it to Falcon. And she didn't want to think about it. "Go an' find the lads. I'll see y' shortly."

"Wot d'ya want me t' tell this lord if I see him?"

Kate turned to go, but Falcon's question stopped her. Looking over her shoulder, she softly replied, "Tell him . . . tell him I'm sorry."

Chapter Twenty-Four

Alec brooded in his study long after Anthony departed. He preferred to bond with his liquor instead of eating dinner. He had moved onto Madeira, having finished all the Scotch.

Tomorrow, he vowed, he would put the dark-haired hellion from his mind once and for all.

Before that time, however, he planned to enjoy his one last bout of self-pity and self-disgust.

He sat in semidarkness with only the slowly dying fire to warm the chill that had settled over his flesh. It couldn't warm the chill inside him, though.

He cursed Kate. And when he thought he could curse her no more, he found other things to curse her for.

In his lucid moments, he told himself that everyone was entitled to a mistake, and Kate, alias the Fox, was his. One, however, he would not make again.

Alec stood up and grasped the back of his chair, a little

unstable on his feet. He would have himself a grand head-ache in the morning. But that would be the last aggravation he would deal with in connection with the Fox.

He needed to find his bed.

He was about to head to his lofty haven when he heard a noise. It was late, and he was sure he was the only one up. He thought that perhaps he had imagined the sound since he wasn't exactly coherent at that moment. But when the noise sounded again, he knew it was not a product of an alcohol-soaked brain.

Alec sobered quickly when he realized that whoever was beyond his study door was attempting, if failing miserably, to remain as covert as possible.

And that meant only one thing. . . .

Someone was in his house who didn't belong there.

Kate? his fevered, sluggish mind thought. Had she come back to turn the knife once more?

Alec dismissed the possibility. She would not be so fool-ish as to return.

Yet she had before.

Ah, but she thought you gullible then. This time it was differ-ent. If it was sweet Kate come back to try to dupe him once more, he would leave an indelible imprint in her mind of what happened to people who crossed him. Three times was a charm, so to speak.

Quietly, Alec positioned himself behind his study door. He wouldn't be the one caught unaware. Whoever had the nerve to step into his house was going to get the surprise of their life.

Slowly, the door creaked open. The person hesitated on the threshold, most likely cataloguing the room's valuables to see if there was anything worth taking.

Alec knew a certain satisfaction when the black-clad fig-ure ventured into the room. He didn't feel like pursuing his intruder through the house waiting for his opportunity to strike.

Stepping out from behind the door, he followed the figure toward his desk. He noticed then that the prowler was rather short and skinny. Could this be one of the lads Kate spoke of so fondly? Had they heard he was an easy target and decided to rob him as well? The thought had him seeing red.

"You've picked the wrong house, criminal," he said in a low growl. "And you're going to be very sorry you made that mistake."

The black-clad figure swung around, startled. The object the intruder was holding crashed to the floor. Eyes of a color Alec could not discern in the dim room widened in fear and alarm. But neither the fear Alec saw nor the fact that he was bigger and taller than the prowler registered until too late. His anger propelled him to action. Before he could stop himself, his fist flew out and connected solidly with his intruder's face. The body went down like a top without uttering a sound.

Alec gazed down at the crumpled figure and then looked at his fist. He could not believe he had hit someone smaller—and defenseless to boot, intruder or not. Frankly, he couldn't believe he had hit anyone.

Christ, what had happened to his calm, unflappable demeanor? His code of nonviolence unless specifically provoked? He had never hit Whitfield, and Lord knew if anyone deserved a shot, it was Anthony. In a short time, he had become a madman. He had never been ruled by his emotions.

Alec knelt down next to the figure, whose head was tilted to the side, the face in shadow, out cold—not surprising with the blow Alec had delivered. God, he felt lousy. Since he had met Kate, his life had spiraled out of control.

Alec was sure his intruder would awaken in a great deal of pain. He cursed himself for his rashness. He couldn't believe he had sunk so low as to start beating up on those who were not his physical equal. He could have just grabbed the scrawny lad and tied him to a chair until the authorities arrived.

He must be crazy, but he thought to put the lad in the guest room, the same one Kate had occupied, until the boy came to. Alec knew he would probably find himself robbed blind in the morning.

He lifted the lad, surprised to find the boy even lighter than he had thought. He shook his head, disgusted that people should have to live the way the boy and Kate and many others like them did. He had always thought there should be some kind of system in place to help the less fortunate. But that was certainly on the bottom of parliament's list of things to do.

The words Anthony had once said to Alec on that day which now seemed so long ago came rushing back to him.

Just what have you done for your fellow man recently?

Alec had tried to help Kate. But perhaps he was just a hypocrite.

Carefully, he stood up with the boy in his arms and headed toward the door. He had not taken more than three steps when a band of light coming from the hallway cast its rays upon his intruder's face. Alec sucked in his breath as he got his first glimpse.

The face he gazed down upon was bloodless. He could see the swelling around the eye as he had predicted. But none of that mattered as he stared in stunned silence.

"Good God," he whispered, his voice raw. "Kate?"

Hurriedly, Alec moved back to the couch and sat down, holding the small, motionless body close to him.

"My lord?" a voice called out.

Wild-eyed, Alec looked up to find his butler standing in the doorway. Holmes stepped into the room hesitantly, his eyes wide as they moved from the shattered vase to the unconscious form in Alec's arms and then to Alec directly.

Finally, as if realizing he was gaping, Holmes shook himself and walked toward a wall sconce.

"Don't." Alec wanted no light to reveal what his fist had wrought.

"But, my lord . . ."

"Goddamn it, Holmes, don't push me!"

"Would you like me to call the doctor, my lord?"

"No," Alec replied, standing up, his captive nestled against his chest. "I do, however, want you to get me a cloth and a bowl of ice water." Then he headed toward the door.

"Is that . . . Miss Kate?" Holmes asked as Alec passed him.

Alec nodded in reply, refusing to look at the damage his rash action had done to Kate's face. "Bring the cloth and water up to the guest bedroom." He started to walk away, but Holmes's words stopped him.

"That's not Miss Kate."

Something in Holmes's voice told Alec that his butler was not picking an inappropriate moment to try to raise his ire.

Stepping into the hallway, Alec hesitated, steeled himself, and then glanced down at the girl cradled in his arms. He winced when he saw the swelling and purpling around the eye with which his fist had connected. But then he noticed the things he had not seen in the relative darkness of his study, things that confirmed Holmes's words.

The girl in his arms was not Kate.

But he would be damned if she could not pass for nearly the spitting image of Kate. The girl had the same smooth skin and delicate features as Kate, the same high cheek-bones and unbelievably long eyelashes. But the structure of the bones was not the same, and the lips were not as full. And her eyebrows were not dark as midnight, but. . . .

Slowly, he pulled off the crude knit cap that covered the girl's hair.

It was not long, silky black tresses that spilled out of the cap's confines, but shoulder-length red hair.

Alec was mystified.

Holmes stepped up behind Alec, trying unsuccessfully to look over his shoulder. Giving up, Holmes moved to his side. "That's not Miss Kate," he repeated.

"I heard you the first time." Alec wondered what the hell was going on. "I can't believe I didn't notice right away," he said more to himself than to Holmes.

Holmes shrugged. "Well, I—"

Alec cut across his words. "Cloth and ice water."

Holmes inclined his head. "Certainly, my lord." He turned to go, but hesitated. "My lord?

"What is it?"

"Well, if that is not Miss Kate . . . then who is it?"

"Bloody good question." And one he intended to have an answer for as soon as the girl awoke.

Alec took the steps two at a time, heading with a quick tread toward Kate's room. He couldn't believe he still thought of his guest room as Kate's room.

He blotted out the thought as he strode into the room and kicked the door closed behind him. He laid the girl down on the bed. He couldn't get over the uncanny resemblance she had to Kate.

The girl groaned then and stirred slightly. She moved her head on the pillow, her hand coming up to touch her face. "Ooh," she moaned, wincing as her fingers brushed over the spot where a bruise was forming.

Alec grabbed her wrist. "Don't touch it," he told her in a firm voice.

The girl's eyes snapped open then. Only one eye opened fully, however, but the fear was evident nonetheless. She did not speak, but struck out at him physically, her small fist swinging wildly. She would have landed a blow to his face had he not ducked his head. His plucky intruder was not deterred in the least as she rallied with her other fist.

Alec grabbed both wrists, but she continued to struggle. "Stop, will you? I'm not going to hurt you."

"Don't touch me!" She squirmed and wriggled. "If y' don't leave me be right now, I promise ye'll be sorry!" And then she proceeded to tell him, in detail, how she would go about making him sorry.

Alec's patience was beginning to wear thin with feisty women. "Will you relax already? My name is Alec. This is my home. You are an intruder. And I punched you. For which you have my apologies. No one is going to lay a finger on you, so just calm down." Something he said must have worked because his small antagonist stopped struggling. "Now, if I release your wrists, do you promise to keep them at your sides?"

She nodded in mute response, her gaze focused on his every move, which was bloody disconcerting.

He decided to take a stern position with her, hoping to get her to speak and, more importantly, to tell him the truth about what was going on.

He narrowed his eyes at her and folded his arms across his chest. "All right. First things first. Who are you? And what are you doing in my house?"

The girl just blinked at him.

"Speak to me, criminal, or you'll find yourself doing your talking to the constable," he threatened, feeling more than a twinge of guilt when he saw her fear double.

The girl swallowed visibly and then stuttered, "B-but the Fox said y' wouldn't call the constable."

Alec's jaw clenched. So Kate had been behind this whole thing? He had been right when he thought she had told her fellow thieves that he was an easy target.

"She did, did she? Well, isn't it unfortunate for you that she was wrong." He refused to feel like a villain when he saw her eyes well up with tears. "I have no tolerance for thieves," he added, although his tone was not as severe.

"I . . . I'm n-not a thief," she refuted, her voice barely above a whisper. Then she amended, "At least not tonight."

"If you weren't stealing anything, then what were you doing sneaking around my house? I don't recall inviting you here."

"The Fox told me t' come," she answered.

"Is that so?"

The girl nodded meekly, a single tear coursing down her cheek.

Bloody hell. Tears.

"And why did she tell you to come?" he pursued, as if he didn't already know the answer.

"Well, she wanted me t' return the vase she took from y'."

Returning the vase? Kate had asked the girl to bring it back to him? Why?

The girl went on in a weepy voice. "Y' frightened me, and I"—she sniffed—"I dropped it."

Alec raised an eyebrow at her. It was his fault, was it? "Perhaps if you had not been sneaking around in my house, it wouldn't have happened."

His chastisement didn't work as his uninvited guest replied, "I told y'. I had t' return the vase."

"Have you never heard of knocking?"

That comment brought a bit of a flush to her cheeks. "Well, it was late. It looked as if everyone were abed."

"Well then, why not come in the morning instead? I could have shot you." Which would have been an interesting feat since he didn't own a gun.

"I had t' come," she persisted, apparently undaunted by the threat of bodily injury.

"Yes, I know. Kate told you to come." He shook his head. "You still have not told me why."

"Kate? She gave y' her real name?" This possibility seemed to amaze her. "I haven't heard that name since we left the orphanage." She narrowed her eyes at him and stared at him as if he had grown another head. "Y' must be pretty special."

Alec ignored the shot of pain in the vicinity of his heart at hearing the girl's words. "Answer the question," he said tersely.

"I did answer it." Her expression changed to one that asked him if he had been listening. "She wanted me t' return the vase t' you."

"I heard that much, what I want to know is why?"

The girl shrugged. "I guess she wanted y' to have it back." She wrinkled her brow then. "Oh, right, there was one other thing."

"Which was?"

"Well, she told me t' tell y' that she was sorry."

Sorry? That one word effectively toppled Alec. "So why the hell didn't she tell me this herself?"

Again, the redhead shrugged her tiny shoulders. "I don't know really." She darted a quick look at him before returning her gaze to the ceiling. "I have t' go," she said abruptly, pushing herself into a sitting position.

Alec put a hand against her shoulder. "Not so fast. You're hurt, remember?" Courtesy of his fist.

"I've been hurt worse than this," she told him without a single inflection in her voice. It was then he noticed the cut on her lip. Had his fist inflicted that damage as well?

"Who are you?" he asked, suddenly realizing he had yet to find cut.

A moment passed in silence before she answered, "My name is Falcon."

Falcon? Whatever happened to real names? "What's your relationship to Kate?"

Slowly, the girl swiveled her head, gazing at him with eyes the same rich shade of blue as Kate's, and he knew. In truth, he probably had known all along.

1 "She's my sister."

Chapter Twenty-Five

"My lord?" Holmes queried as he entered the guest room, his voice sounding like a trumpet blast in the absolute quiet.

Standing at the window, Alec whipped around and put a finger to his lips, nodding his head at his sleeping intruder.

Falcon was piled underneath a mountain of covers, barely taking up a fourth of the bed. He had managed to convince her to stay until the morning after promising her he wouldn't ask any more questions. That, and the lure of a soft bed and a warm meal, was just too good to pass up, Alec imagined. He couldn't help but remember a certain other female who had also succumbed to its lure.

Kate.

All the burdens she had on her slender shoulders, to be put in a position of fending for herself and her sister, and the lads, whoever they may be. She had to be the strong one, the leader as she called herself. Whereas Kate was brave, her sister only appeared to be.

He had seen that strength in Kate, yet he had seen the vulnerability as well, the need for someone to protect her. Alec wanted to be that someone.

Before Falcon had dozed off, she had told him that Kate had been right about him, that he really was different. And as she closed her eyes, Falcon muttered that she knew he would help them. But help them with what, was the question. And where was Kate? He had wanted to shake Falcon awake to get his answers, but he would restrain his impatience for the moment and allow her to rest.

Obviously, Falcon believed everything her sister told her—which made Alec feel like a bloody louse since he had punched her. But he truly couldn't be blamed for that, considering the circumstances. His self-assurances didn't help, however; he still felt lower than pond scum.

But questions continued to nag at him.

Why had Kate taken the necklace? And why had she then returned? Had it been merely to dupe him again? Her actions had made him think she was remorseful. But if she had been, then why had she turned around and taken the vase as if mocking his gullibility?

Alec thought he had her all figured out; then she threw him for a loop by having her sister return the vase—or try to at least. Now it was in a million pieces.

There was one answer that popped into his head every time he asked himself these questions, but he rejected it as being ridiculous.

Kate did not love him.

Besides, he didn't love her. Did he?

Of course not. He was a confirmed bachelor, and she was a confirmed thief. The two elements did not mix. Certainly he felt something for her, compassion, understanding, a desire to help her. Lust. But that was as far as it went.

God, he was sick of thinking about it, but more than that he was sick of himself.

"My lord?" Holmes repeated, but in a whisper this time. "I have the cloth and ice water you requested."

"Just leave it on the bureau," Alec told him distractedly.

Where was Kate? Was she in trouble? Perhaps she needed him, and he was standing in the dark recesses of the guest room doing nothing.

Damn!

Holmes stepped up next to him and nodded down at their sleeping guest. "How is Miss . . ."

"Falcon," Alec supplied.

Holmes raised an eyebrow, obviously wondering where such names came from, but refrained from commenting. Instead, he asked, "Who is she, my lord?"

"Kate's sister."

Holmes stared at the girl assessingly. "Well, that certainly explains the resemblance."

But it doesn't explain anything else, Alec thought grimly.

Holmes's querulous gray eyes focused on Alec's face. "Where is Miss Kate?"

Alec shook his head, turning back to stare out into the night sky. "I'd like to know the answer to that myself."

Kate hid behind a barrel, her eyes darting left and right, trying to discern if there was any activity around the warehouse. All was quiet—perhaps too quiet. She didn't see Drake's motley crew of thugs. It seemed as if Drake's dead body had yet to be discovered. That was to her advantage. She was not going to let Falcon get in trouble if she could do anything about it. She had been protecting Falcon since they were old enough to walk, and she wasn't going to stop now.

Although she was only a few minutes older than Falcon—since technically they were twins—she had always taken the burden onto her shoulders for caring for both of them as part and parcel of being the older sibling.

She had always done the best she could, having not been given much to work with. No parents, no money, no skills—except for one. And a combination of her small size and, on most occasions, her agility helped her to be quite adept at that. It wasn't what most people would call a life, but it had kept them going from day to day, and that was all that really mattered. That was why she was now so ashamed of her wanton behavior with Alec. How could she have forgotten for even a moment about her responsibility to Falcon and the lads?

Yet Kate knew her reasons for coming had not simply been for Falcon. She had also come to get the necklace back. It meant something to Alec, and she wanted to return it. Then the slate would be wiped clean, and she could leave London knowing she had done her best to put everything back to rights.

The thought of leaving London, and Alec, held her immobile for a long moment. Closing her eyes, she waited for the dull pain in the pit of her stomach to pass.

It didn't.

Kate realized the pain was something she would have to live with until she could forget Alec.

But when would she ever forget him?

She took a deep breath and forced the thought aside. Time was of the essence.

Covertly, she crept out from behind the barrels and made her way with catlike stealth across the empty expanse that yawned before the barrels and the door to the warehouse. Her heart beat so fast she couldn't hear herself breathing. Any moment she thought the alarm would go up and she would be caught. But all remained quiet, and she reached the door without incident.

Ever so slowly, she eased open the door. She held her breath, praying it wouldn't creak, and sighed in relief when it made no noise. She paused to listen for shouts or the sound of running feet. But when nothing happened, she stepped inside.

The interior was dimly lit, not surprising when one was intent on carrying out criminal activities, Kate grimly thought, trying to still her trembling. No one was around.

Where were they?

She scanned her surroundings, her eyes lighting on all the stolen items: gold fob watches, silver money clips, a teakwood walking stick inlaid with mother-of-pearl and a lion's head top cast in gold, a pair of fancy tortoise hair combs with winking emeralds, and even some cuff links with diamond chips. All were things that could be stolen while a fine lady or gent spoke to a friend in front of a shop window. Drake must be confident in the fact that no one would dare steal from him to leave such things in plain sight.

Kate didn't care about his booty, though. Somewhere inside the vast warehouse, in the pseudo empire Drake had built, was the big man's suite of rooms. They were quite elaborate from the tales she had heard. She knew the man well enough to know he liked to be right on top of everything—and in this case, he literally was.

After she had left Falcon, Kate had thought of many scenarios regarding what she should do about Drake.

Only one was a resolution.

She would set fire to the warehouse after she had confirmed Drake was dead and she had retrieved the Blue

Water diamond. If she should get caught before then, she would take Falcon's place, confessing to be Drake's killer.

Falcon had been Kate's reason to go on every day. Wit and warmth and compassion had been her sister's strengths, and those things flowed over all who were fortunate enough to be near her. But her sister had always been too fragile for a life on the streets. Kate rarely let her come with her when she went to steal. She couldn't have borne it had her sister gotten hurt.

Very quietly, Kate moved farther into the warehouse, keeping her ears attuned to any noise. She looked for something that stood out, like a dead fat man, for example. But everything was in its place, nothing looking unusual. Still, her senses kept telling her something was wrong.

She came to the stairs that she assumed led to Drake's inner sanctum. She mounted them with more than a bit of trepidation. She had seen many things in her life, but she had yet to come face-to-face with a dead man. And Drake, she was sure, was probably just as hideous-looking in death as he had been in life—even more so, she imagined, trying to keep the bile from rising in her throat.

Reaching the last step, she hesitated, then proceeded down the lengthy hallway. A floorboard squeaked as she passed over it. Under normal circumstances, it would have been inconsequential. But with the danger pulsing around her, and the uncanny silence, any noise seemed magnified and sure to bring disaster.

She stopped for a moment and listened.

All was quiet, so she carried on.

There were many doors lining the hallway, but she knew it was the double doors all the way at the end that she wanted. She figured they would have to be wide to fit Drake's big body. And it also figured they would have to be at the opposite end of the hall, far away from the steps . . .

And her only means of escape.

Reaching the double doors, Kate stilled her trembling fingers, clasped one knob, and eased the portal open. She peered inside, and as with everything else so far, the room was empty. Where was everyone?

More importantly, where was Drake?

She stepped into the garishly decorated room. A huge bed sat back against the far wall sheathed in blood red satin sheets that were rumpled as if the bed had recently been slept in.

Kate conjured up an image of Drake's corpulent body lying within the folds of the bedding, his round stomach like a mountain. She had to look away for fear of becoming physically ill.

The rest of the room was equally as hideous: obscene paintings hanging on the walls, a rug that looked like animal skin at the foot of the bed, a coiled whip hanging from a peg, and mirrors, lots of them. Why would he want to look at himself? If she were Drake, she would paint the walls black and lock herself in.

Steeling herself, Kate ventured into the room.

Her search did not turn up Drake. The man was dead; he couldn't have just up and walked away.

"Well, isn't this a sweet surprise," said a deep, wheezing voice behind her.

Kate whirled around. It couldn't be!

"Hello, pet," Drake drawled as he stood in the doorway. Next to him was his right-hand man, Eli, and behind him were two of his other thugs. "I can see from your expression you were expecting someone else. So sorry to disappoint you. But how could I miss this little party when I have been waiting so long to get you where I want you?" His expression was self-satisfied. "So, what do you think of my love nest?" He asked, waving a hand about the room.

"I think it's as disgusting as you!" Kate spat.

"Now, is that any way to talk to the person who holds your life in his hands?"

"But you're supposed t' be dead."

Drake chuckled darkly. "As you can plainly see, I am very much alive. And I must say that being alive has never been more satisfying than it is at this moment."

"But Falcon—"

"Killed me?" Drake finished for her. "She is such a gullible creature, our dumb, little Falcon. But she has certainly served a purpose. For that I thank her."

He knew! Oh, God, he knew about Falcon being a girl. Kate had prayed they had been able to keep that secret.

Drake chuckled. "Yes, I know that I now possess two sweet doves. I wasn't going to be fooled again. It took a little coaxing to get Falcon to reveal her lush secrets. What a shame to put binding around such lovely breasts. I felt personally responsible for soothing those angry red marks left by the cloth cutting into her delicate skin."

Pain, rage and horror roiled through Kate. "Damn y'! Y' better not have touched her!"

Drake chuckled. "Oh, I touched her all right. But have no fear. Her virginity is intact. Such a gift will bring me a high price." Before Kate could voice her anger, he went on. "Twins, good Lord I've been blessed. The men will certainly like that."

A bead of sweat trickled between Kate's breasts. "Wot men?"

"Why, the men who will be clamoring to bed two identical, sweet morsels like you and Falcon, of course. Certainly you didn't think me fool enough to let you both get away, did you?" He raised a thick, black eyebrow. "Ah, I can see that you did. And here I thought that you, of all people, were smart enough not to underestimate me."

"No!"

He ignored her. "You know that I have a fondness for you, pet. And when you gave me such a lovely diamond, I knew then you were fond of me as well."

"I have a fondness t' see y' dead," Kate hissed. "So why aren't y'? Falcon said she stabbed y'."

Drake put his hand out, and Eli dropped a knife into it. Kate took a step back as he moved forward and dangled it in front of her. "Yes, Falcon stabbed me with this." He turned the knife, pointed it toward his heart and, before anyone could blink, brought the knife down toward his chest. Kate clamped her eyes shut.

The next thing she heard was Drake's evil laughter.

Her eyes flew open. Guffaws spread through the group. Drake took the knife and put a finger to the tip; it retracted up and down. "It's fake. Neat little item, isn't it? I just wanted little Falcon to *think* she had killed me. I was quite melodramatic in my death scene. I believe I could have been an actor." He shrugged. "But thievery is ever so much more lucrative."

Drake straightened his jacket before continuing. "In case you haven't figured it out, my girl, I have a special talent for spotting weaknesses. Your weakness is Falcon. And, lucky for me, Falcon's weakness is you. Quite tidy, wouldn't you say? I knew the little birdy would fly to you, and you, being the protector, would come here and make sure the deed had been done. Did you come to weep over my dead body, pet?"

Kate couldn't hold her tongue. "I came t' spit on y'," she hissed. She should have known Drake's being dead had been a dream too good to be true. "How could I have been so foolish? Even had she stabbed y' with a real knife, it wouldn't have gotten through all that blubber.''

Drake's smug expression quickly changed to anger. His face turned red. "You continue to press your luck, my girl. One would think you knew better.''

Kate clenched her fists at her sides. "So wot do y' want from me?''

"I want a number of things from you, sweet. And I will let you know all of them in short order.''

"Why did y' put on this show?''

Drake shrugged. "I wanted to make sure I got you here. I know how difficult you can be. I thought it important to let you know once and for all who is in charge. You'll do what I want, and you'll do it willingly.''

"I won't do anythin' for y'!''

Next to Drake, Eli growled, the jagged scar on his cheek making him look menacing. He turned to Drake. "Do y' want me t' teach the wench a lesson or two, boss? She won't be speakin' like that to y' again once I get through with her.'' His gaze shifted back to Kate. "Yer gonna be one sorry bitch.''

"Don't worry about her," Drake said. "When she tastes the bite of the whip on her bare backside, she will come around quickly enough.''

Eli's beady eyes gleamed.

Drake added, "You *will* learn obedience.''

"I'll never bow down t' you!''

Drake gritted his teeth. "You will. All in good time. For now, I don't want to mar that silken flesh or my male buyers may be less interested in you." He shrugged. "Then again, they might like the idea of teaching you some manners. That is a very definite possibility.''

Kate's skin crawled, but she refused to let her fear show.

Drake came to stand directly in front of her. "They say

that a fox is one of the most elusive creatures on earth. Did you know that?"

Kate stilled the limbs that wanted to tremble as Drake touched her, tilting her chin up. "Is this goin' t' take long?" she asked with disdain. "If so, I'd like t' sit down."

"Not so long," Drake replied meaningfully, his look implying that other things were sure to come—things that were not going to be pleasant. "As I was saying, the fox is elusive. Perhaps that is why the blue bloods spend so much time hunting them. Winning, you see, means a lot to them. They like their trophies." A pudgy finger caressed her cheek. "People always want what they can't have. I imagine that is why you intrigue me so, my girl." Kate turned her head away. "You are indeed fiery-tempered. I like a woman who will fight me." His finger trailed down her neck and then between the valley of her breasts, where it paused. "I imagine the earl enjoyed the thrill of the hunt," he taunted. "But something tells me he has captured the prize. Isn't that so, my pet?"

Kate forced herself to look him in the eye. "The only thing his high-and-mighty got was duped."

Drake eyed her closely and then shrugged. "Alas, that is true. However, it was a good test."

"What do y' mean, test?"

"How soon you forget everything I say. We will remedy that before the night is through," he said in a low, meaningful voice. Sweat glistened on his face, and he had to mop his brow with his handkerchief. "As I was saying, this was only a test for the earl. I'm happy to say he passed it admirably."

"What are y' talkin' about?" Kate asked tightly, dreading the answer.

"Well, the man never called the constable on you. Doesn't that seem passing strange?"

Kate didn't like the feeling that snaked through her. "It ain't how he does things."

"Not how he does things?" Drake looked to his men and back to her. "You take a priceless, one-of-a-kind necklace and the man does nothing? A smart man like the earl doesn't do things without a reason. In my opinion, it means one of two things. Either you spread your legs and let him slake his lust on you *or* the man loves you." He guffawed. "The fool! Such devotion will cost him."

Drake had twisted the knife more effectively with that one comment than with anything else he had said thus far.

Alec didn't love her. How Kate wished he did. If anything, he felt sorry for her. Intrigued by her, perhaps. And Lord knew she liked how he made her feel, and she thought he liked it, too. But love? No. Alec would never feel that way for her. Too much separated them.

"He doesn't love me."

"If you say so."

"I know so."

"Well, if that is the case, then I imagine you have foiled my plan. But I still have other things in mind for you and Falcon, so all is not lost."

"What plan?"

Eli sneered at her. "Y' still haven't figured it out, y' stupid wench?"

Drake grabbed Eli roughly by the arm. "If you interfere one more time, I will have Gus cut out your tongue," he said brutally. "Do we understand one another?"

Eli very wisely nodded his head and gulped. "Yeah, boss, I understand."

"Good." Drake shoved Eli away and turned back to her. "You could share a similar fate, my dear. It's only because of my benevolence that you remain amongst the living. That could turn at any time."

Kate realized they had reached a pinnacle and a very fine line had been drawn. She had to measure her words from this point on. "So what do y' want from me?"

Drake shrugged. "Well, I had hoped you would be of assistance, but since you claim his lordship doesn't care, I guess you won't be." He shook his head. "Such a shame."

"What does he have t' do with anything?"

Drake's expression changed drastically. His eyes turned cold, dangerous. He was not humoring her anymore. "I realized last night that I could get far more having you than having Falcon. I knew that given time, you would find a way to get the little brat out and that you would take off on me. You're a very clever and resourceful wench. I also knew that even should I thwart you in getting Falcon, you would only succeed in getting me maybe one or two more trinkets from the earl. Then I started thinking you might enlist the man's help. I suspect that regardless of your protestations, he's quite enamored with you. That being the case, he may have caused me some upset. Then I'd have to kill both of you. That wouldn't suit my purpose, you see."

"Alec is a powerful man. Y'd never get away with killin' him."

One greasy black eyebrow rose. "Alec, is it? Well, that's telling."

Kate cursed her quick tongue.

Before she knew what he was about, Drake's hand snaked around her waist, yanking her against him. "You seem to forget that *I* am a dangerous man." His eyes were black pools of twisted evil. "You will serve a useful purpose, and the purpose will be aiding me. As will Falcon. I know she won't go anywhere without you. She doesn't have it in her to make a decision on her own. She lacks your strong spirit, nor does she possess your skill at stealing. And his lordship, as wealthy as he is, is not the only plump pigeon out there on which I could utilize your talent. You see, Falcon alone would never do. A look was all it ever took to cow the stupid chit. A mere touch had her nearly immobilized with fear. That, however, was not a bad thing. It tends to keep one in line." His eyes turned to mere slits as he added, "You would do well to learn a little fear, my dear."

"Y' stay away from her, y' bastard!" Kate hissed.

The arm about Kate's waist tightened, nearly choking the breath from her. Drake's free hand grasped her chin in an unyielding grip. "And what do you think you're going to do about it if I choose not to?"

"I'll kill y'," she replied in a low, harsh voice, her words a vow.

Drake laughed mirthlessly. "You'll kill me? Oh, you have grand ideas, little one. But you'll get no further than Falcon did. But I'm sure you'll keep me on my toes."

Slowly, his grip eased around her waist, and Kate breathed in deeply, willing her dizziness to subside.

Drake turned to Eli. "See, I told you, violence isn't always the answer. Sometimes all it takes is calm logic and reasoning to find yourself where you want to be."

"If y' say so, boss," Eli grumbled.

"I say so." Drake paused. "However, in this one instance, I am sorry to say that violence is a necessary evil." His eyes locked on Kate's. "I hope you'll understand, my dear."

Drake nodded to Eli, whose face lit with evil glee, understanding his boss's silent request. In one quick motion, Eli's hand came up sharply and struck Kate hard across the face with a force that sent her to her knees.

Drake dragged over a chair and sat down. It was too small, and his fat hung over the sides. He put his chunky hands on his knees and leaned toward her. "Finally, I've got you where you belong. If you're smart, you'll stay there. I imagine that we shall be seeing your knight in shining armor shortly."

The blood drained from Kate's face. "What are y' talkin' about? Why would he come here?"

"Why, to save his beloved, of course," Drake replied with a cold smile.

Fear for Alec raced through Kate's veins. She prayed for strength. "And if your little plan doesn't work," she said through her swollen lip. "What then?"

Drake leaned back, eyeing her with malicious satisfaction. "You don't want to know."

Chapter
Twenty-Six

The high-pitched scream echoed throughout the entire house, yanking Alec out of his bed and depositing him unceremoniously onto the floor.

"Bloody hell," he muttered, rubbing his head where he had bashed it against the bedside table. He had just fallen asleep after spending most of the night alternately thinking about Kate and then berating himself for thinking about her. It had become a routine of late, a litany of questions. What had happened to her? Where had she gone? Was she all right?

At the sound of the second scream, he shot to his feet. Opening the door, he ran into Holmes, knocking him onto his backside.

"Has this entire house gone crazy?" he shouted in irritation, his head still throbbing. "What in God's name is going on?" He put his hand out and helped Holmes to his feet.

Holmes steadied himself and replied, "It was the girl."

Alec was already heading down the hallway before Holmes got out the last word. He flung open the door of the guest room. Inside, it was completely dark, not a single taper lit. He heard a whimper a moment before a body came flying at him from out of the blackness. He almost lost his balance as he and the frightened girl staggered out into the hallway. She clung to him like a vine, her body shaking like a leaf.

Alec held the girl for a few minutes, trying to soothe whatever ailed her. Then he attempted to peel her arms from around his neck, where her grip was so tight it was near to choking. For being such a tiny thing, her hold was amazingly strong.

"Oh, my sister!" she cried. "Look at her!"

Alec frowned. "Look at her? Falcon, she's not here."

"Ye've gotta stop them!"

"Stop wot?"

She wailed and hugged him tighter.

"Talk to me, goddamn it!"

"Ye've got t' help her!"

"What's happened to Kate?" Alec urged, trying to calm Falcon enough to make some sense out of her jibberish. "It will be all right, just tell me what's the matter."

Holmes came up to them. "What has happened, my lord?"

Alec looked askance at him. "If I knew that, Holmes, do you think I would still be standing here with a blank look on my face?"

Holmes looked chagrined. "Can I offer some assistance?"

"Bring up a cup of Mrs. Dearborn's *remedy,*" Alec replied gruffly, trying, with some difficulty, to loosen the hold Falcon had around his neck. She was choking off his air supply. She was also soaking his dressing gown as she continued to sob and mutter incoherently.

Awkwardly, Alec headed back into the bedroom. Falcon refused to let him go, so he lifted her feet off the floor. In the process, he slammed his bare foot against the leg of the bed. He cursed fluently as he put his fear-stricken bundle down, finally managing to free himself. She still sobbed, all the while condemning herself for something that Alec had yet to understand.

He lit several tapers and then came back to the bed. "Feeling better?" he asked calmly.

She sniffled and hiccuped. "No," she replied. "I'll never feel better."

Suddenly, she was quiet. She stared up at him, her eyes large and luminous in her small, pale face—a face that looked like, and yet not like, Kate's. But the similarities were enough to have Alec wondering again where Kate was—and if she was all right. As much as he shouldn't care what happened to her, he did.

Alec was hard-pressed not to shake Falcon. He wanted to know what was going on. The tension in the pit of his stomach had begun to build again. He needed answers. And he knew that regardless of Falcon's claims to the opposite, she knew something about what her sister was doing—and where she was. She had five minutes to elucidate or he was taking off the gloves.

Falcon said in a quiet, level voice, "Y' have t' save Kate. She needs help."

Alec grabbed the chair behind him and dragged it over. Sitting down, he leaned forward intently. "What do you mean Kate's in trouble? What kind of trouble is she in?"

Alec thought the girl was going to break down into another gale of sobbing as her eyes began to well up. But she surprised him by remaining cool.

"Big trouble," she answered.

"How do you know she's in trouble?" Then a thought struck him. "Was she here?"

Falcon shook her head. "No, she wasn't here. But I still know she's in trouble." She paused, and looked away. "Sometimes we share a connection."

"What kind of connection?"

"A bond of sorts. It's not constant, an' I think it's stronger in me than in her. Maybe I'm more open t' it." She shrugged her thin shoulders. "I don't know. It's hard t' explain, but I get these sensations sometimes. But tonight, it came t' me in me dreams. That has never happened before. I awoke more frightened than I've ever been, a feelin' of dread hangin' over me."

Alec was not one who believed in any external powers or some kind of mental connections with another human being, but somehow he believed her.

Holmes entered the room with Mrs. Dearborn's remedy, a hot toddy with an extra swig of liquor in it.

Alec took the glass from Holmes and handed it to Falcon. "Here, drink this."

Falcon pushed the glass away. "If y' don't help Kate, they're goin' t' kill her." The look on her face sent a snap of cold fear snaking down Alec's spine.

"Good Lord!" Holmes exclaimed.

"Where is she, Falcon?" Alec asked in a rough voice.

Tears began to run unchecked down Falcon's cheeks. "I knew she would go there," she sobbed brokenly. "I shouldn't have let her. I was a coward. I've always allowed her t' take care of me. Now she's goin' t' die because of me." She buried her face in her hands.

Alec grabbed her arms and shook her. "Where is she, damn it?"

"He's got her. I saw her in me dream. They hurt her

. . . an' she's . . . lyin' on the floor. Oh, God, why did I let her go?''

Alec took her face in his hands and made her look at him. "Who has her?"

"D-Drake."

"Who's Drake?"

"He's dead. I killed him."

It took every bit of Alec's strength to control himself. "If he's dead, then he couldn't possibly have Kate," he tried to reason with her.

"No! I saw him in me dream. Drake has her!" Falcon grabbed his arms, her hold incredibly strong. "An' he's plannin' t' kill her!"

With Falcon's directions, Alec found the warehouse. But that, it seemed, was the easy part.

Outside what seemed to be the only entrance were two large men who appeared as if they were ready to do bodily injury if someone sneezed in their direction.

Alec recalled Falcon telling him that Drake's room was on the second floor of the building. If Kate was still inside the warehouse, that would most likely be where the man would be holding her.

He checked out his surroundings. Besides being dismal, the warehouse seemed impenetrable.

Then he caught sight of a pipe running up the side of the building and some empty crates stacked beside the wall. The pipe was rather slim and didn't appear to have any footholds. But it presented itself as his only option.

Carefully he made his way over to the pipe. He quickly discerned that the crates would be of no help. They were far too flimsy to hold his weight. The pipe, as well, didn't offer much support.

Alec took off his jacket; it would just hinder a climb that was going to prove difficult enough. He rolled up his sleeves and grasped the pipe, pulling himself up, hand over hand.

Coming parallel to the only window, Alec reached into his shirt pocket and pulled out the small knife Holmes had pressed into his hand as he was leaving. Where Holmes had gotten the knife, Alec didn't want to know.

Taking a deep breath, Alec put the blade between his teeth and then let go of the pipe to grab on to the edge of the window. He dangled forty feet from the ground, and if he fell, he would certainly break both legs. But he had no intentions of falling, because falling would mean failure.

Kate was too important to him for him to fail.

What a place to have an epiphany, Alec thought grimly. Nevertheless, he had one while he hung on to the ledge. He realized he couldn't live without Kate. It no longer mattered what she had done or who she was or who he was. All that mattered was being with her. She was a thief all right; she had stolen his heart, and he hadn't even known it. It was probably foolish of him to care. Kate most likely did not return his feelings.

But he loved her, and nothing could change that.

Unless he fell, that was.

With a grunt, Alec slowly pulled himself up enough to look into the room. It was empty. Thank God, he didn't know how much longer he could hold on.

Taking the knife from between his teeth, he levered it beneath the edge of the sill, praying the window would open enough for him to get a hand underneath.

As if it had been oiled, the window came up. He didn't pause to wonder about it. His strength was ebbing.

Putting the knife back between his teeth, Alec lifted

himself up and over the sill. Headfirst, he rolled into the room. He was up on his feet quickly. His eyes scanned the tacky interior.

He heard a noise coming from the side of a massive bed against the wall.

Slowly, he moved toward the bed, his body tense as he came around the side.

Lying facedown on the floor was Kate

"Sweet Jesus!" His voice was a ragged hiss as he knelt down beside her, afraid to touch her, but afraid not to.

Gently, he turned her over on her back. His hands clenched at his sides when he saw what had been done to her. Her face was swollen, one eye blackened, and her lip was bleeding.

Alec reached out his hand to stroke her cheek, wanting nothing more than to soothe her and let her know he was there. She flinched and turned away.

"Well, isn't this cozy?" a voice drawled behind him.

Jumping to his feet, Alec came face-to-face with the man whom Falcon had described in such detail.

Chapter
Twenty-Seven

Alec's hands clenched and unclenched at his sides, the need for physical violence having never been stronger within him. He didn't give a damn that it looked as if Drake weighed twice as much as he did or that the man had brought two of his thugs along. All Alec saw was red, and all he knew was a desire to put his hands around the man's throat and squeeze until his eyes rolled up into the back of his head. But he had to get Kate out of there first.

"You're dead, you sonofabitch," Alec softly hissed.

Drake laughed. "That's a rather amusing threat considering you're outnumbered."

Alec took a step forward, standing in front of Kate's prone form. "If you're smart, you'll get the hell out of my way," he warned.

Drake turned to the henchman on his right. "Eli, it seems his lordship is under the same misguided impression as our dear Fox. He seems to think he's in charge." His gray eyes cut back to Alec. Pointing to Kate, he said, "And as you can plainly see, I don't take well to being told what I can and cannot do."

"With all that weight, your neck will snap quickly when you're swinging from a length of hemp."

"A smart man would know better than to press me. A smart man would also know not to trespass on my property. I could easily kill you—and I would be within my rights."

"You could try." The challenge hung in the air.

Drake eyed Alec from head to foot, the expression of confident arrogance on his round face momentarily wavering. His eyes darted to his men. Alec could see Drake judging his men's strength against his. A smug smile curved one corner of Drake's thin lips.

"I guess we'll just have to see, won't we?"

Alec didn't answer the taunt. "You're a low-life thug," he spat. "Nothing more."

The smile on Drake's face didn't falter, but the look in his eyes shifted with rage. "I'm not going to argue semantics with you. I have you and I have the Fox; therefore, I am in control."

"All right, fat man, if you want to do it the hard way, let's go." Alec waved him on. "Just you and me, right now. I'm going to plow my fist into your face so hard you'll be seeing the back of your head."

Drake's eyes narrowed into slits. "I'll wipe the floor with you."

Alec laughed. "So come on, then. I'm waiting to see what you can do. Waddle your way over here and we'll settle this the old-fashioned way."

"Alec?"

At the sound of Kate's barely audible voice, Alec spun around and looked down at her. Her eyelids fluttered.

Finally they opened, but he could tell she was having a hard time focusing.

He knelt down beside her, mindless of the deadly intentions brewing behind him. "I'm here, Kate," he said softly, taking her hand in his, trying to pour his strength into her.

"Alec?" Kate whispered and then groaned as she tried to move.

"Lie still, Kate."

"What's happened?"

Alec leaned close to her ear and murmured, "Everything will be all right, Kate. I promise."

"This is touching," Drake mocked. "I see my sweet little Fox has found herself a protector."

"Sod off, y' fat toad," Kate told him in a raw voice, touching a finger to her bloodied mouth.

Drake's lip curled menacingly. "I see our behavior lesson didn't take hold as I had expected. We'll try a different method next time. One that I'll enjoy much more." He leered.

Drake's two thugs stepped forward as Alec shot to his feet. "I'll break your bloody neck!"

Drake merely raised an eyebrow and summoned one of his thugs to his side. "Eli, didn't the chit tell us just a short while ago that she didn't like the earl and that the earl didn't like her?"

"She did, boss."

Drake's eyes glittered. "It seems as if I have been lied to, Eli."

"Seems so, boss."

Drake crossed his arms, laying them on top of his massive stomach. "And what do you think I should do about that, Eli?"

"I say kill 'em, boss."

Drake slowly nodded. "I think you have a plan, Eli."

"Thanks, boss."

"Such a shame," Drake sighed. "This has not turned out at all as I imagined." He shrugged his meaty, black-clad shoulders. "I had hoped for cooperation. As well, I hadn't expected you to climb through the window, my lord. Quite inventive. Surprising, too, as I didn't picture you as the type who'd soil his clothing, especially for a tart who hoodwinked you." Smirking, he drew the necklace out of his pocket and dangled it in front of Alec. "Look familiar?"

"I'll shove it down your throat," was Alec's dark promise.

Drake's eyes widened in mock horror. "All these threats to my person. Tsk, tsk, my lord." He pocketed the necklace. "As I was saying, I had expected reasonable behavior from you. *Compliant* behavior. Do as I say, and no one gets hurt sort of thing. Yes, you did indeed surprise me. Ah well, live and learn. The best I can do is cut my losses. Specifically, you, Lord Somerset.

"While it has certainly been entertaining," Drake went on, "the fun is now over. Don't worry about the girl, I'll take care of her once you're gone. Perhaps if she is particularly nice to me, I may even spare her. She is a lush piece after all, and it would be a waste not to use that to my benefit. And as we know, she has more than one talent. She was able to find one ignorant blue blood to steal from; I'm sure she can find another." Drake turned to Eli. "You can take care of his lordship, I presume?"

"Right an' tight, boss."

"Good." Drake snapped his fingers at the two other thugs who had come with him. "Get the girl," he ordered.

Alec blocked their way. "Keep the hell away from her," he growled.

"Alec, don't," Kate pleaded, struggling to sit up. Looking at Drake, she said, "Just let him go. I'll do whatever y' want if y' leave him out of it."

Drake pulled his handkerchief out of his jacket pocket and dabbed at his eyes. "All this mooning is positively maudlin."

"Think about it, Drake," Kate went on, a desperate edge to her voice. "He's a blasted aristocrat, a Peer of the Realm. Y' kill him an' they'll hunt y' down."

Drake scratched his chin. "The first and most important thing I feel I must point out is that no one will know I killed him. I certainly don't intend to tell anyone. Do you, Eli?"

Eli smirked. "Not me, boss."

"And you, Jake?"

Jake shook his shaggy brown head. "I didn't see nothin', boss."

"Gus?"

Gus smiled, showing a missing tooth. "I'll swear on me mother's grave that y' was at yer sick sister's bedside nursin' her back t' health."

"A simple yes or no would have sufficed, idiot."

Gus looked chagrined. "Well, it's no, then, boss."

Drake wore a self-satisfied expression. "Hmm, seems that issue is taken care of."

"His bloody butler will know," Kate persisted, her head throbbing as she tried to rise to her feet. "The man knows everythin' that goes on."

"No body. No crime. And with his lordship's arms and legs weighted down, I assure you, no one will find him. The Thames is particularly murky, which is an added bonus."

Kate prayed for a miracle in that moment. "Drake, just let him go an' I'll start workin' for y' like y' want me to."

"Enough, Kate!" Alec shouted, giving her a warning look. "I'm not leaving here without you."

"I don't want y' here!" Kate lied, knowing that if anything happened to Alec because of her, she wouldn't be able to live with herself. "Just leave me the hell alone!"

"No," he said simply, the set line of his chiseled jaw telling her he meant it.

"Don't be a fool. You're riskin' your life for nothin'!"

"I don't consider you nothing, Kate. If I lose you, I'll lose a piece of myself."

Kate shook her head. She didn't want to hear sweet words. Not after what she had done and the mess she had caused. "Can't y' see we're not right for each other?"

"The way I see it, we're not right for anyone else."

"I believe I'm going to cry," Drake mocked, putting his hand over his heart. "Now, if we are finished with all these declarations of undying love, then I think it's best we get on with the business at hand." He turned to Eli. "If you would please dispense with his lordship as discussed." Flicking a glance at Alec, he said, "Well, at least I have the necklace to console me, so this hasn't been an entire waste of my time. Farewell, my lord. Say hello to the devil for me."

"Y' bastard!" Kate screeched, lunging after Drake.

"Kate, no!" Alec shouted, trying to grab her. She was too quick, and he missed her. Drake's henchman, however, moved faster, grabbing her before she had reached Drake. Eli's hand struck her hard across the face, and she went reeling to the ground.

With a roar of fury, Alec attacked, slamming his fist into Eli's face, sending the man flying back against the wall, hitting it with a satisfying thud. Alec barely had time to get orientated before the two other henchmen came at him, one from each side. He struck one in the groin. The man fell to his knees. The other one he hit squarely in the stomach. That man groaned and doubled over.

Alec's eyes swung to Drake. He didn't waste any time talking. His hands itched to wrap around the man's neck. And if it was the last thing he did, he was going strangle the lowlife.

He knew his only way of winning against the big man was to get him down on the floor. So he put his head down and ran, ramming it into Drake's stomach. They went crashing to the floor and spilling out in the hallway. Unfortunately, he only got in one solid punch before he was pulled off by Drake's men. He did, however, manage to slam his booted foot into the fat man's face. He felt a great deal of satisfaction.

However, the satisfaction didn't last long as Drake's henchmen took him down to the floor, fists flying at his face and body.

Everything happened fast after that, a blur of bodies and shuffling and voices. Alec couldn't put it in any sequence, and could pin only one thing down as a definite. . . .

The deafening roar of a gun as a shot rang out . . . he remembered that with unerring clarity.

Epilogue

Two years later

"The bloody woman is impossible!" Anthony ranted as he stormed into Alec's office—without knocking, as usual, and with Holmes at his heels, also as usual. The only unusual thing was that Holmes had ceased trying to make Anthony conform to the rules of etiquette.

Alec put his pen down and leaned back in his chair, trying to hide his amusement as he watched Anthony head straight for the sideboard to pour himself a liberal drink—a drink Alec knew he wouldn't put to his lips.

Anthony's new bride didn't like him to drink. And Alec was double damned if his friend didn't honor her wishes. Oh, Anthony grumbled a lot, but since his marriage, he had become like a willow in the wind, forever bending.

It dawned on Alec then that he had mellowed considerably toward Anthony. His friend's penchant for untimely interruptions and high drama didn't bother him quite as much. Apparently, he had grown used to it. Perhaps he had merely found an untapped well of patience within himself. Hell, his middle name had become benevolence.

More than that, Alec had come to appreciate his friend. Had it not been for Anthony, he and Kate would have never met. And if they had never met, Alec knew his life would have been nowhere near as fulfilling as it was now.

"What has your hackles in a knot this time, Whitfield?" Alec dryly inquired, trying to keep the amusement out of his voice and failing miserably.

"That woman is liable to drive me insane!" Anthony fairly shouted, but with a decided lack of heat behind his words.

Alec knew his newly wedded friend was quite content with his bride. Anthony groused for the sake of grousing. It made him feel as if he still had some control over his life. He didn't. But Alec decided he would keep that information to himself for a while. Anthony would learn soon enough who ruled the house.

And it bloody well wasn't the men.

Alec shrugged. That was the price a man paid when a woman stole his heart. It was no surprise that Kate's sister had been the one who took Anthony's.

Falcon, like her sister, had a real name. It was Emily. The girl had given Anthony quite a run for his money. Anthony couldn't stand the fact that a woman could be more elusive than he was. He pursued Emily with a relentless vigor, heretofore only shown to his drinking and gambling.

"Anthony!" came his wife's page.

A moment later, Emily entered the room. She was no longer dressed like a hoodlum, but like a woman who was now a duchess.

Putting her hands on her hips, she glared at her husband. Had it not been for the fact that she turned sideways to do the glaring, she would have appeared as reed thin as she had always been.

The protruding stomach belied that possibility.

The baby was due any day, and Kate had insisted her sister move in with them until the blessed event took place.

"Anthony," his wife repeated, this time her tone reproving as she looked first at his face and then the glass in his hand. She said no more, just folded her arms over her chest.

"I wasn't going to drink it," he swore, his expression positively sheepish, to which his wife raised a single, well-shaped eyebrow in doubt. But love showed clearly in her eyes, and a slow smile crept across her lips.

Alec shook his head as he saw his friend melt over that smile like an icicle in the middle of the Sahara Desert.

The drink forgotten, Anthony strode over to her and swooped her up into his arms. She did not resist, but merely smiled brighter at him.

"I guess there is only one way to keep you off your feet, woman," he murmured huskily in her ear.

"I guess so," she softly returned, laying her head on his shoulder.

Anthony headed out the door, mindless of everything—and everyone.

Alec marveled at Anthony's lack of restraint while at the same time wondering where is own wife was. He missed her.

"Poppa! Poppa!" came the excited voice of a one-year-old, clapping her little hands as she toddled quickly into the room.

Alec rose from behind his desk and went to pick up his

daughter, swinging her in the air, her giggles filling his heart with joy. She was beautiful, just like her mother.

"Grace!" his wife called out right before she came hurriedly through the door.

Grace, Kate had decided, was a perfect name for their daughter. She had said that it had been the grace of God that had seen them through their ordeal, and Alec was inclined to agree with her.

Who would have ever thought Holmes would be the one to save them?

Holmes had followed Alec that night when he had gone to the warehouse. He had come up behind Drake when the man had been pulling a gun out of his pocket. A scuffle had ensued between Holmes and Drake, the gun had gone off, and that had been the end of the fat man. His cohorts, having lost their leader, had fled to parts unknown.

Life had gone back to normal—at least as normal as it was going to get with Kate as his wife. It would always be interesting, that much he knew.

Kate stopped before Alec and smiled up at him. Every day with him was as magnificent as flying through a sunset.

With the arm that wasn't holding his daughter, Alec pulled her to him, nestling her closely to his chest. Kate felt protected and loved . . . and home.

Grace laid her head on her father's shoulder, contentedly sucking her thumb. She was Poppa's girl. Kate's heart swelled to bursting at the thought of having this man to love and cherish for all her days. She had indeed been blessed, for nothing in the world was worth more than what she now had in her possession.

The thief had found her heart's desire.